HOPE IN A JAR

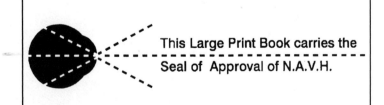

This Large Print Book carries the
Seal of Approval of N.A.V.H.

HOPE IN A JAR

BETH HARBISON

WHEELER PUBLISHING
A part of Gale, Cengage Learning

GALE
CENGAGE Learning

Detroit • New York • San Francisco • New Haven, Conn • Waterville, Maine • London

GALE
CENGAGE Learning™

LIBRARY OF CONGRESS CATALOGING-IN-PUBLICATION DATA

Harbison, Elizabeth M.
   Hope in a jar / by Beth Harbison.
     p. cm.
   ISBN-13: 978-1-4104-2065-7 (alk. paper)
   ISBN-10: 1-4104-2065-5 (alk. paper)
    1. Female friendship—Fiction. 2. Chick lit. 3. Large type books. I. Title.
PS3558.A564H66 2009b
813'.54—dc22   2009027394

Published in 2009 by arrangement with St. Martin's Press, LLC.

This book is dedicated to the girls who navigated the good, the bad, and the ugly from childhood to high school graduation with me. In order of appearance: Tiffany Pruitt, Nicki Singer, Jacki Behrens, Dana Carmel, and Kim Nash.
And to Olivia Nuccio.

ACKNOWLEDGMENTS

Thanks to the many people who made the period during which I wrote this book better. Jim Aylor and Jane Cunliffe Aylor, you have been the best of friends under many circumstances, but never more so than during that frightening January week in Children's Hospital, when you dropped everything to join us and had the presence of mind to ask the doctors questions we were too flustered to ask.

Also Annie Jones, whose prayers and support during that same frightening period offered so much comfort and hope.

Everyone at Children's National Medical Center in Washington, D.C., whose work that long week allowed us to leave with smiles instead of tears. Thank you.

Thanks also to Scott Hicks, Elaine McShulskis, Jacquelyn McShulskis Taylor, Mike Kowalski, Mimi Elias, Connie Jo Gernhofer, Rusty Gernhofer, Jen Enderlin,

Steve Troha, Courtney Fischer, Anne Marie Tallberg, Matthew Shear, Sara Goodman, Tori Hajdu, Mindy Rabinowitz, Meg Ruley, Annelise Robey, Mike McCormack, Dani Klein, Marty Hawk, Dave Miller, and Charlie Plunkett. If I started outlining how grateful I am to each of you for all the different reasons, this would get way too long, so I hope you'll accept a blanket *thank-you!*

John, Paige, and Jack, you are the lights of my life.

And a million thanks, always, to Connie Atkins, aka "Mommy," for the love, support, loans, babysitting, dogsitting, psychology, editing, and rides to the airport and train station.

ONE

I can bring home the bacon, fry it up in a
    pan,
and never never never let you forget
    you're a man . . .
           — ad for Enjoli perfume by
                Charles of the Ritz

The only thing worse than finding out your boyfriend is cheating on you with a beautiful woman is finding out he's cheating with an average woman.

Allie Denty learned this the hard way, when she got off work early and walked into her bedroom to find what appeared to be a seal flopping under the covers of her previously made bed.

It was hard to say who became aware of whom first, or who was more surprised. At almost the moment Allie entered her bedroom, a woman she'd never seen before popped her head up from under Allie's 450-

thread-count Martha Stewart sheets and screamed like a banshee.

"But —" Allie began in shock, as if they'd been in the middle of a conversation.

She didn't have time to finish the thought, whatever it might have been, because the woman leaped off the bed, stumbling to pull the sheet around herself, only to reveal Kevin, whose hands were bound over his head with his Jerry Garcia necktie.

The tie Allie had given him for Christmas last year, even though it cost more than all the other ones at Macy's.

Every muscle in Allie's body clenched and she looked in alarm from the banshee to the boyfriend she'd so foolishly — and so *completely* — trusted.

"What the —" Allie tried again. "Kevin! *What* is going *on?*"

The woman had stopped screaming, but her breath continued to sputter out in ragged gasps.

"Allie," Kevin said, but it sounded like he was trying on someone else's voice. He cleared his throat and tried again. "Allie, this isn't . . ." — it was clear halfway through his sentence that he knew how lame it was — "what it looks like."

"It looks like you're fucking some other woman in my bed," Allie said. To hell with manners. She'd just discovered that she was less attractive to her boyfriend than a woman who, now that she got a better look, could have played the *before* in an ad for just about any diet, exercise, or lifestyle cosmetic ad in *The National Enquirer.* Her light brown hair was lank and shapeless; her eyes were the same dull shade as her hair; her mouth a thin pink line, too small in a somewhat doughy face.

And her butt — which Allie unfortunately got a good look at — was even more cottage-cheesy than Allie's.

Granted, she had a perfect, straight nose. But was that what Kevin was attracted to? A model-perfect nose on an otherwise completely unremarkable face?

"Well," Kevin said, struggling out of his bindings. "It's complicated . . ."

Allie didn't remember what came after that. Not a denial exactly. How could he deny it? Good Lord, the condom was still hanging off his shrunken skipper. Wasn't what it looked like? It was *exactly* what it looked like.

Nothing complicated about it.

"I should go," the woman said, hastily pulling her clothes on.

"You think?" Allie gaped at her. Then horrible realization came over her. "Wait a

11

minute, aren't you the one who brought those paper samples to the office last month?"

"Your order will be ready on the seventh!" the woman said defensively. "There was a delay with the printer for the watermark."

This was surreal. The unremarkable woman who had sold them Kevin's new letterhead at a deeply discounted price, the woman who had asked to use the restroom and who had then — Allie couldn't help noticing — taken a very long time and emerged with a bit of toilet paper stuck to her shoe, was now in bed with Kevin and marking the end of Allie's past two years.

"Allie, we can work this out." Free of the necktie, Kevin got out of bed, just like Allie had seen him get out of bed naked a million times before. Only there wasn't usually another woman in the room.

Fortunately, Paper Girl didn't wait around; she just thundered from the room and a moment later the front door slammed.

Fine.

One gone, one to go.

"Really, Kevin? The discount paper vendor? Seriously?"

"She didn't know about you," Kevin said in defense of the one person whose emotional stake in this was the smallest.

12

"What, did she forget I was the one who placed the order with her a few weeks ago? When she got here, did she miss the pictures of *us* all over the place? My stuff in the bathroom? Is she *blind?* She shouldn't have been here, Kevin" — her voice shook with anger — "but more than that, *you* shouldn't have *brought* her here —"

"I know."

"— so now *you* get out."

He was maddeningly calm. "Let's talk about this —"

"Get *out,*" Allie said, and her voice grew stronger as she said it. *"Get out!"* She picked up his jeans from the floor, his underwear, his stupid *Star Wars* T-shirt. "Get the fuck *out!*" She hurled his clothes at him and pushed him out of the bedroom toward the door.

"But —"

"You can get your stuff out of here later. Or I'll send it. Just" — she shoved him toward the front door — "get" — she picked up his damn Hanes 32 briefs and threw them into the hall, hoping modesty would make him go after them like a dog — *"out!"* She slammed the door and turned around.

Immediately she heard a noise in the hall.

A woman's voice.

Oh, God, she'd been waiting for him.

Coconspirators, keeping secrets from Allie, comparing notes, hooking arms and leaving together. It was disgusting to contemplate.

For a long moment Allie stood there, listening to the murmuring voices through the door, fearing she might hear a giggle or an outright laugh. But all she heard was talking, then shuffling footsteps, the ding of the elevator's arrival, and then . . . nothing.

Nothing except for the low moan that rose in her own throat, a moan that slowly rose to an explosion of sobs. She hadn't seen this coming. That had always sounded so stupid when it was other people saying it, but it was the honest-to-God truth. She'd never dreamed Kevin would be anything less than faithful to her, just like she was — unquestioningly — to him.

Come on, it wasn't like he was some sort of hot-stuff hunk with movie-star looks. He was an average Joe. An average Kevin. With a high IQ and a decent personality. Every once in a while he'd made her laugh. Well, chuckle anyway.

For two years — two long, ignorant years — Allie had given up the dream of finding a soul mate because she believed Kevin was so good for her. They'd just moved into her apartment together, and were looking for a new place. A bigger place they could buy

14

together.

She'd thought they were on the path to a pretty good life partnership.

Instead, he was sleeping with another woman when he thought Allie wasn't going to be home.

Who *was* he?

If he wasn't who she'd thought he was, who *was* he?

And what had happened to the guy she thought she knew? Did he just . . . not exist? Could she have been that wrong?

"Allie!" Kevin's voice was faint outside the window but it still startled her. "Allie, please!"

She stood motionless, like an animal frozen with indecision. Cross the road or run back in the woods?

"Can you at least throw me my wallet and my keys?"

Her eyes fell on the bedside table. There they were. Just like every night. Evidently that was his bedtime ritual, no matter what he was going to spend his time doing in bed.

And no matter with whom.

She considered throwing them in the incinerator. That would certainly create a moment of great satisfaction.

Revenge was always tempting. However, it was seldom satisfying and almost always had some stupid ramification you didn't think of. In this case, she'd probably have to endure an hour and a half of him sitting out there, waiting for AAA to come open his door, or for Lexus to cut him a new key and bring it to him, and then there would be calls from his credit card holders, and — she didn't want to deal with it.

She grabbed the wallet and keys and went to the living room, where there was a tiny balcony.

He was standing in the grass below.

"You want these?" She held them up.

"Yes, Allie. Please."

"Then take them." She hurled the wallet, and enjoyed the solid *thump* when it hit him in the forehead. That was one good thing about having had an older brother growing up — she didn't throw like a girl. "And don't forget your keys." She raised them in her hand.

"Not in the face!" he shrieked.

Even in her anger, the pool of betrayal and hurt feelings, she wished he would be a little more of a man about it.

What would the neighbors think?

She dropped the keys over the railing instead of hurling them. There. Let him climb through the azaleas to find them. He was no longer her problem.

She went back to the bedroom, stripped the sheets off the bed, stuffed them into the washing machine, set the water to hot, and dumped in half a box of soap. After a moment's hesitation she added several cups of bleach.

Then she went to the bathroom to wash her hands. She spent a long time at it, scrubbing as if she could wash the last hour away, to make it so it had never happened.

Finally she gave up and stood in front of the mirror, gazing into her own confused face. What had just happened? Where had she gone wrong? And when?

The woman gazing back looked like she'd given up a long time ago. The hair was dry, and where once it had been a silky light blond, now it was brassy from home coloring. Her cheeks looked soft . . . no, doughy. The lines by her eyes, which didn't bother her most days, looked, today, like they were carved in with the sharp edge of a putty knife.

Worse, by far, the optimism that she'd always taken for granted in her soul had gone to sleep somewhere along the way — maybe a long time ago, now that she thought about it. There was nothing happy in her eyes. She looked defeated.

She *felt* defeated.

She was defeated.

Allie sank to the floor, her body suspended not by bones but by deep, heaving sobs. She couldn't believe this was happening. Had happened. Had probably been happening for a long time and she just hadn't noticed.

Stupid.

Stupid stupid stupid.

She hated Kevin.

But when it came right down to it, she knew this was her fault. It wasn't the other woman she couldn't compare to — it was herself. Where had *Allie* gone?

Somewhere she'd let go of her dreams and, at the same time, she'd let go of her hopes. She'd settled for a life of tedious temp jobs and a rented apartment and a man she didn't really love, a man who clearly didn't *deserve* her trust.

Allie had settled for all of that.

And for that she hated herself most of all.

"Noah, it's me. Again. I'm sorry to be a pain, but I just . . ." Allie swallowed, trying to keep her voice from wavering. She didn't want to sound pathetically needy.

Though, given the fact that this was the third message she was leaving on his cell phone — and the fact that he would see she'd called about a dozen more times without leaving messages — she was already in the first-class section of the Pathetically Needy Train.

". . . just wanted to talk to you," she ended lamely.

Where *was* he anyway? Noah was a workaholic — she could *always* get ahold of him because he was always at his architectural drafting board, either at home or the office, working.

Then again, he had mentioned he was seeing someone "newish" so maybe he was out with her, whoever *she* was.

Allie disliked her already.

The poor girl didn't stand a chance. And Allie was feeling just uncharitable enough to hope that Noah would dump her soon so Allie could have him to herself again.

Not "have him" have him, of course. There wasn't anything romantic going on. Never had been. They'd been friends since eighth grade, as soon as it was no longer taboo for boys and girls to talk to each other without making dramatic gag noises.

Not that it would be hard to feel for a guy like Noah. Allie and her friends used to joke that he looked like Matt Dillon's better-looking brother back when Matt Dillon was a current reference (and not long after Allie's room had been plastered with magazine cutouts of Matt Dillon). At six foot, he was a comfortable four inches taller than Allie, and he was broad enough that she felt feminine next to him (as opposed to Kyle Carpenter — from the summer after college — who, at five foot nine, had made her feel like an Amazon).

But despite the fact that he looked like her teenage crush and was the *perfect* height for her, Allie never even hinted at having a Thing with Noah because she didn't want to lose their friendship.

Really.

He was her best friend and the only person she could call in the middle of the night with a question about, say, *Green Acres* and get an answer that was (1) correct and (2) didn't involve expletives about calling in the middle of the night with a question about *Green Acres.*

That wasn't the kind of friendship a person should risk.

So instead Allie had dated a series of guys who weren't *quite* right for her: from Luke Dashnaw, who quit his job as an investment banker to become a clown ten months into their relationship; to Stu Barker, who was a Buddhist and spent one day every week in complete silence, meditating and fasting; to Kevin, who had sex with the paper salesgirl in Allie's bed when Allie wasn't home.

Allie was beginning to wonder if she'd be better off by herself.

She was also beginning to worry that soon she wouldn't have much choice. Despite very frequent and *very* concerted efforts to the contrary, she knew she wasn't as pretty as she had once been. Her thirty-eight-year-old face was starting to sag a little; the years of indulgence had puffed out her chin and hips; the summers at Tally-Ho pool in Potomac, languishing under the sun with only a thin film of baby oil between her skin and the UVA and UVB and UV-Whatever-They-Discovered-Next rays, had etched lines into her face that wouldn't otherwise have been there.

Thinking about it now, Allie felt her spirits dip even lower.

There was only one thing she could do to feel better. It would cost her, of course, but sometimes you couldn't put a price tag on mental health.

Or, actually, you could, and if you considered that it was $150 per hour and maybe once a week, a little shopping trip was nothing.

So she went to Sephora.

It was like taking a short trip to paradise; a place where everything was pretty, everything smelled good, everything was tempting, and all of it promised to ease life's little problems.

Immediately upon walking into the overlit, glistening black-white-and-red that was her personal heaven, Allie felt better.

Not that she came here that often. To the contrary, she usually settled for the drugstore brands, but every once in a while she just couldn't resist going.

Now was one of those times.

Because not only had she just ended a relationship — one of the top three reasons to go straight to Sephora — but she had her twentieth class reunion coming up. Come to think of it, that had to be in the top three, too. In fact, she'd stand her ground in saying *either* of those were a better reason to splurge than a wedding.

Anyway, here she was.

"Can I help you find something?" a girl who was *almost* half her age *and* half her size asked Allie.

"Yes." Allie was prepared. She had a wallet full of credit cards. "Show me all of your favorite things."

The girl looked confused. "What exactly are you looking for? Like, mascara, or" — she looked Allie over — "microdermabrasion?"

Under any other circumstances, Allie might have been insulted, but she'd been as low as she could go this week, self-esteemwise, so she was willing to admit she needed help.

"I want to know about anything you have that will make me look better," she said. "Show it all to me."

The girl was like an obedient dog, tentatively moving toward the hamburger that had dropped on the kitchen floor. "Are you sure?"

"Yes. Absolutely."

"Cool. Because we just got this moisturizer that everyone is saying gets rid of fine lines in, like, days . . ."

For the next hour, Allie followed the waif through the store, trying mascaras, foundations, creams, lotions, perfumes, even tooth whiteners. There was Dior, Lancôme, Fresh, Urban Decay, bareMinerals, LORAC, and a hundred other brands Allie wouldn't normally have even considered because their prices were so high.

She wasn't able to get it all — a hundred and twenty-five bucks for an ounce of skin potion was still too much, no matter how desperately unhappy she was — but she got enough to make for a very satisfying walk back to the car and drive home.

She'd realized, as she'd shopped, that her anguish wasn't really all about Kevin. In fact, very little of it probably had to do with Kevin. Every time she tried to fit him into the puzzle piece of her heart that felt missing, he didn't quite fit.

Yes, he'd cheated on her, he'd betrayed her, he'd made her feel like a loser and a fool, but maybe she understood why. At least a little bit.

She and Kevin had a very *companionable* relationship. They went on nice dates together, liked the same restaurants and the same wine. But at night when they came home, more often than not Kevin would stay in the living room, watching the Biography Channel, or Discovery, or something while Allie went into the bedroom and watched *Sex and the City,* or *Six Feet Under,* or *Big Brother.* Something that Kevin would regard as far too lowbrow for his tastes.

And while they *did* have sex regularly, it was just that: It was just *regular* and, frankly, it was just *sex.*

There were no fireworks.

There weren't even pathetic little sparklers.

On paper, Kevin had made a lot of sense. He was an attorney with a firm that had a reputation for moving its junior associates up to the top of the ranks quickly. He loved D.C., just like Allie did (even if he didn't love it for the same reasons), and had every intention of staying and making a life here, in one of the better northwest neighborhoods. He worked harder than everyone else at his firm to get further faster, and to make his goals reality.

As a matter of fact, that was how Allie had gotten stuck in the hamster treadmill of just doing temp work. Kevin had needed her help to get all that extra work done, so despite her English degree from Rutgers, she'd worked as his paralegal, researching with him, well into dawn on many nights, and picking up temp work for the cash to contribute to the household.

In retrospect it looked like a really foolish thing for her to have done, but she'd truly believed in Kevin, even if she didn't love him passionately, and she'd believed they were building a life together.

Turned out they were.

His life.

So as she came home from Montgomery Mall, with her expensive little shopping bag of treats, she found that she was much more interested in getting her*self* back than in getting *him* back.

It was a good feeling.

The next several hours of exfoliation, conditioning, blow-drying, and makeup were good ones. Positive steps in what had been a negative rut.

It wasn't a movie makeover, of course. It was home maintenance, though high-quality home maintenance. Plus, she still had these extra fifteen pounds or so to deal with, and she was not excited about going to the class reunion with them.

Not that she had been a *gazelle* the last time they'd seen her. She'd never been Audrey Hepburn, but at five foot eight she had been athletic and strong, and had had big boobs so it was generally acknowledged that she was pretty hot once.

Built, they said back then, though that weird little expression had come and gone pretty quickly.

Anyway, Allie's curvy physical assets had earned her a lot of privilege throughout high school and college: She'd never lacked a boyfriend, something that was terribly important at the time; more than one restaurant meal had been free; she'd flirted her way out of three speeding tickets; and one summer night, when she'd been wearing a particularly excellent dress she'd gotten from The Limited, a guy had offered her a million bucks to sleep with him. That was when *Indecent Proposal* was in the theaters, so it was neither a sincere nor original offer, but it was a nice sentiment.

Yup — those were the glory days when curves and boobs were acceptable and a Big Mac wasn't a sin.

Then Kate Moss had come along and ruined all of that. And Vincent Gallo did those stupid Calvin Klein heroin-chic shots that fed the trend that did not eat. Sure, everyone complained about it but nothing changed. Thin had been in now longer than any other trend in recent history. Even Tyra Banks argued against ultrathin models one day, but named ultrathin models on *America's Next Top Model* the next.

Because, upon reflection, even *without* the extra fifteen, Allie might have gone to her reunion feeling unfashionably fat. But now? She felt like Mama Cass would have taken her in hand, muttering, *Come over here, Allison, let's have a ham sandwich while they choose teams for Reunion basketball.*

The truth was, even when she'd gone to Liz Claiborne the other day to try to find some new clothes that might flatter her and lift her spirits, everything she'd tried on in her previous "fat size" was too small and she'd had to go up yet another size.

But Allie was dealing with what she had,

and she was doing her best. At this point, the plan was still to go to the reunion and if she couldn't miraculously drop a bunch of weight then maybe the makeup would draw attention to her better assets so no one noticed the worst.

That was what the salesgirl had said anyway.

Once she was all dressed up with nowhere to go, Allie got herself a glass of wine and decided to test the waters of the reunion by looking at the Web site Cindy Barlow — yes, the always overachieving reunion chair had actually purchased a domain name — had set up.

Allie went to the message boards at Classmates.com and clicked on the board labeled *WINSTON CHURCHILL HIGH SCHOOL — 20-YEAR REUNION — WHO'S COMING?* A bunch of people had already checked in:

Peter Ford: Bulldogs still rul!

Peter Ford was a jock who could barely count to ten, but who made himself a hero by establishing a record in yards run on the football field.

What Allie remembered best about him was that he pulled her shirt up in front of everyone during gym in seventh grade.

Lucy Lee: Will definitely try to make it. Anyone know what happened to Paulina Sams?

Lucy had been the smart girl who had the unusual distinction of also being really popular. She was an anchor on the local news now.

Allie had always felt like a complete loser in comparison to her. It seemed ominously clear that she would continue to feel that way.

Yancy Miller: Paulina Sams lives in Seattle now. She has two kids and she's pregnant with number 3. Her husband is an exec with Starbucks. She probably won't be able to come because of the baby.

That figured. Yancy Miller had been the biggest gossip in school. Allie wasn't even sure she'd been friends with Paulina, yet there she was with all the information.

Allie looked on. Then she saw it.

Victoria Freedman: I'll be there — watch for me!

Of course she'd write something like that.

Vickie had been the bitchiest girl in school, from sixth grade right on through twelfth. She'd grown up a few doors down from Allie and they used to play together when they were very young. But once Vickie's father had struck it *very* rich, they'd moved out of Fox Hills and into the much pricier Potomac Falls neighborhood. After that Vickie went out of her way to make it clear she'd never had anything to do with Allie or anyone else who wasn't in the popular group.

Watch for me.

Allie figured it was wiser to watch *out* for Vickie. And she would, that was for damn sure. They wouldn't have any contact unless Vickie saw Allie before Allie could hide.

Yancy Miller: Saw you on MSNBC talking environmental law, Vickie! Way to go!

Suck-up.

Wilhelmina Fram: Cannot attend.

Who was that?

Allison Denty: Will attend with guest.

That was all she'd written. Allie Denty

will attend with guest.

And now they could scratch that guest.

Noah Haller: Will be there.

Thank God.

Even if he wasn't actually going *with* Allie, she was so glad he was going to be there. One friendly face in the crowd, one person who would get it when the Vickie Freedmans and Lucy Lees walked by all high-and-mighty.

Thank God for Noah.

Allie looked at the bottom of her glass. There was only a stain of wine left. She decided she could either refill the glass and take the chance on being really sorry tomorrow, or she could opt for herbal tea.

The latter seemed wiser.

In the kitchen, she took out a box of Bigelow's Red Raspberry tea and heated the water in the microwave. She opened the tea bag and the smell of raspberry drifted up into her memory. It had been years since she'd had this stuff. When she saw it at the grocery store last week, she couldn't believe it was still for sale. She got two boxes of it but hadn't thought to actually have any until right now.

When she dunked the bag into the boiling

water, the smell took her back, through her twenties, and back to her teens when she and Olivia used to make raspberry tea lemonade at home since Snapple was so expensive.

Allie paused. Olivia. There was the one person she'd been trying not to think about. The one person whose memory brought back actual pain.

And the one person she was both hoping and hoping *not* to see at the reunion.

The relationship was completely unresolved. They'd been best friends for years, then had one blowup, and Olivia had left and that had been the end of their relationship. Poof! Like it had never happened, no matter how much Allie thought about it or missed it.

Olivia had left in a hurry halfway through senior year. It had been February. Her mom had left that bum she was married to (way more than a day late and a dollar short), packed a suitcase for herself and one for Olivia, and she'd taken her daughter and disappeared into the night.

Well, maybe it hadn't been *night* exactly. Allie wasn't sure. It had happened after she and Olivia had had the Big Blowup and they weren't speaking at the time. All Allie knew was that Olivia, her former best friend of half a decade, was in school one day and gone for good the next.

It had been awful, of course. Confusing and upsetting and the source of a lot of speculation. Yet privately, though she never admitted it out loud, Allie had been a *little* bit glad. Since they'd stopped being friends, it had been very hard to figure out exactly what they *were.* It had been even harder to figure out just how to act in this new, undefined state.

It was painful to pass Olivia in the halls and have to squelch the urge to run to her, giggling and gossiping — or maybe whining and complaining — about whatever had happened in Ms. Rosen's music class, or what dumb thing George Riggs had said this time.

It was even more painful to see Olivia instead acting all chummy with Vickie Freedman and her ilk, ignoring Allie just like the rest of them did.

Just like the rest of them used to ignore Olivia, too.

She turned into one of *them,* so it was something of a relief when Allie didn't have to face *that* every day anymore.

But in the privacy of her room, without Queen Bees and Bullies to contend with, the heartache of losing her best friend was almost too much for Allie to bear. Everywhere she looked there was a reminder — pinups they'd swooned over, records they'd sung along with, collages of words and pictures significant only to them, mixed tapes of their songs. So much of their time had been spent in Allie's room that once Olivia was gone it felt like something was missing.

She could only guess it was considerably easier for Olivia. After all, she'd left and hadn't even bothered to say good-bye to Allie. She'd never given Allie a chance to defend herself, and she certainly hadn't given her the benefit of the doubt when it came to believing her.

She'd just dumped her. And the years dissolved like cigarette smoke in the front courtyard during lunch hour. There wasn't a hint of their friendship left in Olivia's eyes.

Supposedly no one knew a forwarding address, although it had taken Allie months to screw up the courage to casually ask Vickie and her friends during yearbook signing at the end of the year.

Eventually, Allie worked up her own anger. What kind of person, no matter how mad she might have been at Allie, and no matter how wrong she was, just up and left after nearly six years without so much as a good-bye?

So, to the point, why would Allie want to see her again now, after all these years?

She didn't.

Fortunately, there didn't seem to be any point in sweating it, either. Olivia had graduated from a different school. Someplace in California, Allie had heard, though the information wasn't reliable. Wherever it was, Olivia had probably made friends there, in her new life, and didn't have any intention of coming back here.

It was, Allie reminded herself, a relief.

Now. If only Vickie Freedman felt the same way . . .

But no, Vickie was still local. And if she was anything like she used to be — and there was nothing in her personality to suggest she wouldn't be *exactly* how she used to be — she would do something to make Allie's life just a little more miserable.

Two

How un-sweet it is.
— ad for Sour Grapes Lip Smackers
by Bonne Bell

"I'll trade you Watermelon for 7UP," Allie offered, hoping Olivia wouldn't see the trade as obviously unbalanced as she did. Come on, the 7UPs were *always* sold out at Woolworth's, while there were racks and racks of Watermelon.

"I don't know." Olivia examined the fat 7UP-flavored Lip Smacker. She'd dumped the entire contents of her new purse — they only started using purses this year and barely had anything to put in them — onto Allie's patchwork bedspread. She wrinkled her small, irritatingly straight nose, then shook her head. "I like 7UP."

"You do not! You never, ever, *ever* have 7UP. You *always* have Coke."

Olivia fired back fast. "They don't have Coke-flavored Lip Smackers and besides it

36

doesn't really *taste* like 7UP."

"Yes, it does, it tastes *exactly* like 7UP. That's why they call it 7UP."

"Then I guess I like 7UP."

Allie gave an exasperated sigh. If she hadn't gotten Olivia into Lip Smackers, she'd still be trading Hello Kitty puffy stickers and Wacky Packages with fifth graders.

Now suddenly Olivia was this big Lip Smacker expert.

Please.

Allie looked at the things she'd poured out of her own purse. Four Lip Smackers (Watermelon, Sour Grapes, Dr Pepper, and Piece a Cake, which she was *never* going to trade), a roller bottle of Love's Rain Scent perfume, a broken Snoopy pencil, a Hello Kitty sticker she'd put on the outside of her purse but that was now a gummy mess, a "teen-sized" Tampax tampon (hope sprang eternal), and two dollar bills.

Fifty cents more, plus tax, and she could just go to the mall and buy her own 7UP Lip Smacker, if they had them.

Unused.

"Fine," Allie sniped, tossing her light blond hair, which she knew Olivia envied. She walked over to the mirror and looked at her image in between pictures of Scott Baio, Shaun Cassidy, and Robby Benson, which she'd taped around the perimeter.

She didn't really like Shaun Cassidy as much as everyone else did but it would have been embarrassing to admit she still liked David Cassidy, now that he was ancient.

"I don't want the stupid thing anyway," Allie said. "I was just trying to help you." It was mean. She knew it was mean and she didn't *want* to be mean, but Olivia was being such a stubborn jerk. "It makes your lips silver."

"It does?" Olivia's image appeared in the mirror next to her. Right under Shaun Cassidy's crotch. Her red hair was parted in the middle and lying lank down both sides of her head, framing her pale white face. Allie had tried over and over to get her to use a blow-dryer and some Body on Tap shampoo to give her hair some bounce, and maybe a little bit of blush, but Olivia was determined to stay mousy, apparently.

She smeared some of the lip gloss onto her lips, then frowned. Her brown eyes met Allie's blue eyes in the mirror. "No it doesn't."

"Yes it does." Allie brushed her hair and put it into barrettes on each side of her head, like that picture of the model Cindy Harrell in the latest issue of *Seventeen*. "Totally silver. They're not even lip color anymore. I don't want it." She turned and flounced back to her bed, bouncing down onto the softness.

Olivia wiped her mouth with the back of her hand, looked at it for a minute, obviously seeing the very sheer frosty tint, then joined Allie on the bed.

For a moment they lay in silence, staring at the ceiling. It still had thumbtack holes from when Allie had experimented briefly with putting a picture of John Travolta from *Grease* over her bed. It had gotten really creepy, really fast.

"I'm still not trading," Olivia said after a few minutes. "I like it."

"Fine." Allie leaned back against her pillows, half admiring Olivia for finally standing up for something, yet half seething that she was standing up for keeping something that she hadn't even cared about before Allie wanted it. "By the way, I want those two pictures of Leif Garrett back."

"Why?"

The wind rose outside, bringing the springtime scent of the viburnum blossoms under her window into the room. "Because I like him again."

"You said he looked like he smelled funny and he had lizard eyes."

"Well, now I don't think so." But he did.

He totally looked like he smoked pot and smelled like pee. "You can have your Parker Stevenson back." She gestured idly at the picture of Parker Stevenson that was taped to her closet door. Top right, over in the corner, because she didn't really like blond guys that much, including Leif Garrett. She'd only done the trade because everyone else thought he was cute and wanted the picture and since Allie was Olivia's best friend she got first dibs.

"You're just saying this because I won't give you the 7UP," Olivia said, exactly right.

But Allie wasn't about to admit it. Olivia *always* had her figured out. Allie was sort of sick of it. "That's not true. I'm just saying it because I want the pictures back. You said we could trade back if I wanted to."

Olivia thought about it for a moment. "Well, you *can't* have them."

Allie was surprised. When they'd made the trade, Olivia had said she was only doing it as a favor and she didn't like Leif Garrett. "Why not?"

"Because I don't have them anymore."

Allie couldn't believe it. Those things were like gold in the trading arena of Cabin John Junior High. No one with any brains at all would trade them without thinking *very* carefully about it. Unless, of course, they were trading them to their best friend, who said they could have them back if they wanted. "What did you do with them?"

Olivia's face went pink, which totally made her lips look even more frosty by contrast. "My mother used them to line Flicker's cage."

Allie's jaw dropped. Flicker was Olivia's cockatiel, and there was never a messier, or meaner, bird in the history of the world. If Leif Garrett had been at the bottom of that cage for even two minutes, he would be unrecognizable now. "Are you *serious?*"

Olivia nodded, pressing her lips tight together.

"Did you *tell* her what she'd done?"

Olivia nodded again, her face growing redder until finally she burst out laughing. "If he didn't smell funny before, he does now."

Allie gave a shriek of laughter. "Oh. My. Gosh. Do you know what Vickie Freedman would have given you for those pictures? Like, anything you wanted! She is *in love* with Leif Garrett." In truth, that was probably the reason both Allie and Olivia had tried to like him and had stopped at nothing in their fights to get the pictures everyone else wanted, even if they didn't.

"Vickie Freedman wouldn't talk to me even if I had Leif Garrett himself with me."

41

It was probably true. "You're *lucky* she won't talk to you. Today she asked me if I was wearing Toughskins jeans in front of, like, everyone. And I'm not, they're Zena. But now everyone thinks I still wear Toughskins and Underoos."

"Underoos?"

Allie nodded miserably. "I heard her say that while they walked away."

"She's such a jerk. Just because she has Sassoon jeans she thinks she's so cool."

Inspiration hit Allie and she sucked in her breath. "You should give those Leif Garrett pictures to her now."

"But they're a mess!"

"Exactly. Stick them in her locker anonymously." She had the entire picture in her head, folding the pictures, wedging them through the vent holes in the locker, hearing them drop to the floor on the other side . . .

They dissolved into fits of laughter again.

Allie was relieved. She didn't like fighting with Olivia. School sucked bad enough without having her best friend mad at her.

"Do you really think the 7UP Lip Smacker makes my lips look silver?" Olivia asked, when they had calmed down.

"Well . . . only if you use too much of it." Allie got up and took Olivia by the arm.

42

"Come here. Let me show you." Unlike Olivia, Allie was an aficionado of *Teen* and *Seventeen* and, when she could get away with it, occasional issues of *Glamour* and *Mademoiselle*. She knew *all* about makeup and what worked and what didn't.

She sat Olivia down at her dressing table, dipped a Kleenex in Pond's cold cream, and handed it to Olivia. "Wipe your face clean and we'll do a makeover."

Olivia did. "But not too much makeup. My mom and Donald will kill me if I come home looking like a hooker." Donald was Olivia's newish stepfather, and the reason she and her mom had moved to Potomac last year. He owned a gas station by Montgomery Mall and had a girl working behind the cash register who looked *exactly* like a hooker, so Allie doubted he would care if Olivia wore makeup.

"I'm *not* going to make you look like a hooker. God." Allie put her hand on her hip. "Why would you even say that? Do you think *I* look like a hooker?"

Olivia frowned and looked at her. "Are you even wearing makeup?"

"No" — her mother wouldn't let her wear it out of the house — "but I mean when I do put it on. Do I look like a hooker then?"

Olivia screwed up her face. "Well." She let

out a short breath. "There was that one time —"

"Apart from then."

"Oh." Pause. "No."

"See? I know exactly what I'm doing." She took a sip from the Orange Shasta can that had been sitting there since they came upstairs an hour ago. She held it out. "Want some?"

Olivia took it, while Allie opened the drawer and riffled through the old cosmetics her mother had given her to "play dress up" with plus the Butterfly Collection she'd seen advertised in *Seventeen* and had begged for until her mother finally relented under the condition that Allie didn't tell her father. Some of the stuff wasn't too bad. She started with a Merle Norman cream base in Bisque.

"That's too dark!" Olivia objected, looking for her image behind Allie's arm.

"Right, so I'm using it to make you look tan. Trust me." Now she had to put her money where her mouth was, as the Close-Up commercials said, and somehow make this dark, streaky mess work.

"Okay. You're right." Olivia sat back after some time. "I *do* look tan."

"Yup." Allie spread the base over Olivia's sharp little face, blending and blending, just like they said to in *Teen,* until finally the dark color approximated a tan. At least until just under Olivia's jawline. She had to stop somewhere. Olivia was so pale that in order for this color to look completely natural on her, Allie would have to paste it over her entire body.

But she was making a point, not a prom queen.

Next she took out a tube of Bonne Bell red gel cheek color and swiped it across Olivia's cheeks.

It shouldn't have surprised her, but she marveled at how pretty Olivia's face looked with the strategic coloring instead of the early-spring, still-in-school pallor they both had.

"If I had enough money," Allie said, "I could get the good stuff. You know, the things they sell at those glass counters at Hecht's? If you're rich enough, you can just buy yourself pretty."

"Do you really think so?"

"I'm telling you, they make stuff that performs miracles. Seriously."

"I wish I were rich."

"Me, too." Allie stepped back so Olivia could see in the mirror properly. "All right, now, see how you look like you've been at Ocean City for a week?"

45

Olivia's eyes widened and she put a thin hand to her cheek. "You're pretty good at this."

"You could be, too." Allie was confident she would still be better at it, though. "It's just like art. Only instead of drawing on paper, you're doing it on your face."

Olivia laughed. "Too bad I suck at drawing people."

"Yeah, but the face is already there. You're just coloring it in." In a final gesture of truce, Allie took out Olivia's 7UP Lip Smacker. "Now when you put this on" — she spread it on Olivia's lips — "the shimmery color makes you look even *more* tan. See?" She had to admit, she'd impressed even herself with this experiment.

It had taken her a while, but she'd figured out the tan skin/pale lip trick while studying a picture of Farrah Fawcett in a Fabergé Organics shampoo ad when she was trying to make her hair look like Farrah's.

"Cool." Olivia turned her face side to side, watching herself, then raised her chin. "But there's a line."

"I know." Allie squeezed onto the chair next to Olivia. Outside the window behind the mirror, the cherry tree waved its green spring leaves in the breeze. "I didn't have enough to do your whole body so I had to stop there."

Olivia giggled, looked at their images together, then handed Allie the 7UP Lip Smacker. "You should have this. I never get tan, no matter what I do, but you're like Malibu Barbie all summer. It will look great on you."

Allie wanted to snatch it before Olivia changed her mind, but her conscience stopped her. "You don't have to do that. I just showed you how good it looks on you."

"But I'm never tan."

"You can *get* tan." Allie took the Shasta again. "We should lie out."

"No, I just burn."

"Then fake it. Use QT or Sudden Tan."

"No, they make you orange." She thrust the Lip Smacker at Allie. "Take it."

So she did. "You can have my Piece a Cake one," she offered, halfheartedly.

"Really?" Olivia squealed.

Uh-oh. There was no getting out of this now. If Allie admitted she was just being polite, then she'd look like a total jerk.

"Sure."

Olivia ran to the bed and picked it up. She had the lid off and the tube halfway to her lips when she paused, hand in midair. "I can't."

"Huh?"

"You got this when you went to Florida. You can't even find this flavor here. You should keep it."

Allie was so moved by Olivia's thoughtfulness that she almost cried. She could never be that nice. No matter how she tried, or how much she wanted to be, she would never be the kind of person who could give up something she really really wanted, right when it was in the palm of her hand, just because someone else wanted it, too.

But she *could* be the kind of person who could share.

"I have an idea," she said, rummaging through the drawer of makeup. There she found two old Lip Smackers that were used right down to the bottom of the plastic casing. She hadn't thrown them out because she could still use a pen cap or a Q-Tip to get the last of it out.

Instead, she went to the bathroom and came back with a length of dental floss, which she used to cut the 7UP Lip Smacker and the Piece a Cake Lip Smacker right in half. Then she put the halves in the old tubes and handed one to Olivia. "You'll just have to remember that the one that says Bubble Gum is actually Piece a Cake."

Olivia looked her in the eye. "Thank you."

Why was it that Olivia sometimes seemed

so much older? She was a good three inches shorter than Allie — though, granted, Allie was tall — and she only weighed ninety-three pounds. It was so weird how she was able to make Allie feel like a guilty little kid sometimes.

"You know, you really should be a model," Allie said knowledgeably.

Olivia's cheeks turned pink. "I could never be a model!"

"Yes you could. Did you look at yourself?"

Olivia screwed up her face. "You're the one who's really into that stuff anyway. When I grow up I'm going to travel the world."

"I don't think you can do that for a living," Allie said. "Travel the world."

"I don't care, I'll find a way to get paid for it. Maybe I'll work as a waitress in a whole bunch of different cafés or something and just earn money as I go."

"That sounds fun," Allie said, but she didn't think it did at all.

Olivia nodded, though, clearly determined. "Or maybe I'll be a photographer. But one thing I'm *not* going to do is get a regular job that goes every day so I'm home only like three hours a week the way my mother is."

"I thought your mother liked her job." Al-

49

lie would have liked to work at Hecht's. Then she'd get a discount on everything, including the cosmetics department.

Olivia shrugged. "She never goes anywhere, never does anything, never sees anything. The other night she said she's never been out of the United States. Ever."

"Neither have I."

"Well, me neither, but I *want* to."

"Okay." Allie thought about it. "Hey, maybe you could be a stewardess and fly all over the place."

"I don't know." Olivia frowned, thought, then gave a slow nod. "Maybe so."

"You should think about it. Seriously."

The squabble over, Allie went to her record player, picked out their favorite Blondie record, and put it on. The record skipped, so Allie had taped some quarters onto the needle, which stopped it from skipping but slowed it down a little.

They sang "Call Me" to their own drummer.

Allie hated gym class more than any other class, including history *and* biology. It wasn't the activity she disliked — she'd always enjoyed playing games outdoors — it was the fact that they had to go to the locker room and change into completely different clothes in order to go to gym.

For one thing, the locker rooms were depressing. The school had been built in the fifties and the locker rooms hadn't been changed since then. They smelled of old pipes and mildew and the misery of every other girl who'd hated gym class.

It seemed like there were a lot of them.

Plus, it was embarrassing to have to change clothes in front of everyone else. Like, *really* embarrassing.

When Allie had talked to her mom about it, her mom had patiently pointed out that everyone probably felt similarly about it and so everyone had their own worries and weren't thinking about Allie's.

For a while that thought had helped Allie a lot.

Until the day It happened.

They were changing back into their day clothes after class. Allie was struggling to pull her jeans on because they were getting a little too small. So it was when she had them wedged around her thighs that she heard Vickie cry, "Oh, my God, Allie has poo on her underpants!"

For a moment, Allie froze.

What Vickie had said was that Allie had *Pooh,* as in Winnie-the-Pooh, on her underpants because it was true. In an uncharacteristic moment of whimsy, Allie had let her mother talk her into the adorable underwear and undershirt set. She'd pictured herself wearing them to sleep on hot summer nights, but in fact they made her so happy every time she saw the little bear's picture that she actually wore them whenever she felt a little down.

But that didn't matter now — and it certainly wasn't going to cheer her up in the future — because what everyone else heard Vickie say was that Allie had *poo* on her underpants.

"What?" someone asked.

With hands that suddenly felt like they were made of mashed potatoes, Allie fumbled to pull her pants up.

"She *does?*" someone else asked.

It was like the voices were coming from everywhere, and nowhere. Allie was so blinded by tears she didn't want anyone else to see that she kept her focus forward, yanking the zipper up and grabbing her shoes in hand.

"Oh, my God!" Giggles erupted. A *lot* of giggles.

Allie could have stopped and showed them that it wasn't *poo* but *Pooh,* but she wasn't sure that was any better. It might, in fact, just double the stories that were bound to go around.

"I do not!" she yelled heatedly, focusing her attention on the person who had started it all.

"Yes you do!" Vickie was red in the face from laughing so hard. "And you know it!"

"Liar!"

"If I'm a liar, pull your pants down and show everyone."

"No!" Allie sniffed, hoping no one saw the tears. "I don't have to prove you're a liar, everyone knows you're a liar."

Vickie was completely unfazed by the argument. She'd won and she knew it. And with every word Allie spoke in protest, she just proved Vickie's point to everyone else.

"What's the matter, Pooh-pants?" Vickie taunted.

Poo-pants, everyone else heard.

"Are you going to cry, Pooh-pants? Maybe you should go to the nurse and take care of your little problem." There it was. It had taken a minute for Vickie to get the misunderstanding she'd created but once she did she wasn't going to let it go. "Maybe you can get some new pants there."

"You're a bitch!" Allie cried.

There were gasps and then a silence followed.

At first she wasn't sure why. It wasn't like

no one had ever used the word before.

But when she heard Miss Stein's voice behind her — *"I beg your pardon, Miss Denty?"* — she knew exactly why everyone had finally stopped taunting.

And she knew she had lost in more ways than one.

THREE

Olivia Pelham listened to the tiny *click click click* of the Bulova wall clock opposite her desk. It was the electronic mantra to her end-of-day meditation. A routine she went through every day as sort of a cooldown. If the clock ever *stopped* ticking, she'd probably go mad, like some character in an old *Twilight Zone* episode.

She loved this time, late in the evening, when everyone else had gone home and she could enjoy the quiet, watching the lights of Manhattan slowly click on and off in the honeycomb windows of the buildings across the street. She loved the sound of the traffic below, even the incessant honking of the taxicabs.

To Olivia, it was a lullaby.

She could have gone home and gotten the

same kind of quiet, of course. And the view from her Upper East Side apartment was arguably prettier than the one she had now of Madison Avenue.

But it wasn't *alive.*

It was empty.

She was empty.

Not that she was *lonely* particularly — she wasn't. Whatever was missing in her life was a lot bigger than romance. It was . . . She couldn't say.

The clock continued to tick in the semi-darkness.

She wanted to open the window and fly away. She wanted to fly all over, to see everything, smell everything, taste everything.

She wanted to get out of the small room her life had become, if only for a little while.

All the way through college, she'd been sure she would find a way to at least take a year off and travel the world before entering a Serious Career, but money was tight. Money had always been tight.

So traveling the world was a pipe dream that had just gone up in smoke.

Sure, she'd been to Paris, Milan, London, all the big fashion spots, but she'd never seen much outside the walls of her hotel rooms or the runways there.

In Olivia's life, going abroad was more claustrophobic than staying in bed.

And leaving her job to go off and experience the world fully was impossible. She couldn't travel with her job but she couldn't afford to travel without it.

She was stuck.

Trapped.

Pushing that thought aside, she forced her mind back to work. It was far more comfortable than contemplating her dissatisfaction.

An hour ago, her date for the evening, David Weiner, had called to cancel. Well, *date* might be stretching it a little bit — David and Olivia had a "relationship of convenience," meaning a couple of times a month they got together and . . . well, *got together.*

It was amazing how little emotional connection she felt to a man who knew her body inside and out, but Olivia told herself that was because she was at a place in her life where commitment could only make things muddy.

Of course, Olivia had been in that place all her life, so she wasn't sure she could envision a time or place when that wasn't true.

She tapped a pen on her desk. She wasn't sure what to do with herself now. She'd planned her time out for the evening with three hours at David's. Now she had a three-hour gap and she didn't want to spend it sitting at home.

She put the final touches on her notes on the layout for the November party makeup feature for *What Now* magazine, where Olivia was the senior beauty editor, and set it aside in the out bin. If she counted her success by the number of issues she'd herded to publication, this was her fifty-sixth accomplishment.

And she was pleased with that at least.

The clock ticked on. Hypnosis.

God. She didn't want to go home. It was like resisting a magnetic force to try to get up from her desk and haul herself down the elevator, outside to the waiting car, and home to her apartment only to come back in again in, what, fifty hours. Hm. Maybe that was stretching the idea of *working late* a bit too much.

Her phone rang, startling her.

That was the other thing about the quiet. Nice as it was most of the time, it sometimes made her jumpy.

"Yes?" She didn't take the time to look at the caller ID. "Olivia Pelham."

"Olivia." It was a man.

"Yes?"

"Are you still at work?"

"Yes." Even if she wasn't, it would be the correct cautious answer. *Yes, I'm still at work, surrounded by people and protected like Rapunzel in the tower by the security guard in the lobby.*

"Do you ever leave?"

Finally she recognized the voice and sat down in relief. "Noah," she said. "As a matter of fact, I was about to do just that. Why? Feeling guilty about being a slacker?"

"Not tonight." He laughed. "It's Friday. I know you don't normally keep track of that sort of thing, but this is a night that a lot of people choose to go out and enjoy themselves. You remember that, right?"

She smiled. "I enjoy work."

He laughed. "Man, I give up. You are a workaholic. You need help."

"Point taken." She leaned back in her leather executive chair and it squeaked. She had to get some WD-40 to take care of that. Ages ago, her friend's father had told them about the many uses of WD-40 and she'd never forgotten it. "So what are *you* doing tonight? Or is giving me grief your form of entertainment?"

"Of course it is. But that's not why I'm calling. I just wanted to ask what time you want me to pick you up from Union Station tomorrow."

59

She drew a blank. "What?" *Union Station, Union Station.* There was *Union Square Café* downtown, but Union Station . . . Oh! That was in D.C. Where Noah lived, but still — what had she forgotten? "Why?"

"Are you kidding?"

She shrugged, even though he couldn't see her. "No. What the hell are you talking about?"

"The reunion."

"Oh." Now she remembered. "Shit."

"That's right, *oh, shit.* Most people have been dreading this for weeks, marking the days on their calendars like condemned men going to the gas chamber. I can't believe you forgot."

"Blocked it out, most likely."

"Don't blame you. So when do you want me to pick you up? Or do you want me to at all?"

She leaned back. "You know, I'm not sure I'm going. Tomorrow? Huh."

Noah laughed. "I don't have a lot of patience for the traffic by Capitol Hill, so if you don't lock in quick my offer may expire. Better decide, Ms. Pelham."

"Noah, I can't go. I'm just" — she looked over her neat-as-a-pin desk — "swamped."

"Bullshit, you're not too busy to come down for one night. At least tell me the truth, that you don't want to."

"It's not that. I *am* busy," she lied, feeling a growing dread at the very idea of going back. "I really am. Look, I know I said I was going to go, but you caught me after three martinis, and I wasn't really considering everything I have to do." Guilt swept over her. "But it's not like you'll be all alone there, right? Are you still in touch with anyone from high school?" She doubted it. She knew very few people who were, even among those who had had good experiences.

"You don't need to set me up with a substitute friend, Olivia. I can fly without you holding the strings."

"Of course. Sorry."

"But I still think you should come."

"Why?"

He let out a long breath and said, "Because high school sucked, and going back sucks, so I think we should do it together. It's sort of a ritual in moving on."

"Twenty years later."

"It *is* a little depressing, isn't it? Twenty years."

There was a silence while she thought about what he'd said and he, presumably, thought she was a scaredy-cat, afraid to go back and face her past.

"Would you go?" she asked, vowing that she would lock in with his answer. "If you were me?"

He laughed. "I don't want to answer on the grounds that it might weaken my argument to get you here."

"In other words, you wouldn't."

"Probably not."

"But you think I should."

He hesitated. "Hell, Liv, I have no idea if you *should.* I just wish you would."

"Is anyone I know going to be there?"

"Undoubtedly. Lots of them. And plenty of people you hoped you'd never see again."

She sighed. "Obviously. Stupid question." She pictured herself going, checking into a hotel in D.C., dressing up, and walking into a room filled with some of her worst memories. "Listen, I just don't think I can make it this time. But, hey, there will be another one in five years or so, won't there?"

"I'd bet on it."

"Then I'll go to that one. I *promise.*"

"You may be on your own there."

"No way," she said flippantly. "I'll hound you into coming so badly you won't be able to say no. None of this *letting your friend off easy* stuff for me."

He laughed. "I've always been too easy on my friends."

"For sure."

"All right, well, since you're not going, I may as well tell you that I'm going with —"

Her call waiting beeped on the line.

"What?" she asked. "Sorry, you were beeped out."

"I said that I'm taking —"

The phone beeped again. She *loathed* call waiting but in her business it was, occasionally, a necessity. Enough so that she couldn't strike it completely from her phone service. "Wait, hold on, okay? Just for a sec."

"Sure."

She clicked over. "Olivia Pelham."

"Olivia," a weepy female voice said on the other end of the line. "It's —" Sob. "It's me. I hope I'm not bothering you."

"Mom." *Oh, no.* "You're not bothering me. What's going on? Is something wrong?" Dumb question. Clearly something was wrong. "What is it?"

"I'm having a bit of an emergency and I didn't know who else to call."

"Wait, Mom, hold on." She clicked over to the other line. "Noah?"

"Yup."

"I've got to take this call. It's my mother and something's up. God knows. Can I call you back later?"

"Sure. Of course." He sounded concerned, no longer messing around with her. "Good luck."

"Thanks. I think I'm going to need it." She clicked back over to her mother, who was in midsentence, apparently having missed Olivia's instruction to hold.

"— so there is, at least, *that,* but now that I've left I just can't see going back. Especially after" — muffled crying — "after he'd do that to me. With *her,* of *all* people."

So, even having missed a little chunk of the diatribe, Olivia was able to tell what had happened.

Again.

And now her mother had left husband number . . . four? Five? Caroline Pelham O'Brien Lindon Katz Libitzky, Olivia counted silently. Five. Jesus, at this rate she was going to go through enough husbands to form a football team before she died.

"It's terrible," Olivia said, because it *was* terrible, even without knowing the details or who the *her* was in this case. What was more terrible was her mother's taste in men.

In fact, Olivia truly couldn't bear to think of some of the mistakes her mother had made.

Yet here she was, faced with another one, fighting the urge to yell, *Why the hell don't you just learn from your mistakes? You're* sixty-five years old. *That is too fucking old to be moaning that your boyfriend is cheating on you again!*

Maybe it's time, she wanted more than anything to be able to say, *that you try taking care of yourself for a while instead of always looking for a man to take care of you.*

But she couldn't.

Or at least she wouldn't.

"I know it is. I just can't believe this has happened again." Her mother drew in a shuddering breath. "But I didn't call you to whine and cry."

"You didn't?" Olivia's shock at this little snippet of self-awareness made her more frank than she meant to be. "What is it you need, then? How can I help?"

"I'm going to get a new start," her mother announced. "On my own. No fellas for a while."

Olivia's jaw dropped. "That's wonderful!" Although her mother had been married five times, she'd moved for men even more than that. Olivia counted the moves she'd had to make with her mother, then stopped at six when her mother went on talking.

"It's worth a try. I've never done that. You know, just for a little while."

Olivia nodded enthusiastically to herself. "Absolutely. Amen to that, Mom. I am so proud of you."

"I was hoping you'd feel that way."

"I do. I absolutely do."

"That's good to hear because, as you might imagine, I'll be needing a little help. Just at first, you understand. I wouldn't want to put you out."

A small swirl of dread coiled in the pit of Olivia's stomach. Another shoe was going to drop. A boot. A steel-toed work boot. Size thirteen, men's. "How do you mean?"

"Oh, honey, isn't it obvious? I need to stay with you for a little while."

Need not *want.* A subtle difference but enough to make Olivia a pretty bad person if she refused.

"Just a little while, like I said," her mother went on. "Long enough to get back on my feet again. You don't mind, right?"

No matter what she had on them, Manolos or Wal-Mart, Caroline had never stood on her own two feet. It might be more of an undertaking than she expected.

"I guess not." Olivia swallowed. "What were you thinking?" she asked, imagining a learning curve that would last approximately as long as rehabilitation from paralysis. "For how long? And when?" She hadn't meant for her apprehension to ring out quite so clearly but she couldn't help it.

"Now," her mother answered, but it sounded like a question. *Now?* "I'm at La-Guardia Airport."

"You're at *LaGuardia?*" Olivia repeated. She stood up and started pacing in front of the window that, a few minutes ago — or had it been days? — had seemed to represent such a pleasant peace and solitude. "God Almighty, Mom, why didn't you call me *before* you got on the plane?"

"Oh, I don't know. I was afraid you might try to talk me out of leaving. Pull the old Dr. Joyce Brothers routine and suggest talking and confessing, and all that kind of nonsense before just giving up on the marriage."

Dr. Joyce Brothers might have said that thirty years ago, but Dr. Phil would tell her to leave the bum today and Olivia wouldn't have disagreed.

Or would she?

If she had honestly known the next step her mother would have taken was to hop on a plane and fly from Oregon to New York to move in with her, would she truly have encouraged her to leave? Or would she have given in to that small temptation, which would undoubtedly have been there, to tell her to stick it out, try to make it work.

Stay out of my world.

67

Guilt tightened Olivia's hold on the phone. "You did the right thing, Mom," she said. Because even if Gary Libitzky hadn't slept with *her* (whoever *her* was) this time, he was a domineering, bossy, nasty old piece of work and no one should have to live with an SOB like that. "Listen, save your cell battery for now. Hang up and I'm going to send a car for you. Are you at the baggage claim?"

"Yes."

"What airline? Do you know which baggage claim?"

"AirTran Airways," she said. "I think this is baggage carousel two."

"Stay put. I'll send a car." Olivia snapped her phone shut and took a deep breath.

Baggage carousel two. It sounded so festive.

Too bad it was anything but.

Three hours later, Olivia had gone through three cups of Bigelow Orange Spice tea and her mother had gone through half a bottle of cheap airport chardonnay and all the nasty details of the last week of marriage to Gary Libitzky.

The finer points were different, but basically it was the same story Olivia had heard many times before. He seemed so nice at first, he was so generous and solicitous when he was courting Caroline, but then, almost as soon as they tweezed the rice out of their hair from the wedding reception, he'd begun telling her what to wear, whom to talk to, etc., etc., etc.

Had she left right then she would have spared herself a lot of heartache, Olivia thought. Or Gary would have straightened up. Probably the former. Either way, it would have been better.

But Caroline hadn't left then. She stayed until long after the party was over, just like always, and now her crisis was Olivia's, as well.

Just like always.

"It sounds like you did the right thing," Olivia said through a yawn. She looked at the clock on her mantel. This one was quiet, informative, not the brightly colored, loud Bulova she had at the office. It whispered that it was one-thirty A.M.

No wonder Olivia was so tired. She was *never* up at this hour.

"Now why don't you go and get some sleep?" she said, standing up and hoping to shepherd her mother into the spare bedroom. "I'm sure things will look better" — she paused — "or at least more optimistic in the morning."

"Oh, I barely sleep anymore," Caroline said, waving a hand at the notion. Her hands looked old, Olivia noted. Crepey. She had age spots. Her face had aged, too, of course, and in much the same way.

For a long, long, *long* time Caroline had somehow managed to maintain youthful, fiery-haired Maureen O'Hara looks. People had commented on how attractive she was throughout Olivia's entire high school and college career and beyond.

Had she suddenly aged, or was Olivia only now noticing? How long had her hair been so brittle? Had those lines appeared on her face all at once or just a few with each passing year?

"One of the perks of getting older," Caroline went on. "So what do you say you and I get up and have breakfast at the Plaza in the morning before we go to New Jersey to see Aunt Cassandra?"

"Whoa whoa whoa." Olivia was awake now. Wide awake. She'd rather go to Hades to see Lucifer himself than trek to New Jersey for a visit with Aunt Cassandra. The old hen. "Before we *what?*"

Caroline clicked her tongue against her teeth. "I know you're not that fond of Aunt Cassandra, but she's going to hear I'm back and if I don't go and hold my head high she's going to hear about this from someone and gloat. We can't have that."

"Why can't we have that? We never see her."

"Because I will *know* she's gloating and I just can't stand that, that's why."

Aunt Cassandra was Olivia's father's much-older sister, but she felt like a distant relative. And she was also one of the most unpleasant people Olivia had ever met in her life.

And she'd met *lots* of people at this point.

"Mom, she's got to be close to ninety now. She's probably not paying as much attention to the society pages as she is to the obituaries. As long as she doesn't see you *there,* you should be all right."

Caroline shook her head. "I've already called her and told her we were coming. I'm nipping this one in the bud. And I'm telling you, the old bird is as sharp as a tack. She knew who I was before I even said, and we haven't talked in more than a decade. Can you imagine?"

Olivia could imagine. That was just the sort of person Cassandra Pelham was. Held on tenaciously to everything, whether it was a memory of someone else's humiliation, the purse strings to the family fortune (such as it was), or, apparently, life itself. "Well,

I'm sorry, Mom, but I can't go. I have plans."

"Plans?" Her mother looked at her sharply. She had a bit of the old Cassandra spirit herself. "What plans? You didn't mention anything like that before."

"I didn't have time." Olivia was irked. Less than four hours and her mother was already driving her nuts. Worse than that, she was driving Olivia to have to choose the lesser of two evils. She *hated* that.

"Tomorrow's my twentieth high school reunion. I'm going down to D.C."

Caroline frowned. "Didn't you graduate from high school in California? Or was that college?"

"No, it was high school, Mom" — Olivia's jaw felt tight — "but only because we moved there halfway through senior year. I spent the rest of the time at Churchill in Potomac, remember?"

Caroline's expression darkened. "Of course I remember."

She should.

"Though I barely ever saw you." Caroline pursed her lips. "You used to hang around with that Denty girl all the time, eating meals at their house, sleeping over —"

"I'm going to bed." Olivia was through being patient and indulgent. "If I'm gone when you wake up, help yourself to whatever you want in the kitchen and make sure you lock the door when you leave. I'll leave a spare for you."

"Shall I send your regards to Aunt Cassandra?" Caroline asked, either to jab her point home or to attempt a joke to lighten the mood.

But it was too late for Olivia to bother trying to figure out which it was.

It was just time to end this conversation and go to bed.

"Good night, Mom."

"Good night, honey." This time the voice was not joking. It was just small, and tired. And maybe a little bit defeated.

FOUR

Go from dull to darling.
       — from "That Gal" by Benefit

Allie was certain she didn't want Kevin back.

Her eyes were a little puffy from wallowing in self-pity, her skin was pale from too little sleep, and her expression wore the horror of facing her twentieth high school reunion alone like a Halloween mask, but at least she had confidence that she'd done the right thing about Kevin.

So . . . there was that.

But the class reunion still hung over her head like one of those swinging blades from a James Bond movie, and the prospect of going without her arm prop (Kevin could hardly be called "arm candy" even before he turned out to be such a jerk) just seemed dismal.

"I don't want to do this," she said to

herself over coffee. It was the first of many times she'd say the same thing that day. "I don't want to go to this stupid reunion."

Really, what was the point? She didn't want to go *at all*. She didn't want to see anyone, she didn't want to be seen by anyone, she didn't want to get dressed up, go out, drive downtown, try to find a place to park, haul her considerable butt into the building, and find the room where the people responsible for ninety percent of her most miserable days and nights were.

She didn't want to do this.

"I don't want to do this," she said to Noah on the phone shortly after noon. "Don't make me."

"Do what?"

"The reunion."

"Whoa, I'm not making you do that."

She groaned. "Then why am I going?"

"I don't know. Because you secretly want to go?"

"How do you figure?"

"Because you're dying to know what everyone looks like right now and how successful, or not, they are."

It was completely true. "But that's just mild curiosity. You can report back to me."

"That's true."

"No it's not, you're terrible at reporting

things back."

He laughed. "And here comes the Reagan story again."

"You stood next to him at a urinal, for God's sake, Noah! It seems like you would have remembered at least a pertinent detail or two."

"I was ten! He wasn't even the president yet."

"He was the governor. He was an actor. Don't tell me you didn't see *Bedtime for Bonzo* at some point in your youth. Anyone else with any sense would have looked —"

"How many times are we going to have this conversation?"

She gave a laugh. "As many times as it takes for you to either remember something or pretend to remember something."

"This is stupid."

"Fine. Meet me at the Tastee Diner in Bethesda at seven instead of the reunion and I'll never make you tell the Reagan story again."

"That actually sounds really good," he said, a little wistfully. "Even though I don't believe you about not talking about the story again."

She leaped on that. "Then let's go!"

"I can't."

"You can!"

"No," he said firmly. "I really can't."

"Noah, you're acting like you don't have any control over this. It's just a stupid reunion. If you don't want to go, and I don't want to go, then why the hell are we going? Let's get some beer, go over to Hains Point to watch the airplanes take off, and sit and bitch about the people we remember instead of going and *talking* to them."

He hesitated, longer than someone who disagreed with her should have. "I see the appeal, there, Al, I really do, but I've committed to going tonight. Tori wants me to take her and I said I would."

Allie heard the sound of a record scraping backward in her head. "*Tori?* Who the hell is that?"

"You know. Tori. The woman I've been seeing."

"I do not know." But wait — Did she? Noah *had* mentioned he was seeing someone a while back, but she hadn't heard him mention her again.

He gave a short laugh. "Well, I guess you'll see at the reunion."

"Oh, come on, Noah. Who is she? Where did you meet her?" *What does she look like?*

"We met through work, and I told you this already, I'm sure."

Allie wasn't sure enough to disagree with

that. "And she wants you to take her to the reunion as a *date?* How pitiful."

"Not completely. She went there, too."

"She *did?*" Tori, Tori, Tori. Allie concentrated but no Tori came to mind. Rather than admit she was that oblivious to others around her, though, she simply said, "Then, good, you have a date. You don't need me to go."

"Fine." He let out a long pent-up breath. "Go to Hains Point and raise a Bud for me. Just make sure you take a cab."

She frowned, and adjusted her grip on the phone. "So you're saying I'm off the hook? I really don't have to go?"

"Not as far as *I'm* concerned."

"But you're still going to the stupid thing."

"Yup."

She sighed. Noah had never been manipulative, but if he were, this would have been one of his better tricks. But he wasn't, which meant that he really wanted her to be there but he didn't want to be a pushy asshole about it.

Like Allie would have been.

Besides, she was kind of curious to get a look at this Tori person. Noah never dated anyone for long, so this might be her only chance to meet one of his girlfriends.

So she relented. "Okay, fine. Fine. I'm going."

"I'm glad."

"This better not suck."

There was a smile in his voice. "I know."

They hung up and Allie set about trying to figure out what she was going to wear now that she was actually going to the stupid reunion.

It was funny, but up until this moment she hadn't really planned on going. Yeah, when Kevin was around they'd talked about it, she'd RSVP'd, but in the back of her mind, she'd thought that RSVP'ing — especially with *guest* — was better than just being one of those lost or forgotten classmates.

And going *with guest* gave her the perfect excuse to leave early, with that guest, without looking like she'd bailed.

Now she was going *without* guest and she had just about five hours to get herself together and actually *go.*

First she needed to lose that damn fifteen pounds.

She went to the mirror and stood looking at herself, trying to be objective.

Okay, there was no way to drop fifteen unsightly pounds in the next five hours. Unless, as one of her high school classmates might have suggested twenty years ago, she cut off her head.

And even then, didn't the human head only weigh like eight pounds, according to that kid in *Jerry Maguire*?

So that was no help.

But the new makeup she'd gotten really *did* look good. No one was going to mistake her for a movie star, God knew, but she looked pretty good, given the circumstances.

At least it wasn't so bad that she'd have to hide under a paper grocery bag or something.

The phone rang and she welcomed the interruption. "Tell me you've changed your mind," she said, certain it was Noah. For God's sake, the fact that she'd even *thought* of hiding under a grocery bag was probably a sign she shouldn't go, right? "Let's not do it at all. We'll run away, what do you say?"

The awkward pause that followed told her it wasn't. She looked at the handset to try to read the caller ID but the number was gone and instead it showed *talk* and a running timer.

"Isn't . . . I mean I'm not sure that's practical," Kevin's bewildered voice said. "Not that I'm complaining. Far from it —"

"I thought you were someone else," Allie said, without patience. Just hearing his voice, even those brief few words, brought back the full force of his betrayal.

Bodies, sweat, tongues, skin . . . the asshole.

And he thought she'd *forgiven* him?

"Who?" he challenged.

"None of your business, Kevin. Did you call for some reason or just to question me about my private life?"

"A week ago you wouldn't have said that."

She gave a single, mirthless laugh. "What a difference a slut makes."

He took a pained breath. "Charlotte isn't a *slut* —"

"I meant you." Oh, God. Her name was Charlotte. She had a name. Now she was real. "*And* her. How *dare* you defend either one of you to me!"

"It just . . . *happened.* I swear it's never happened before . . ."

Never happened before. That hadn't even occurred to her. As he blathered on with his meaningless nonapology, Allie thought back on the past few weeks. Maybe it *had* happened before. Perhaps even more than once. Had there been another time when he'd come home before her? Behaved strangely? Smelled of perfume . . . or worse?

". . . and I promise you it will never happen again, if you'll just give me another

81

chance."

Allie frowned and shifted her weight, considering the intent of his words, though not his proposal. "*If* I'll just give you another chance. Hm. What if I don't?"

"I . . . don't follow."

"You said it will never happen again if I'll just give you another chance. What if I don't?" she challenged. "Do you and *Charlotte* have a relationship of some sort? If I won't let you come back — and by the way I won't so this is all hypothetical — does that mean things will go on with her?"

"Allie, don't try to argue the case. We can get tied up in semantics all night —"

"Funny, until recently I didn't know you liked being tied up in *anything*."

He was silent for a moment before saying, "That's not fair."

"No. It wasn't." She couldn't breathe. She didn't want to be having this conversation. "It wasn't pretty, either. Jerry Garcia is probably spinning in his grave. He's probably just a blur."

She didn't want to be living this reality. The betrayal was bad enough, but to now be in charge of the choice to be alone at thirty-eight years old had its own difficulties.

It would have been so easy just to say

okay, come on back. They could pop some popcorn, watch *Lost* on DVD, talk about their days and their coworkers and their plans for the future.

But she couldn't forget what had happened. She couldn't forget that maybe it wasn't the first time. Maybe it already wasn't the last time. Who knew?

Allie didn't.

Allie never would, because she would never again feel like she could believe anything that Kevin said to her.

It was a terrible feeling.

"What color is the sky, Kevin?" she asked.

"What?"

"The sky. What color is the sky?"

"Green," he said, which was a mistake because on some level she had been giving him one last chance to tell an absolute truth and it didn't matter that he was being sarcastic. "What the hell do you mean, *'What color is the sky?'* I'm trying to talk to you about the rest of our lives, Allison. This isn't the time for flippancy."

No, it wasn't. And yet, when she'd asked him one half-assed question, when she'd *handed* him the opportunity to give her one indisputable truth, he hadn't done it. In fact, he'd done the opposite. It didn't matter that he was kidding.

If he was kidding.

See? She didn't know.

"Kevin," she said, trying hard to stop the quaver in her voice. "There is no *rest of our lives.* Not together."

"But we had *plans!*" He wasn't pleading, though on paper it might have looked like he was. No, he was complaining. Had *she* inconvenienced *him* by being mad? "You can't let one little indiscretion ruin all of that!"

"*I* can't let one little —" She caught her breath at the sheer injustice of it all. "You're trying to say this is *my* responsibility?" She bit her lip, trying not to cry because this *so* did not deserve her tears. The anger was so much more appropriate than crying and was infinitely stronger.

But.

Even on the heels of an explosively stupid statement like that, she *wanted* to forgive.

Not because he deserved it, because God knew he didn't, but because it would have been easier.

She just couldn't.

"Allie," he soothed, using the voice that had carried her through everything from work mishaps to late-night panic attacks. "Come on. This is me you're talking to. Don't do this."

"I didn't do this," she said, steadying her trembling voice as much as she could. "I. Didn't. Do. This." She sniffed, but held her head high, knowing what she had to do. "*You* did this." She swallowed. "I'll be gone for a few hours tonight. You can come then and get your stuff out of here. Anything you leave behind is going to the Purple Heart."

That was good. She felt good about it. It was perfectly fair to offer him five hours to come in, with whatever friends — or girl-friends — he could muster and pack his four suits, twenty-five T-shirts, thirteen pairs of underpants, seven pairs of pants, drawer full of mismatched socks, razor, Thicker Hair shampoo, and Springsteen's *Born in the U.S.A.* CD. Maybe the coffee-maker. They'd bought that together, but he drank more coffee than she did.

She wouldn't begrudge him that.

She'd begrudge him the years he'd taken from her, the dignity, the confidence, but not the coffeemaker.

"Should I leave the key?"

"Oh, for God's sake, obviously, Kevin. Put it on the kitchen counter. I'll be gone seven to midnight. Please make sure you're gone before I get back."

She heard him take a long breath on the other end of the line. A long *steady* breath.

Nothing rattled him. Or if it did, he wasn't about to show it. It was one thing that made him a good attorney.

It also made him a particularly crappy ex-boyfriend.

"Do you want the coffeemaker?"

Surprise. "No."

"What about the bread machine?"

The *bread machine!* With everything that was happening, she hadn't even remembered they had one, but he was going through a mental inventory of everything they had together, no matter how inconsequential.

"You can have it," she said, though she wanted to keep it.

"How about the DVD —"

"Take whatever you want!" *You asshole.* "Just leave the key when you're through. And never *ever* call me again."

Living well probably *was* the best revenge. But looking good came in a *really* close second. And since Allie didn't have the option to go with the former at the moment, she decided to do her damnedest to achieve the latter.

She already had the new makeup. Now she needed to do a serious upheaval from the basics up.

First, she needed to bathe. To exfoliate. To condition.

In short, to do everything she could for the foundation she had to build on.

She turned the shower on to a nice, steamy temperature, and got in, wincing at first when the hot water touched her skin. But soon it was soothing, pounding down on her tense muscles.

She had a huge assortment of shampoos and conditioners to choose from. Kevin used to joke that she was a shampoo whore. It wasn't so funny now. Anyway, she settled on Pantene's Ice Shine shampoo and let it sit while she used Basin's slightly-too-expensive-at-twenty-five-bucks salt scrub all over her body to smooth, exfoliate, and leave a shimmering and slightly dangerous (for the shower floor) sheen of moisturizing oil on her skin.

Then she got out, went to her sink, and took out an old packet of St. Ives soothing face mask. She couldn't tell what kind it was anymore — too many other products had spilled over the name and something acidic had evidently bled the letters — but it smelled like cucumber.

More important, it didn't sting. Allie was ultra-aware of that kind of thing right now. She knew that anything she put on or in her . . . self . . . could create a reaction.

So she put the face mask on, then slathered Hi-Protein Hair Repair conditioner onto her hair.

Then . . . she waited.

Everything was supposed to take a mere twenty minutes to perform miracles, but when you couldn't lean back or lie down, for fear of getting gooey products all over your sofa or sheets or clothes, twenty minutes could pass like hours.

So she decided to take out her nail polish set and do a pedicure. No sense in doing a manicure tonight. She was too nervous; she would inevitably scratch all the polish off her nails and end up looking like a mess.

Limiting the polish to her toes seemed like a good idea, and she even had the perfect peep-toe sling-back Carfagnis to wear, so that was perfect.

If only she had the perfect outfit to go with them.

There were plenty of dress pants in her closet, and various tops that she *could* pair with them, but with varying results. For instance, the black Chico's pants went with almost everything . . . except for the midnight blue, gold, and *different* black Anne Klein top she had, the one with the more flattering sweetheart neck. If the Chico's made her ass look smaller and the Anne Klein top made her shoulders and bust and — please, God — her arms look smaller, which one was the better choice?

Together they were a cacophony, so there was no doubt about that particular combination.

The question was, which illusional reduction was more important to her?

Eventually she decided on the top. It was better to be a big-assed girl than a linebacker, and anyway people were more likely to look at your face, hair, and torso than your hips.

At least she *thought* that made sense.

So she went to the shower, rinsed her face, rinsed her hair, tried to rinse that man right out of her hair, and then dried her oversaturated body with Egyptian cotton towels.

She looked in the mirror.

Disappointment.

These rituals used to make a difference. She could remember being young, and considerably more fresh faced, and using the apricot scrubs and Mudd masks and coming out of the shower looking pink and glowy.

Now she looked blotchy.

She toyed with the idea of canceling, again, but that would just be ridiculous. Not even with a friend as easygoing as Noah could she reveal herself to be *that* much of a flake.

Fortunately, she had her new makeup. And it was better stuff, probably up to the challenge.

It only took fifteen minutes or so, but she emerged from the bathroom with Dior lashes, MAC eyelids, Bare Minerals cheeks, and Nars lips, and, frankly, she felt fairly good about it.

Good enough to go for a little while. A *little* while. She'd get dressed, go, endure an hour or so, and come home to watch reruns of *Seinfeld.*

In just a few hours all of this would be over.

The Acela Express train didn't feel very *express* today, Olivia thought, looking out the window as Wilmington, Delaware, passed in a blur of old buildings, graffiti, and spindly weeds growing by the train tracks.

Since it was Saturday, there wasn't a huge crowd of people on board, fortunately, but even without all the stops the weekday Metroliner made between New York and D.C. the trip seemed to take forever.

She leafed through an issue of *Vanity Fair*

but couldn't concentrate on the articles.

She was not looking forward to the reunion. True, it hadn't been up to her to move away from Potomac when she and her mother did, halfway through her senior year, but by the time everything happened and they fled, she could not have been more happy to go.

Afterward there had been time to think. On the long drive to California there had been time to think. In fact, there had been a lot to try to work through in the ensuing years, but regret at leaving Maryland, or the impulse to return, had never crossed her mind.

It might be the one move in her life that she was certain had been the *right* move.

Now she was going back, and for the worst of all reasons: an event designed exclusively to see people and places that would remind her of the most painful time in her life.

Why on earth had she said yes to this?

She couldn't blame Noah. He wouldn't have remembered those last terrible weeks before she went; at least he wouldn't remember them with the clarity *she* remembered them with. For him, this was a high school reunion, somewhat melancholy, somewhat fun.

Nothing more.

But, damn it, Olivia *knew* what it would feel like to go back. It would be melancholy and dark and sinister and familiar and unfamiliar. It would be altogether disorienting.

And she should have known better than to agree.

Was there something else going on deep in her subconscious? Was it morbid curiosity drawing her back? Some deep Oprahesque need to face her past and purge it from her present?

Maybe.

Then again, maybe this was just going to be an exercise in misery.

Wilmington disappeared behind the train and suddenly the tracks were rattling over the unexpected appearance of rural America — green grass, green trees, red barns, and blue lakes. Nondistinct, generic nature, soothing in its greens and blues.

The train barreled on toward her past.

Noah would be there, she knew. Obviously.

But what about Allie?

Once, she would have thought the prospect of seeing Allie after a number of years apart would have been a wonderful one.

Then, after that, she would have imagined dreading it. Hating her. Avoiding her.

But all of that had been ages ago and never would she have imagined having strongly contrasting feelings about it twenty years later. She had always imagined "nearly forty" as being synonymous with "peace of mind" and "knowing who you are and where you're going" and, especially, "not even remembering the crap that happened in high school."

Turned out that wasn't true. As much as Olivia had accomplished in the interim — and it had been a long road — she never quite forgot the stupid teenage angst.

Yet now she was going to come face-to-face with at least some of it.

She set her magazine down in her lap and leaned her head back against the hard headrest, turning to watch the scenery and clear her mind.

Or so she hoped.

With no building or development on it, the landscape outside her window had probably looked exactly like this twenty years ago. It didn't matter. It would have been exactly the same.

In her melancholy mood, she couldn't help it, she had to remember; she had to ask herself where she was twenty years ago. Before the world had blown up in her face.

Before everything had changed.

FIVE
EIGHTH GRADE

You can try hard or you can try soft.
Soft will get him every time.
— ad for Love's Baby Soft

"Did you *see* the new boy?" Allie asked excitedly, throwing her book bag down by the hall table. "Oh, my God, it's so hot in here." She fanned herself with her hand.

It was the second-to-last week of school — a terrible time for a new student to be starting — and it was as hot and sticky as August. Unfortunately, Allie's dad was too cheap to run the air conditioner unless it was a dire emergency, so inside the house it felt like a sauna.

"I just saw him from far away." Olivia threw her book bag on top of Allie's, her books falling heavily and slipping out. She'd pick them up later. There was no hurry to tidy up, like there would have been at her house. She liked it that way. "Is he cute?"

"Ooh." Allie feigned a faint over the edge

of the sofa and onto the soft cushions. "He is *so* cute. I swear he looks like he could be Clark Brandon's brother. Dark hair, light blue eyes, this *perfect* nose, and, oh my God, he's got the greatest mouth. His lips aren't too thin but they also aren't too big and girly."

"I hear he came from somewhere in the South." Olivia sat on the sofa next to where Allie was still lying. "Bet he's got a cool accent. Sort of like the guys on *The Dukes of Hazzard.*"

"He does! But they're not as cute."

Olivia shrugged. "I don't know. I like older guys."

Allie sat up and grinned. "G-ross."

"Well, not *that much* older."

"Those guys on *The Dukes of Hazzard* are totally *that much older.* They're like thirty."

Olivia shrugged. She would not be swayed from her John Schneider and Tom Wopat love. She had the Daisy Duke cutoffs to prove it, though they were stashed in the back of her closet and she would never, ever wear them out in public, even if her mother would let her.

Which she wouldn't.

"Want a Steak-Umm sandwich?" Allie went into the kitchen. Like she needed to ask. They had Steak-Umm and cheese sandwiches, like, daily.

Olivia looked back at her from the sofa. "Yum!"

Allie went to the stove and put a big silver pan down, then she took the Steak-Umm box from the freezer and pulled three flattened pieces off. Two for her, one for Olivia, who always wanted just one piece of bread and one Steak-Umm. "I hear the new guy's name's Noel," she said, as the meat started to sizzle around the edges of the pan.

Olivia shook her head. "Noah. Like in the Bible."

"Really? Like Noah's ark?"

Olivia nodded.

"Hm. That's a weird name." Allie considered this as she picked up the TV remote from the counter, where her mother probably had it while she was watching *As the World Turns* and preparing dinner. She pushed the on button. It made a heavy *ka-chunk* sound and the TV sprang to life. "I wonder if he likes animals."

After a thoughtful pause, Olivia said, "It would be weird if he didn't."

"It would, wouldn't it?" Allie watched Dinah Shore for a moment, interviewing Burt Reynolds. "I think they're going out."

"Who?"

She gestured at the TV. "Dinah Shore and

Burt Reynolds."

Olivia wrinkled her nose and looked more closely at the TV. "No way. He's like a thousand years younger than she is."

"So? You'd go out with a guy a thousand years older than you, you just said so." She went back to the stove to check on the Steak-Umms.

"He's kind of short."

"Burt Reynolds?"

"No, Noah."

"Oh. I know." Allie turned the meat over and sprinkled some Season-All over it. "Why are the cute guys always so short?"

"They grow slower. Or later. I think that's it, they grow later than girls do."

"Maybe." She set bread on plates, added a slice of Kraft American cheese to each slice of bread, then got a spatula out and lifted the greasy meat onto the bread before fanning herself with the spatula. "But you know, Phil Crans's brother? He's, like, a junior at Churchill and he's shorter than me."

"But you're tall."

Allie snorted and folded Olivia's sandwich in half the way she liked it. "Not *that* tall. Anyway, he's like four feet tall. He *never grew* past a certain point." She gave Olivia a knowing look. "This Noah kid could be the same way."

Olivia grimaced, although privately she thought Noah was pretty cute just as he was and maybe it wouldn't matter if he didn't get much taller. Then again, she wasn't as tall as Allie so things like that bothered her less.

"Anyway." Allie assembled her sandwich and took a bite as she walked back over to the sofa. "He's one to keep an eye on. Trust me, he's gonna be a fox."

It turned out to be easy for Olivia to keep an eye on Noah, at least during fifth period, because he sat directly across from her during Mr. Horner's geography class.

When he asked her if she wanted to be partners during study time, she was surprised but flattered.

"Sure," she said, and as they walked over to the table in the corner by the open window to study for tomorrow's quiz, she decided that he was just the right height for her.

"I hate this class," Noah said as he plunked his books onto the table. "Mr. Horner is so lame."

"Yeah." She agreed, even though she was terrified of getting caught and being sent to the principal's office.

Noah was worth that chance.

She put her books down more quietly than he had and sat down. It smelled like pencils and old textbooks.

"He's worked here since, like, the sixties," she went on, looking down at the table while she spoke so that the teacher wouldn't see her lips moving. "Or before." Someone had written LYNARD SKYNARD RULES on the table in heavy black pencil. Probably Peter Ford; he was always talking about Lynyrd Skynyrd and he was the only person she could think of, off the top of her head, who would be interested enough to write it down but dumb enough to spell it wrong.

"I bet he's been here longer than that," Noah said. "He probably doesn't even know Hawaii is a state."

They laughed and immediately got barked at by Mr. Horner, which, of course, made them laugh even more, if quieter.

"So you're friends with that blond girl, right?" Noah said after a while. "Allison?"

Olivia got an uncomfortable feeling in the pit of her stomach. "Allie," she corrected, as if *Allison* had been completely off the mark. "Yes. Why?" She took a pencil sharpener out of her bag and turned her pencil in it.

"She's cute." He gave a one-shoulder shrug.

"I guess." She kept turning the pencil. The shavings were coming out onto the desk. It smelled like wood.

"So is she going out with anyone?"

It was on the tip of her tongue to say *we don't really "go out" at this school,* but that was patently untrue and he'd find out soon enough and think she was a liar. Plus, if she made out like *she* didn't want to go out with anyone, he'd never ask her out.

So she said, "I don't know. She sort of likes Brian Poska." Strictly speaking, it was true. Allie had told her she'd danced with Brian at Outdoor Ed two years ago and she'd had half a crush on him for the rest of the year. Olivia hadn't been here then, but she couldn't say for sure that Allie didn't still harbor lingering feelings for Brian.

But she knew she didn't *dislike* him, so by default she *had* to like him.

"Oh, that guy." Obviously, Noah had noticed that Brian was one of the few kids who had hit a growth spurt. He was almost six feet tall and some people said he already shaved.

A lot of the boys looked at him with envy.

"Yeah, they've known each other, like, forever." Olivia nodded, cementing the idea that, yes, Allie and Brian were really really close. "It's hard to bust up something like

100

that." The tip of the pencil she was sharpening got so sharp it broke and she had to start over.

"Is that the kind of guy she usually likes?"

"What, tall?" Ugh. She could have slapped herself for that. She hadn't meant to say it, she was just looking for something undeniably different from Noah, but she didn't mean to insult him. "I mean, he's so tall it's weird."

Noah looked at her funny and she knew she'd gone around the bend with this one.

"At least for me," she added, and the pencil broke again. She gave up and threw them both down.

"We better study before Horner decides to give us a pop quiz now as punishment for talking," Noah said, not quite meeting her eye.

"No kidding." She gave a laugh, though she'd never heard of a pop quiz as punishment in the entire year and a half she'd gone to school here. "He's such a jerk."

Noah nodded his agreement and opened his book to the pages Mr. Horner had written on the board.

They didn't talk for the rest of the period and later, when they passed each other in the hall, Noah gave a nod but Olivia couldn't help noticing he still looked a little embarrassed.

"Guess who asked me to be study partners today in geography," she trilled later, as she and Allie trudged up the hill by the basketball courts on the way home. The grass had just been cut and little pieces were clinging to her feet and her Dr. Scholl's.

The air all around them smelled fresh and green.

Allie looked interested. "Who?"

Olivia metered her response, pausing just long enough to let Allie's curiosity pique before announcing, "Noah Haller!"

"Really?" The only giveaway that she was jealous at all was that she bit down on her lower lip for a moment before asking, "What did you say?"

"I said yes, of course!" Olivia shook her head. "What do you think I said? No? Come on! The guy's the perfect height for me!"

"What?"

As she'd said it, Olivia had realized she was going just a little too far. And why was height, of all things, the only thing that came to her in the way of compelling arguments? "I mean he's not that short. Remember how we were talking about that the other day and you were saying how he was way too short for you?"

Allie frowned. "Yes. Sort of. But you also said you weren't interested in him." She didn't say *and you know I am,* but she might as well have for the way the fact of it seemed to echo around them now.

"Anyway" — Olivia pretended not to be aware, as they trudged on, across the soccer field — "when we were standing together I noticed he's like an inch taller than me. Which, I'm sorry, makes him way shorter than you."

"It only makes him a couple of inches shorter than me," Allie countered, defensive about her height. She'd confided to Olivia once that it made her self-conscious in elementary school, though there were taller kids around now in junior high. "And you yourself said he'd grow."

Olivia shrugged. "It doesn't matter because he's got a crush on someone else." If she'd known she was going to lie her way down the road to hell like this so soon, she would have made a nice, decorated handbasket in home ec instead of that stupid crumble-top coffee cake that tasted like soap.

Allie stopped. *"Who?"*

"Who what?" She was buying time. She hadn't gone too far quite yet.

"Who does he have a crush on?" Allie

asked impatiently. "You know that's what I'm asking. Is it you? Are you telling me he asked you out?"

For a moment, looking into her friend's eyes, she wanted to tell her the truth. *No, it's you!* she'd say, and Allie would be over the moon.

Then she'd start going out with Noah, and talking to him on the phone all night, and Olivia would be left out in the cold, no best friend, no boyfriend, just her mom's old cat, Simon.

Besides, Allie *always* got that kind of news. The boy always liked her, the puppy was always for her, she always got the A on her crumble-top coffee cake, even though it tasted as much like soap as Olivia's did. Maybe even more.

So, no, Olivia was *not* going to give Allie's ego another big reward.

"Vickie Freedman," she heard herself say.

If she'd been aiming to turn Allie off Noah for good, she'd made a direct hit. "Are you *kidding?* Yuck! I thought he was *way* smarter than that!"

Olivia gave a half shrug, implying agreement. Inside, a small, burning guilt attached itself to her stomach, but she barely noticed it for the glee that was jumping around her chest shouting, *Success!*

"How could he — how could *anyone* be stupid enough to fall for her act?" Allie was railing. "She's such a fake!"

"Peter Ford likes her."

"Peter Ford has the IQ of a gnat. Besides, she's a cheerleader and he's on the basketball team, so he sort of *has* to like her."

Olivia shrugged. She was going to be outmatched in this conversation. There was no way to make it seem okay for any normal person to like Vickie Freedman. "So what do you think about Brian Poska?"

Allie looked at her as if she'd just asked what she thought about drowning puppies. "What about Brian Poska?"

"Well, you used to like him, right?"

"Sort of. In *elementary school.* Why?"

"Because he's cute." Olivia forged forward, even though she could see the objection gathering in Allie's expression like storm clouds. "And you said yourself you wanted a boyfriend, so why not go out with him?"

"For one thing, he's going out with Rena Dromerick."

Ouch! Rena had pale blond hair down past her waist, bright blue eyes, a pert little nose, and she was one of those girls who was clearly destined to be a high school cheerleader and date the cutest guy on the football team.

No one in their right mind would want to try to steal a boyfriend from Rena Dromerick. They'd just look like an idiot for even trying.

"I didn't know."

Allie snorted. "You would if you'd seen them sucking face outside by the music hall after lunch." She pulled a face. "It was really disgusting. I mean, I'm not a prude or anything, but I don't need to see those two slobbering all over each other and tongues flying and all. George Michael, yes. Brian Poska, no."

Olivia could picture it, thanks to Allie's vivid description.

She was glad she hadn't had to witness it.

"Who else is there, then?"

Allie considered this for a long moment, wiping the sweat from her brow before walking on and saying, "There's always Peter Ford. He dumps a girl every week."

"So that would be something to look forward to. Besides, he's gross."

"I know." Allie sighed. "You know what we need?"

"What?"

"We need new images."

"Really?" Olivia was intrigued.

"Yeah. Summer's practically here. I think

we should get really really tan, grow our hair long, maybe put in some highlights like Rena Dromerick's hair."

"Your hair would look like Rena's," Olivia said. "Mine would look like Cruella De Vil's."

"Never mind that. If we put Sun-In on you, your hair will lighten up until it's almost blond but it will be natural. No black roots."

"Are you sure?"

"Trust me." Allie gave a confident, if sweaty, nod. "By next fall, we'll be completely different people."

"I'm going to the Barbizon School of Modeling," Vickie said to her friends, loud enough for Allie to hear. She was doing it on purpose, and Allie knew it, because way back when they used to play together, Allie had confessed that she wanted to go to the Barbizon School of Modeling because the girl who played Cissy on *Family Affair* was on the commercials for it so it must be good.

"Are you going to be a model?" Stephanie Lowenstein asked excitedly.

There was *no way* Vickie could be a model — or *just look like one,* as the commercial went. For one thing she was too short.

"Well, I *guess* so," Vickie said, comfortable enough to be coy. "See, they've been writing to me and asking me to come for a while."

"I got one of those things in the mail, too," Allie said, as she walked past. "All you need is money."

"Then it's too bad you don't have that, isn't it?" Vickie snapped.

Her friends laughed.

"But even if you did," Vickie went on, "there's no way they'd take you. You've got *terrible* skin."

Allie felt heat flush over her. Lately her skin *had* been bad. Ever since she'd gotten her stupid period. She should have known she couldn't give any guff to Vickie without having it come back at her a hundred times worse.

Vickie stopped and focused on Allie. She may as well have been shining a spotlight on her. "What's the matter? Cat got your tongue?"

"I'm just trying to think of a reason I'd want to go to the kind of modeling school that would take *you*." Lame. It was better than nothing but it was lame.

Vickie kept a mean gaze on her for a moment, then gave a single nod. "You are such a loser, Allison. I don't even have anything to say to you. You're just jealous, as usual."

"I don't blame her," Stephanie said, aligning herself with Vickie physically, shoulder to shoulder. "If I had zits like that, I'd be jealous of you, too. I'd be jealous of almost everyone."

They walked off together, laughing at that and then laughing at something else. They seemed to make a point of laughing the whole way down the hall.

Meanwhile, Allie was stuck in place, like the humiliation had melted her right into the floor.

She should never have tried to cross Vickie, especially not in front of people. This was an embarrassment she'd never forget.

Six

Calgon, take me away!
— ad for Calgon Bath Salts

The reunion was being held across two conference rooms at the Shoreham Hotel on Calvert Street in D.C. The prom had been here, too, which seemed ironic. That marked the only other time in Allie's life that she'd been here, so even though the hotel had been updated and changed along the way, the place felt disconcertingly familiar.

Regardless, she walked in with the same sense of *how do I look?* and *who else will be here?* that she had back then.

Except back then, she'd been pretty confident that she looked good in her Jessica McClintock dress, she smelled good because she'd borrowed her mother's White Shoulders, and she had felt pretty good with Ben Paroby by her side, whereas this time she

110

was unsure that the Liz Claiborne Elisabeth dress she was wearing did anything to mask her extra weight, the walk had probably made her smell more like sweat than Clinique's ironically named Happy, and she had *no one* with her to hide behind if it didn't.

Fortunately, the lighting was low, and pretty flattering. Years before, the prom committee had hung lots of tacky decorations and blown up photos of the more popular kids and those who had gotten senior superlatives, like Most Likely to Succeed, Best Looking, Class Clown, and so on. Thank God the reunion committee had resisted the urge to rehang the same pictures so that people could make unfortunate comparisons.

And, looking around the room, Allie could see that she wasn't the only one who looked different from how they had in high school. An hour or so of light mingling just proved it. Peter Ford, one of the first people she saw, had a considerable paunch now, whereas Bucky Kincaid, always *the fat kid,* K–12, was svelte and handsome. Alex Hartner was as pillowcase blond and gorgeous as ever, like she'd been frozen in time, so that was one more person to feel crappy in comparison to. Thank goodness Marlene Newman's curves had expanded in all directions, but Allie already knew that because she seemed to run into Marlene *everywhere.*

"Oh, my gosh, fancy meeting you here!" Marlene gushed, sloshing red wine over the lip of an overfull glass.

That looked pretty good right now.

"Marlene, hi." For once, Allie was glad to see Marlene because it meant she wouldn't have to stand on her own looking awkward. "Yeah, imagine running into you here, of all places."

"So are you having fun?" It was clear that Marlene was as happy as if she'd just been named Reunion Queen.

"It's great," Allie said limply. Then, trying to perk it up, she added, "I can't believe how many people showed up."

"I know! Where's your boyfriend? I saw you were bringing a guest on the Web site. Is it that guy I saw you with at the airport in Florida?"

That's right, the airport in Florida. Kevin and Allie had gone on an impromptu trip to Disney World after clicking on an Internet advertisement for it late one night after too many beers. They'd arranged a 7 A.M. flight out of Orlando and, in an airport that had felt practically empty, they had run into Marlene and her sister, who were there for some Tupperware convention or something.

"Yes, he was going to come but actually . . ." Actually she didn't owe Marlene or anyone else an explanation. "He wasn't up to it."

Marlene rolled her eyes. "My husband, Louis, tried to tell me he wasn't up to it, either, but I told him he'd better *get* up for it, or he wouldn't need to get up for anything else for a while, if you catch my drift."

"Caught." Thrown back. Ew.

"Speak of the devil."

A gray-haired and gray-bearded man hurried up to them, looking, honest to God, so much like Walter Huston in *The Devil and Daniel Webster* that it gave Allie a start.

Then the three of them stood there for a moment, the wheels of thought almost audible as everyone tried to think of something to say besides, *Jeez, you look like Walter Huston.*

"Oh! Oh, I'll be damned!" Marlene exclaimed suddenly, startling both Allie and Louis, who exchanged looks and, for just a fraction of a second, understanding. "Look who it is. Olivia Pelham. Wow, she looks amazing!"

Allie looked in what felt like slow motion. Sure enough, it was Olivia, though she was surprised Marlene had pegged her that quickly. No longer the thin, gangly colt she'd been in high school, Olivia was, even from this distance, a knockout. From her glossy auburn chin-length bob, right down to her burgundy leather peep-toe stilettos, she was perfect.

In high school, Allie had been the pretty one and Olivia had been the smart one. Allie could live with that particular imbalance because she knew perfectly well she was smart and she'd rather be perceived as the good thing people could see than the good thing people had to figure out.

Now, undeniably, Olivia was the pretty one and Allie . . . ? Well, Allie was the fat one. Or the dumpy one. Or the unsuccessful one.

And the drunk one, if she had to stay here much longer.

"Aren't you going to say hello?" Marlene was actually poking Allie in the back. "You two were inseparable in high school."

"We haven't —" Allie stopped. She had to break this bad habit of telling people more than they needed to know. She didn't need to explain the breakdown of her friendship with Olivia to Marlene any more than she needed to explain her breakup with Kevin to her.

All she needed to do was politely excuse herself and go to the ladies' rooms, where she could feel weird in private. "I think I will," she said to Marlene. "Louis, it was great to meet you. Marlene, I'm sure I'll see you soon." Someplace odd, undoubtedly. Like Cirque du Soleil or something.

Allie made a beeline for the lobby. The heck with Noah, she'd talk to him later. She just wanted to go home and spend what was left of the evening with Ben, Jerry, and the complete third season of *The Gilmore Girls.*

The idea was so appealing that she didn't pay enough attention to her surroundings, so when someone said, "And there's Allie Denty now! What a coincidence!" she was caught off guard.

She looked up to see a very large woman gesturing toward her. Claire something. What was her last name? She looked *exactly* the same as she had in high school. And next to her, making them look like a cartoon of Laurel and Hardy, was Olivia.

"We were just talking about you!" Claire said. "And here you are! Your ears must be burning."

"What were you saying?" Allie asked, with a little less levity in her voice than she'd been aiming for.

"That you were here," Claire answered simply. "And so is Olivia. You two were inseparable in high school. Allie, doesn't

Olivia look wonderful?"

Allie and Olivia locked gazes.

And for one moment, time spun crazily. Olivia's eyes were the same, though they were more artfully enhanced than they had ever been in junior high or high school, and something deep in them was so painfully familiar to Allie that she caught her breath.

Claire excused herself, probably to go point David out to Goliath, and Allie and Olivia were left alone.

"Hi, Allie," Olivia said stiffly. She sounded like a grown-up now, no surprise there, but again there was a note of familiarity.

"Hey," Allie said, sounding a bit too bubbly. "It's great to see you. How've you been?" It was such a small question to ask after such a big gap of time and emotional distance.

"Good. And you?"

"Really good." She hadn't meant for it to sound like one-upmanship but it did. Especially when she added, to fill the silence, "Just great, actually."

The silence pulled at the seconds like taffy, stretching into long, awkward gaps.

"So what do you do these days?" Olivia asked, all confident, willowy, and casual.

"I'm between jobs." Technically true. She just didn't add that, with her temp work, she was almost always between jobs. "What about you? What do you do?"

"I work for *What Now* magazine."

"You do? How interesting! What do you do there?" She'd almost said, *You never liked English or writing very much,* but then she would have been one of the very people she'd just been thinking of disdainfully. To remember that Olivia had hated English class implied an active involvement with the past that Allie didn't want to cop to.

"I'm the senior beauty editor." Olivia gave a quick smile. It was only slightly reminiscent of the smile Allie remembered. Her mouth shape was basically the same, but her teeth had been straightened and polished to a very white sheen. Not crazy one-hour burn-your-enamel white, but natural-looking, perfectly shaped white.

"Wow. That is impressive."

"Thanks, Allie."

Had it not been for the crowd around them, they could have heard crickets.

"So . . ." Whenever she was nervous, Allie had the annoying tendency to blather on through otherwise awkward silences. Had she kept her damn mouth shut, maybe Olivia would have moved on to someone chattier and Allie could have hit the bar, hard. Instead she was left to try to make

117

conversation, to paraphrase Air Supply, out of nothing at all. "How's your mom?" *I guess she and Mr. O'Brien didn't get back together.*

"She's doing great," Olivia said, with a hair too much enthusiasm. Her perfect white teeth seemed to clench over her words. "In fact, she's at my place right now."

"Alone? Or is she still with . . ." Oh, God. Why couldn't she just keep her mouth shut? This was none of her business.

"No," Olivia said unceremoniously. "She left Donald O'Brien a long time ago." Her jaw tensed for a moment and she added, though not directly to Allie, "Just about twenty years ago now." She clicked her tongue against her teeth. "Just about exactly."

Of course. It was why Olivia and Caroline had left town.

Although Caroline had always been nice enough to Allie, Allie had always held it against her that she wasn't a better mother to Olivia. Even to Allie's young eyes, it had seemed like Caroline Pelham O'Brien had been a lot more interested in some giddy schoolgirl idea of romance than she was in taking responsibility for herself and her child.

On some level, those memories had

haunted Allie and talked in echoey voices in the back of her mind now and then when she found herself coming too close to settling for the wrong relationship.

In that sense, Allie had Olivia's mother to thank for mustering up the strength to kick Kevin's cheating ass out instead of giving in to the temptation to take the path of least resistance. Conflict, heartache, starting over . . . all of that was resistance.

Another tense silence ballooned between them.

"I really like your lipstick," Allie blurted, unable to come up with anything else. "Not to sound weird or anything . . ."

Olivia laughed. "That's not weird. It's just the kind of thing I notice, too. This is Shiseido. Raisin, I think is the name. I just got a sample and tried it."

"I guess you get to try all sorts of things like that with your job," Allie said, making a mental note of the brand and color. It really was fabulous. Like that lipstick Monica Lewinsky wore in her Barbara Walters interview; everyone had wanted to know what color it was rather than how far she'd gone with Bill Clinton.

"I do." Olivia nodded and quirked her Raisin lips. "It's quite a perk."

"Lucky you." Immediately Allie worried

that she sounded bitter. *Lucky you* sounded so much like *fuck you,* under the right — or wrong — circumstances. "Seriously. I'd love a job like that." She was filling in awkward silences now. Babbling.

She wished this wasn't so hard. It wasn't supposed to be. Once upon a time, she wouldn't have believed it would be hard to talk to Olivia.

But that was a very long time ago.

"So have you seen Noah Haller?" Olivia asked at last, glancing behind Allie. "I'm supposed to be meeting him here, but I left his number in my hotel room."

Noah had mentioned seeing Olivia once a few years ago. He hadn't said anything about it since, so it hadn't occurred to Allie that they might still be in touch.

Then again, he might not have mentioned it because she'd made such a big deal of it.

Did she say anything about me?

Did you *say anything about me?*

How long did you talk?

What did you say?

Her interrogation had been pretty lengthy, now that she thought about it. It probably wasn't surprising that he'd decided not to bring it up again.

"You're meeting Noah?" Allie asked, as casually as she could manage.

"Yes." Olivia smiled and shook her head. "Somehow he talked me into coming tonight."

"Did he tell you anything about his date?"

Olivia frowned. "I don't think so. Why? Who is it?"

"I don't know. Her name's Tori and she went to Churchill at some point, but I don't remember a Tori from our class, do you?"

After a moment, Olivia said, "The name doesn't really ring a bell. But you and I were never the sort to know everyone in school."

"That's for sure."

"For example, did you know we went to junior high with Lucas Vanderslice?"

"Who?"

"Big indie filmmaker. Wrote and directed *Highway Twenty-one*."

"Oh, my God, are you serious?"

Olivia nodded. "We didn't get out much. Oh, look, there's Noah now."

Allie followed her gaze and saw him walking toward them from across the room. There was a woman by his side, slim and sexy, with long, glossy dark hair and full, sensuous lips. All the things you'd see in a Cover Girl ad.

"Oooh," Olivia said. "And that's Tori."

"Presumably."

"My God, what a lot of work she's had done."

"Her?" Allie looked at Olivia then back at Noah's date. Did Olivia know Tori?

Olivia laughed. "Can't even say her name, huh?" She turned her attention back to the approaching two. "I'm going to guess cheek implants, subtle collagen enhancement of the lips" — she looked over the woman like she was a horse — "Restylane, obviously, to get rid of lines without that frozen Botox look." She clicked her tongue against her teeth and shook her head. "I think there may even be an eye lift there. But it's excellent work, I have to hand it to her. I hardly recognize her, but as a woman on the street she looks pretty natural."

Allie was completely confused. "How long have you known her?"

Olivia opened her mouth and looked surprised, but she didn't have time to answer before Noah was there.

"I see you two have caught up," he said. He looked a little ill at ease. "How's that going?" When he asked, he looked straight at Allie.

"Great," Allie answered, as if it were impossible to imagine there could be any other answer. "This is just so much fun."

"Hold on to your hat, sweetie, it's about

to get more fun," the woman with Noah said with a white smile that made Olivia lean forward a little bit.

More admiring assessment, Allie figured. She'd know exactly what it took to have a smile like that.

Money, most likely.

The woman did look a bit familiar. Was she a TV personality or something? There was such an air of expectation around them that she felt like she couldn't ask without insulting her.

Allie opened her mouth to try to nudge them to remind her but she didn't get the chance.

Noah straightened in the woman's coiled arm. "Olivia, Allie, you remember Tori, right? She's been dying to see you again."

Who the hell was this person? The only Toris Allie could think of were Spelling and Amos and this was not either one of them.

"Of course." There was an unmistakable chill in Olivia's voice and the facts clicked into place for Allie as Olivia spoke. "Vickie Freedman. How could I ever forget?"

SEVEN

Does she or doesn't she?
— ad for Miss Clairol

Good Lord, it looked like Allie was going to pass out or throw up. Maybe both. Olivia had seen this same look on her face after they'd tried Southern Comfort at that Eagles concert at the Capital Center in Landover, Maryland, a thousand years ago. It had since become a shopping center, which made Olivia a little sad, even though she wasn't going to revisit it no matter what it was.

"Vickie?" Allie repeated, her voice a sharp arch.

"I go by Tori now," Vickie said, disdain dripping from her voice as she looked over Allie. "Goodness, Allison, you look just like your mother! It's amazing!"

Noah's jaw dropped, as did Allie's posture.

"What?" Allie asked weakly. It was plain

to see she'd been caught off guard.

"Of course, I haven't seen your mother for *years,* but she was just darling then."

Allie's mom was wonderful, but she'd also had two kids and been a superb cook, all of which had taken a bit of a toll on her waistline. To Olivia, Mrs. Denty had embodied every wonderful thing you might associate with the word *mom,* but there was no way around it, and there was nothing insulting about it: She'd looked like a mom.

No girl wanted to hear that she looked like her mom.

Probably not even Alexa Joel wanted to hear she looked like her mom.

More to the point, Vickie had obviously not meant it as a compliment, no matter how she tried to dress it up as one.

"I'm sorry." Vickie's forehead moved slightly downward, and Olivia suspected that was as far as it would go, thanks to a very skilled plastic surgeon. "Did I say something wrong? Your mother is" — genuine *oh, shit* flashed in her eyes — "she's still with us, isn't she?"

Allie gave her an impatient look. "Yes, Vickie, she's still hobbling around at sixty-three, *barely* hanging on. It's funny, though," she went on. "Because you don't look like your mom at all. Or your dad. Come to think of it, you don't even look like *yourself.* What happened?"

Now *that* was the tart-tongued Allie Olivia remembered.

Vickie's face colored. "I guess I was just lucky enough to age well," she said crisply. "Allison, if I said something that somehow offended you, I didn't mean to. I remember your mother as a lovely woman, and I'd think you would be proud to resemble her, but if there's some reason that's an insult, I am sincerely sorry you feel that way."

Olivia cringed inwardly. She hated the *sorry you feel that way* "apology." "Noah," she said, trying to lift attention somewhere — anywhere but here. "When we last spoke, you were getting ready to redesign the pavilion down in Fredericksburg. How did that go?"

"Oh, Lord, do we have to talk about *work?*" Vickie moaned.

"Why didn't you say something before tonight?" Allie asked Noah, keeping her eyes fastened on him.

"About what?"

"About *this.*" She gave the slightest nod toward Vickie.

"We'll talk about this later," he said pointedly.

The intensity between the two of them

126

was remarkable, Olivia thought.

"How did this happen?" Allie sounded like she was trying to re-create some sort of terrible accident scene. "Who else have you been seeing?" Her voice rose. "Olivia, Vickie . . . Honest to God, who else? Is Mr. Horner on your speed dial? Is Principal Massi on your Internet joke list?"

Noah took a step forward, allowing Vickie's arm to drop awkwardly.

It was like they didn't really realize anyone else was around.

"How did you two meet up again?" Olivia asked Noah, trying to divert this impending car wreck of a conversation.

"We met at a project site in Urbana back in March," Vickie said to Olivia. She was so confident, so cocky, that she didn't seem to notice the intense arc of energy that spanned the space between Noah and Allie.

"Noah had been instrumental in drawing the plans for a new Towne Center and I was working on behalf of the state historical society to ensure that the integrity of the nearby Civil War battlefields wasn't disturbed."

"How interesting," Olivia said, although this wasn't the conversation she wanted to have or the person she wanted to have it with, but since neither Noah nor Allie spoke it was incumbent upon Olivia to keep it going. "So you work for the local government?"

"I work for whoever hires me," Vickie said.

The brief pause she left was just enough time for Allie to produce a sarcastic scoff.

Vickie ignored it and said to Olivia, "I'm an environmental lawyer. I work with the Cohen, Hahn, and Everett Environmental Team on K Street."

"That must be very interesting," Olivia said again, since she could think of absolutely nothing else to say.

"It *is*," Vickie agreed. "A lot of people assume it's just about pollution and landfills and tree hugging, but you would be *amazed* how much the protection and preservation of the environment affects everything around you."

"I would imagine so." Olivia wouldn't have expected altruism from Vickie, but she was willing to open her mind to the possibility that she'd changed.

"The smart politicians are starting to see that now, so that's where the power is — in *not* blatantly exploiting the environment. It's the exact opposite of the way things were just a few years ago, and a lot of the old boys haven't figured it out yet, so the smart money is in my field right now."

"What a coincidence that you and Noah should run into each other."

Allie sighed.

"Actually, it's a surprise we didn't run into each other sooner. One of the architects, not Noah, had plans for a tower office building that obscured the battlefield skyline behind it. Now that's just plain stupid, to put up one large tower and piss everyone off when you have an expanse of land that will allow for three smaller buildings, ample parking, and the potential for more revenue from leasing the office space *and* charging for garage use." She shook her head with what was probably the same condescending smile she had given the poor sucker who had tried to get that one past her. "It's just foolish. Fortunately, Noah was just brought in to keep the shops in the center the same neotraditional style every other subdivision is using now."

"Noah does beautiful designs," Allie said defensively. "They're not like every other subdivision."

"Oh, they look nice," Vickie granted her. "All those places do. But again, he could get a lot more done, for a lot more money, in a lot less time if he concentrated his efforts on some of the rebuilding down in Southeast." She elbowed Noah in a way that suggested this was a conversation they'd had more than once.

"Maybe he's not just in it for the money," Allie said.

"Allie." Noah's voice held a warning.

"What?" Allie snapped.

"Let's step outside for a minute and talk, okay?" He glanced over his shoulder at Vickie and Olivia. "We'll just be a minute."

He led Allie away, and Olivia could see she was talking animatedly as they went.

"I honestly thought she'd be over the old jealousies of the past," Vickie said on a sigh, all but clicking her tongue at the retreating figures. "For me, high school seems like it was another lifetime, but to look at Allison you'd think it was just last week."

"She's really close to Noah," Olivia said. Their body language showed that. "Surely you know that."

Vickie waved the notion away with a thin but wiry arm. "We don't talk much about women from his past."

"Well, it looks like she's part of his present, too," Olivia said, quiet but firm. "They're friends."

Vickie wasn't to be swayed. She just shrugged her slender shoulders. "On some level, I suppose, yes." Then she gave a laugh. "Not the level *she'd* like, though, you can tell that."

There was no point in pursuing this conversation. Vickie wasn't about to agree that Noah's friendship with Allie meant a thing and Olivia wasn't in any position to give an impassioned denial about Allie's feelings toward him.

She wasn't close to either of these women.

What struck her was that this man she'd thought was so logical and intelligent had somehow fallen for a woman who had spent her early years building a solidly shrewish, catty, mean foundation.

Granted, Olivia wasn't a psychologist and she didn't even have the advantage of parenthood to inform her opinion, but she couldn't see how someone who actively sought to make others miserable and then took genuine pleasure in seeing those plans succeed could have grown up to be the kind of human being Noah Haller could fall for.

"Tori?" They were interrupted by none other than Lucy Lee, who looked no different from how she had as a senior in high school. She walked up with her arm hooked in that of an extremely, and unimaginatively, tall, dark, and handsome man.

"Lucy!" Vickie leaned in and gave her the fake kiss near the cheek that Olivia herself had given countless times. She then slid her eyes to the man, blinked, and said, "Todd."

"Tori, how are you?" He leaned in and gave her a kiss, this time a real one, and she raised her hand to his shoulder, where it lingered for just a fraction of a moment longer than seemed appropriate to Olivia.

Admittedly, it had been a while since Olivia had actually *experienced* intimate contact, so she might have been hypersensitive to it, but she watched the two with interest.

"Lucy, you remember Olivia Pelham," Vickie said.

Lucy turned a frozen smile to Olivia, looking at her as if considering a purchase. "No, I'm not sure I do . . ."

Olivia let her off the hook. "We didn't really travel in the same circles. I'm not sure we even had a class together."

Lucy smiled. "It's good to see you anyway! This is my husband, Todd Reigerberg." She held out her left hand, revealing a blinding fiesta of brilliant-cut diamonds wedged onto her narrow finger.

"It's nice to meet you." This was about where the evening ended for Olivia. She'd reached her limit of empty smiles and meaningless small talk. From this point on, all she needed to do was find an opening, make her excuses, and go back to the hotel.

"Oh, my gosh, there is Sue Ward!" Lucy exclaimed finally. "Shit, she looks great. I've got to go say hi. You two take care of yourselves, would you? Oh, and Olivia, it was nice to meet you."

Olivia nodded. She was about to make her own exit and had even gone so far as to say, "Well, Vickie," when Todd caught Vickie's eye and nodded toward the door outside to the terrace. She gave the tiniest nod of assent before they both turned to Olivia. They must have thought they were in some sort of privacy bubble that they could invoke and dissipate at will. It was totally strange.

"I'll be moving along now, too. Good to meet you, Olivia." He barely looked at her before turning back to Vickie, sucking in a small sharp breath, and adding "Tori" with a nod.

Olivia watched him go in utter amazement, then turned back to Vickie without bothering to hide it. "You two seem close," she said, letting the unsaid *really close* hang in the air.

"What, Todd and me?" Vickie feigned surprise. "Oh, no. God, no. We hardly know each other."

Olivia almost laughed. "Really."

"We met once when Lucy interviewed me for a piece on an ancient eminent domain case. Todd's the six o'clock anchor here, you know."

"No, I didn't know."

Vickie nodded. Her gaze traveled around the room, locked on something — Olivia would have been willing to bet it was Todd — then returned to Olivia. "Where were we?"

"I was leaving," Olivia said. She couldn't have taken the edge off her voice if she'd tried. "Good to see you, Vickie. Tell Noah I'll talk to him later in the week."

She walked away without giving Vickie the chance to pull her back into conversation. When she'd gone far enough, she turned around and watched Vickie hook up with the unmistakable figure of Todd Reigerberg. It was like a bad spy movie. Vickie walked past him, slowing as she did so; his mouth moved slightly and then it was as if he counted to three before following her outside.

Olivia was tempted to slip out after them and see what they were up to. It could have been anything, of course. She might be an informant for a story he was working on, for example, or an anonymous source. For that matter, it could have been a drug deal. Or maybe he was selling his car.

But as far as Olivia was concerned, it

looked like it was very obviously a romantic rendezvous.

Should she tell Noah? Twenty years ago, there would have been no question, but he was a grown man and she had enough faith in him to trust he knew what he was doing. Maybe he and Vickie had an open relationship. Maybe they didn't even have a *relationship,* per se, so much as an *arrangement.*

Olivia had had arrangements before.

Whatever the case, she couldn't picture a scenario in which she wouldn't embarrass Noah and herself by speculating wildly about his girlfriend.

Chances were very good that he would tell her to mind her own damn business and he would be right.

Besides, this relationship was obviously a passing thing. He didn't take it seriously enough to tell his friends about it before now. If she knew Noah — and she thought she did — he was way too smart to be fooled by Vickie Freedman.

"I'm sorry," Allie said, through unattractive sniffles. "I don't know what's wrong with me. Of course it's your life and if you want to fuck the whole thing up by dating a parasite like Vickie Freedman, you have every right to."

Noah laughed softly. "Thanks, pal. I knew you'd understand."

"Oh, Noah!" She threw herself into his arms. He smelled good. Just like always. Like soap and water and some sort of Mountain Fresh laundry detergent. How could he be so stupid when he smelled so sensible? "I'm sorry I can't be a better friend." She pulled back and looked into his eyes.

"You're a great friend, Al. Maybe not to *Tori* —"

Allie made a noise of disgust. *"Vickie."*

He ignored that. "But since you're not the one seeing her, it doesn't really matter. It's not like you'll ever see her."

Allie gave him a look.

"Tonight's an exception," he said.

"It's not about whether *I* see her," Allie said. "I'm worried about *you.* You're dealing with a psychopath."

"You or her?"

"Not fair. Look, you have no idea who she is. You haven't even seen her for years."

"Neither have you! Jesus, Allie, you need to get out of the past."

"I'm not *in* the past, but I remember who she was and what she did."

"In the past."

"Yes. Fine. So what? Don't you remember

what she was like? Have you forgotten what she *did?*"

"Well . . . yeah. I guess so. I actually don't remember her that well at all from school."

"Are you kidding me?"

He shook his head. "We traveled in different circles. In fact, when we first met up again, I didn't even recognize her."

"That probably had *something* to do with the fact that she's had her face completely overhauled."

He crossed his arms in front of him. "Allie, this is stupid. This is a stupid conversation."

Tears burned in her eyes. "I know." She did know. He was oblivious. High school had been a million years ago, and what had happened to Allie back then had been her problem, not his, and he had every right to be duped into thinking this admittedly pretty woman was a hot find.

How could Allie make him see the truth when he thought he was looking at it right now?

She fixed her eyes on the cars passing on Connecticut Avenue. "Just tell me" — she turned her gaze to Noah — "please tell me what you see in her."

"Jesus, Al, we're just dating. We've been dating for like five minutes. This drama is too much."

"You hardly ever date, though, Noah. Not with your schedule. If you've been seeing her for three months, that means you think there's something there and I'm here to tell you there *can't* be."

"Bullshit."

"What?"

"I don't mean to offend you, but honestly, Allie, you don't know much more about the outside world than you're saying I do. You and Kevin were swimming around in mediocrity together for, what, two years?"

"Yes."

"And before that?"

"What's that got to do with *anything?*"

"Not a thing." His expression softened and he tapped his temple with his index finger. "Think about it."

"I just don't want to see you make a huge mistake, and I swear to you, Noah, if you get serious with this girl it's going to be a huge mistake. You'll be sorry."

He looked at her for a long moment, then said, "We're just dating."

She swallowed with such an effort that it felt as if pride truly did have mass. "I'm sorry," she said quietly.

Something here wasn't right. The feeling she had in the pit of her stomach told her she was losing something and that she couldn't stop it.

Olivia was on her way out through the lobby when she saw Allie come in and head for the ladies' room. Noah followed in a few seconds and, when he saw Olivia, came to her.

"Hot as hell out there," he commented, slipping two fingers in his collar and tugging it. "So do you want to tell me how awful Tori is, too? I'd like to get it all out of the way."

Tori. That was going to take some getting used to. Unfortunately, it seemed she was going to have time to do that. "Is that what Allie did? Told you Tori was awful?"

He fastened his gaze on something in the distance and Olivia noticed the muscle in his jaw moving like a small, tight guitar string. "They didn't get along, I gather."

"She didn't get along with a lot of people. Vickie, I mean." She took a short breath and corrected herself. "Tori."

"I don't buy this business about who you seemed to be two decades ago meaning shit about who you are today."

"Were you so different then?" she challenged.

To his credit, he looked like he thought

about it before dismissing the idea. "I wouldn't want anyone who knew me then to expect me to be the same person."

"You still have the same friends."

"Some of them." He looked in the direction Allie had gone. "Or I did."

This was none of her business, but she had to say, "Be patient with Allie. This is obviously freaking her out for some reason and I don't think it's because she prefers you to be miserable."

"I don't know what the hell she wants. She'll probably be back with that jerk Kevin before you know it anyway."

"Kevin? I don't know who that is."

Noah waved it away though the heat in his expression made it clear this Kevin was no friend of his. "Doesn't matter. Are you going back in to the reunion?"

She shook her head. "I have an early train. But it was good to see you, Noah. It's been too long."

"You'll just have to come back soon," he said, obviously knowing she wouldn't.

"I will," she said, knowing he knew she didn't mean it.

Then they hugged good-bye and Olivia joined the long line out front for a cab. After ten minutes the line still hadn't moved and she felt the first drops of rain start to fall on her.

"Do you need a ride?"

Olivia turned around to see who it was, the voice both familiar and unfamiliar at the same time.

"Where are you staying?" Allie asked, taking her keys out of her purse. Her face was blotchy from crying but she was clearly making an effort to sound normal.

"Wardman Park."

"Come on, I'll give you a lift so you don't have to stand in the rain."

"No, really, I don't want to take you out of your way."

"It's not out of my way." Allie leveled her clear blue eyes on Olivia, and, under the circumstances, it was more uncomfortable than looking into the eyes of a former lover. "Don't be stupid."

Olivia had to laugh. She'd been half expecting a soft plea, a request for a few minutes to apologize or somehow try to put the past to rest. What she got, though, had been pure Allie.

Don't be stupid.

"Okay, then." Olivia smiled and joined Allie for the short walk through the drizzle to the street.

"I totally scored, parkingwise." Allie held

her key fob out and a blue Toyota Camry beeped to life. "God knew I'd need a quick getaway."

"You didn't enjoy yourself?"

Allie looked at her as if she'd just asked if she ate chipmunks for breakfast. "No."

Olivia turned her gaze to Allie. "I don't know who really enjoys reunions."

They got in and Allie put the key in the ignition and started the car. "Masochists. Egotists. Vickie."

Olivia shrugged and looked at the road as they pulled out into traffic. "Noah doesn't remember her. He doesn't know what she was like."

"Convenient."

"She didn't matter to him."

Allie drew to a stop at a red light and tightened her grip on the steering wheel. "She seems to now," she said, looking straight ahead.

Olivia studied her profile. "I don't know. I have a feeling this is a passing thing."

"Really?" Allie jumped on that. "Did Noah tell you that?"

"Not in so many words."

"Then what do you mean?"

A car behind them honked and Allie stepped on the gas.

"It's just an impression I got," Olivia said

at last, then clammed up, clearly unwilling to elaborate.

A few blocks passed in silence, with nothing but the quiet double swish of the tires going through puddles to add punctuation to the long stretches of nothing.

Finally, Allie asked, "So what's new in makeup, then?"

Olivia laughed. "Mauves."

"Mauves aren't new."

"They are every five years or so."

Allie smiled and tapped her fingers on the steering wheel. "Well, good. Mauves actually work with my eye color."

"That's true. A strong-hued mauve, close to purple, will make your eyes look green. Of course you'll have to wait until fall. Right now we're still in pastels. Yuck."

Allie nodded enthusiastically. "I *hate* pastels. The other day, I tried this peach color that was supposed to look good on everyone and I looked like a corpse. Seriously."

"Was that the Juno Peche Glow?"

"Yes!"

Olivia nodded. "Bad information. That looks horrible on almost everyone."

"Thank goodness it wasn't just me."

"Nope." The conversation, which had had a spark for a moment, was petering out.

"Not just you."

The silence that followed was so thick with things unsaid that by the time the Wardman Park Hotel came into view, Olivia felt like she couldn't breathe.

Allie drew the car up in the fire lane in front of the hotel and put it in park. "Here you are." Was that relief in her voice? Or just the lack of anything else to say that put tension into her syllables?

"It was good to see you again, Allie," Olivia said. It would have been normal to make a token gesture at staying in touch, but she couldn't do it.

"You, too," Allie said. "Thanks for the makeup tips." She looked sad. It was as if the familiarity they'd once shared hung like a fog over them but there was no way to access it.

So it wasn't really real.

"You've done really well for yourself," Allie went on. "You must be proud."

"Thanks." It was strange, but this might have been the first time anyone had ever acknowledged Olivia's hard work and accomplishments. That was sad. There was nothing more she could think of to say. "And thanks for the ride." There was a silence, then she said, "Look, I really do appreciate the ride. I don't mean to make things awkward. It's just been so long and . . . after what we went through, hating each other and all . . ."

"I never *hated* you," Allie objected, then was instantly offended. Olivia might as well have stood next to her in front of a mirror and said, *God, we look so fat.*

Allie knew, obviously, they'd had a falling-out.

But she'd never known Olivia felt actual *hatred* toward her.

"I guess I'll be going now," she said, trying to move Olivia on.

But Olivia felt the awkwardness she had created. "I didn't mean *hate*," she said. Then, on a sudden impulse, she dug in her purse and pulled out her business card. "Here's my card. Drop me a line sometime, let me know how you're doing."

Allie took the card. "Sure. Okay. Thanks."

When hell froze over she'd call.

Too bad she didn't know the weather forecast.

Eight

Sometimes you need a little Finesse,
sometimes you need a lot.
— ad for Finesse shampoo

Olivia hated the days that Allie had piano lessons because instead of their usual routine of walking from school to Allie's, eating junk food like Steak-Umms and HoHos, and watching *General Hospital,* she had to go to her house.

She walked through the crisp fall air alone, kicking the fallen leaves in front of her as she went. She liked the shushing sound and the earthy smell of them. They smelled gold and red, and all the fiery colors of a Maryland autumn.

When she got to her house she turned the key in the lock and pushed the door open. In contrast to the golden afternoon outside, everything inside seemed gray and cold. It wasn't like the warm Technicolor explosion of the Dentys' house.

146

She flipped on the lights in the foyer and the hallway — ignoring her stepfather's voice in her head, chastising her about wasting electricity — and went to the kitchen.

"Hey, Flicker," she said as she passed the birdcage. Speaking of things that set Donald off, Flicker was high on the list.

That goddamn bird stinks.

How long do those goddamn birds live?

I wasn't through with the sports page before you put it in the goddamn cage!

Olivia walked through Donald's house, trying to block out his voice from her mind.

She was hungry. That was more important than Donald's echoes.

The fridge offered little choice. There was some raw broccoli that was going brown on the ends, some sugar-free yogurts that gave Olivia a headache, lunch meat that had turned bad a few days ago, and that strange artificial orange juice that Donald O'Brien preferred to the real thing. The freezer wasn't much better but at least she was able to find the Birdseye mixed vegetables she liked with the buttery sauce, so she took that out and heated it on the stove while listening to Luke and Laura fighting with a Cassadine on *General Hospital* in the other room.

"What is this garbage?"

She narrowed her eyes and stopped stirring for a moment. Who was that? Luke was still talking so it was obviously a different character . . .

Then all the sound snapped off and a figure came around the corner into the kitchen.

"Why are all the goddamn lights on?"

Olivia was so startled she dropped the wooden spoon she'd been using on the floor.

"Oh!" She glanced at him furtively. "Donald." She bent to pick up the dropped utensil.

"It's not like you to be clumsy," he said, also moving forward to pick up the spoon, too close to her for comfort.

It was as if there were heat waves rippling off him.

Olivia took a step back. "I'm sorry, I didn't mean to be." She took the spoon in shaking hands and went to the sink to rinse it.

"Why so skittish?" Donald asked, stepping up behind her. Once again, the heat of him came at her like an affront.

"I'm not." She turned and walked across the room to return the wooden spoon to its holder, even though she wasn't quite through with it.

"You jumped like you'd seen a ghost," he said.

Far from it. His skin was deeply tanned — he liked to keep it that way because he thought it made him look rich — and his age had carved deep lines into his features that looked menacing to Olivia, although she'd heard other women refer to him as handsome. He also wore his hair too long for a man his age, though he evidently thought it was cool.

Olivia found him repulsive.

But she couldn't say why he made her so jumpy. She'd always been a bit nervous, trembling at the sounds of the house settling at night and imagining people would jump out at her from the darkened corners. Perhaps she'd caught too many suspenseful *Movie of the Week* specials on TV.

On top of that, she and her mother were living in Donald O'Brien's house, and even though they'd been here almost two years it still felt like it was *his* house. Olivia wasn't allowed to put things on the wall of her room with thumbtacks because they would leave holes, and she shared a bathroom with Donald's cranky old mother from Atlanta, who was a frequent visitor, and any other guest who needed a place to wash up. Therefore, signs of Olivia's permanent

149

residence were also forbidden there, and she had to keep her toiletries in a blue bucket in the closet.

The house looked clean, that was certain, but she preferred the disorganized, cluttered, warm mess of Allie's house. Thank God she had that one place in the world where she felt as if she belonged. She could even add items to Mrs. Denty's grocery list.

"So, again, I ask you why you're so skittish," Donald repeated, narrowing his eyes with implicit accusation. "Are you on something?"

"On something?" She looked down at her feet, as if she'd misunderstood him. "I don't —"

"Drugs," he snapped. "Have you taken something? Smoked something?" He looked absolutely certain that he'd caught her at something.

"No!"

"I won't put up with that in my house, you know."

She straightened her back and faced him even though every instinct in her was to kick him in the nuts and run away. "I don't take drugs. No one I know takes drugs."

He nodded, scrutinizing her. "That better be the truth. For your sake *and* for ours."

"It is." She wanted to sound strong, to

intimidate him as much as he intimidated her, but to her own ears she sounded like Smurfette. On top of that, she hated how he and her mother were *us* and *ours,* as if Olivia were just some outsider who had stumbled upon the house and forced them to take her in. "Do you know when my mother's going to be back?"

Still watching her, as if she were going to whip out a joint if he looked away for so much as a second, he said, "She's working until closing tonight because of the preholiday sale this weekend. I don't expect we'll see her until around eleven."

Oh, God. Olivia's mother worked at the Hecht's department store at Montgomery Mall. It was only a couple of miles away but through so many lights and major roads that it might as well have been a hundred miles. On the nights she had to help prepare for a big sale, she was usually stuck there well past closing. Sometimes she didn't get home until after midnight.

Olivia couldn't stand the thought of being in the house with Donald alone that long. Not that her mother made things any more comfortable, but at least when she was there Donald had something else to focus on besides everything Olivia was doing wrong, messing up, or in the way of.

"I can take some steaks out of the freezer for dinner," Donald said, as if it were a generous offer. "Do you know how to cook them?"

"Not really." Not unless they were Steak-Umms. "And I'm sleeping over at Allie's so I won't be here," she said, though they hadn't specifically talked about it yet. She slept over at Allie's almost every weekend, so it was a safe bet, and even if she didn't, she'd rather stay out as long as she could and risk his wrath later if she had to than sit here and eat dinner with him in stony silence.

"Allie's," he echoed, walking heavily to the freezer. "Allie, Allie, Allie. I hope her family doesn't mind that you're there so much. They've already got two kids of their own, you know."

"I know." It was just like him to try to inject even more doubt into Olivia's self-esteem. *You know your friend has her own family and they don't want you, don't you?* She didn't even think he did it on purpose. It was just his personality to automatically default to the negative.

"They invited me," Olivia said, defensive. "Her mother invited me. So I guess it's okay."

"I guess so." He didn't look at her and

instead began to whistle quietly as he plunked a frozen steak onto the counter and took a tomato out of the fridge. "I expect you to behave yourself when you're there. I don't need the goddamn neighbors talking about what a hellion my wife's kid is."

Maybe it was the fact that she'd been agitated around him for so long, or maybe it was that he was attacking her now when all she wanted to do was leave so they wouldn't be around each other, but Olivia's temper flared. "I'm not a hellion!"

"Watch your tone, young lady."

"I'm not a hellion," she said again, although a little bit more quietly.

He shrugged. "What do I know about what you do when you're not here?"

"Nothing!" Anger swelled in her chest. "But if I were doing all these things you're accusing me of, you probably would have heard about it by now."

He stopped and looked at her. His voice was low and icy and there was definitely a warning in it. "Watch your tone."

"I'm sorry." She hated herself for apologizing. "I didn't mean to yell."

"Don't do it again."

"Okay." She couldn't think what else to say or how to get out of this. "Um, I've got to go now." She looked at the clock then. It was only four-thirty. Allie wouldn't be home for almost an hour.

"Make sure you let your mother know where you're going," Donald reminded her. Far be it from him just to tell his wife himself when he saw her.

"I'll call her," Olivia said without looking back. "As soon as I get to Allie's."

"Olivia."

She stopped, took a short breath, and turned around. "Yes?"

"Make sure it's okay with Peggy Denty that you stay over."

"She said it is —"

"I'm asking you to confirm." He was like a drill sergeant. "You don't want to impose. Am I right?"

She hung her head. "Yes. I'll make sure."

She ran to Allie's house like there was a ghost at her heels. And, in a way, there was. In her imagination, Donald was everywhere, regardless of how hard she tried to get away.

He hadn't done anything or even said anything overtly mean, but his words felt like blows. Everything about him that made her feel bad came from the stuff behind and between his words, and in his gestures.

It all added up to one fact none of them could ignore: She was an intruder in his house, the unfortunate price he had to pay for marrying her mother. She owed him something, but she wasn't sure exactly what. Probably just gratitude and undying subservience.

Allie's house was six up and across the street, around a bend. If the street were straight, they probably could have seen each other's bedrooms at night, maybe sent signals with flashlights.

Knowing Allie was still at her piano lesson, and that her older brother, Ross, was probably the only one home, Olivia went straight around to the backyard to wait until Allie got home. As long as the sun stayed out, it would remain pretty warm. It didn't really cool down these days until dusk.

She sat on the trampoline and looked at the back of the house. The wide picture windows upstairs were open, and Olivia could see the curtains inside stirring with a breeze she barely even felt. The kitchen window, bottom left, was open, too. Olivia could smell coffee, very faintly, mingling with the earthy smell of fallen leaves around her. Mrs. Denty always had a pot of coffee on.

Often, when Allie and Olivia came in from school, Mrs. Denty would have a friend over, too, and they'd be sitting on the porch, drinking coffee with sugar and cream, and eating the buttery melt-in-your-mouth shortbread cookies Mrs. Denty made.

Olivia leaned back on the warm canvas of the trampoline and looked at the sky. White, puffy clouds moved very slowly, changing form gradually. Mickey Mouse became an elephant and then a giraffe and then expanded into blue nothingness.

It was soothing.

"Olivia?"

She shot upright.

Mrs. Denty was standing in the middle of the yard, her hand over her eyes like a soldier's salute, blocking the sun. "I thought that was you!"

"I'm sorry!"

"Why are you sorry?" Mrs. Denty came over to her. She wore pleated tweedy brown pants with built-in suspenders, and a puffy-sleeved white blouse. Olivia had seen those pants at Hecht's and they were pretty expensive. "Good heavens, you didn't do anything wrong. I was just wondering who the dead child on the trampoline was."

Olivia laughed. "Just me."

"And that's fine if you want to be out here for some reason, but wouldn't you like to come in?"

"I didn't want to bother you. Actually, I

thought Ross would be the only one here, and I *really* didn't want to bother *him*." Ross was a senior in high school and had *no* time for irritating little "rug rats" like Allie and Olivia.

Mrs. Denty chuckled. "Loud as he plays that stereo, he probably wouldn't even have heard you." She put out a hand. "Come on. You're never a bother. You come talk to me while we wait for Allie Cat to come home. I assume you're staying over tonight?"

"Yes, I was planning on it," she said, then her conscience poked her. "Donald wanted me to make sure it was okay with you for me to be here."

A dark look crossed Mrs. Denty's face. "It is *always* okay. Honestly, I have told him that myself countless times."

"I think he just wants to be sure. He has a big fear of people talking about him. Saying bad things, like that his wife's daughter is a cling-on or a hooligan or something."

"You?" Mrs. Denty laughed outright. "He doesn't have a clue how good you are."

Olivia nodded. "I know." Then she was glad to feel Mrs. Denty's warm arm around her shoulder.

"People who don't have their own kids sometimes have trouble relating to them at all." Mrs. Denty gave her a squeeze. "I hope you know it's not your fault."

"I know." Olivia swallowed the hard lump in her throat. She did know, or at least she was pretty sure, it wasn't her fault. But still, it was hard to feel completely at home anywhere these days, and Mrs. Denty being so nice to her was reassuring but at the same time it made her feel sort of guilty.

Like she didn't deserve it.

"Now you have a seat and I'm going to pour you some of this wonderful hot chocolate I found at the Giant today."

Allie came bursting into the house then. "I'm home!" As soon as she saw Olivia, she cried, "Oh, my gosh, you are in *trouble!*"

"Me?" Dread filled Olivia's chest, much, much more than Allie could have realized or even imagined.

Allie nodded. "I just went by your house to get you and Mr. O'Brien was there and he said he thought you were with me, and I said I was just at piano, and then he looked really mad and said he was going to go look for you, and that if I saw you I should let him know." She took a moment to catch her breath. "He looked totally furious." She shuddered. "He is such a jerk."

Olivia bit her lower lip. What was she going to do? The idea of an enraged Donald O'Brien driving around looking for her was terrifying. "I'd better go," she said, defying every self-preservation instinct she had.

"No!" Mrs. Denty never yelled, at least not as far as Olivia had ever known, but this was close. "I'm sorry, Olivia, but please let me call him." She bustled to the phone, taking large, hard strides to the kitchen.

Olivia was profoundly grateful for the offer. She did not want to talk to him herself.

It took long minutes after she dialed before Mrs. Denty finally spoke. "Donald? Yes, hello, this is Peggy Denty. Listen, I'm calling to see if my daughter has come to your house, by any chance. Olivia's here and we've been waiting for her to get back from piano and —"

Allie giggled but Olivia tensed.

"— she was?" Mrs. Denty went on. "Just now?"

Olivia felt a sense of relief rush through her like cool water.

"Then I suppose she'll be here — Oh, for heaven's sake, here she is right now, coming in the front door." She gestured at Allie, who picked up the cue with relish.

"Hey Mom, Liv." She called it out while running across the room away from the phone, then came back and added, "Oh, Liv, Mr. O'Brien wants you to call him right away."

Mrs. Denty winked at her daughter approvingly and Allie gave a silent, squealy smile.

"What's that?" Mrs. Denty asked into the phone. "Yes, right here. We've been having hot chocolate together and chatting. Did you want to talk to her?" She paused, then shook her head at Olivia. "It's no bother at all, honestly, Donald. I've told you that before. We love having her. Right. Okay, then, give my best to Caroline. We'll send Olivia home in a day or two. Okay. Byebye." She hung the phone up and looked at it for a moment, less than pleased, before turning back to Allie and Olivia with a smile.

"Was he pissed?" Allie asked.

"Don't use that word," her mother said, then sighed. "He was angry at first, but when he found out Olivia was where she said she'd be, he cooled down." She shook her head to herself, then said to the girls, "I don't condone lying, but sometimes you just have to know how to deal with people. If I'd called and simply told him the truth straight-out, he'd have thought I was covering for Olivia."

"Like she'd ever do anything wrong," Allie scoffed.

"I've done things wrong before." Olivia was feeling vaguely protective of her mother for some reason. Maybe of her mother's choice in men.

"Bull," Allie said, before her mother could say something more gentle.

"My point," Mrs. Denty stressed, silencing both of them, "is that sometimes the only way you can get someone to believe the truth is by using a little white lie. Now, how about we have that hot chocolate I was telling you about?"

NINE

Make yourself happy with a little tickle.
      — ad for Tickle deodorant from
                               Bristol-Myers

Allie wasn't tired after dropping Olivia off at her hotel. In fact, she was wired. And the idea of going back to her apartment and the pile of mail on the table, the half-eaten chicken and cashews from China's Good Fortune in the fridge that she wasn't sure was still safe to eat, and thirty-eight minutes of the latest episode of *America's Next Top Model* (the first thirty-eight minutes — she'd sat on the DVR remote without realizing it and had shut it off so now she wouldn't know how it ended until next week) didn't appeal to her at all.

So she took the long way back, popping in a depressing old Jackson Browne CD and driving up Woodley Road to the National Cathedral singing along about a photograph that captured the moment right after a smile. She pulled up in front of the old herb cottage and put the car in park.

This was probably stupid. Perhaps even dangerous, given the town she was in and the hour. But this was a place she'd loved since she was a child and her grandfather used to bring her to the Flower Market here the first Friday of every May. She couldn't come here without feeling nostalgic and yet, in some way, warm.

She got out of the car, ignoring the voice in her head that told her not to do this.

That voice was *always* in her head, telling her not to do pretty much everything. *Don't drive on the highway,* it told her, *it's too dangerous. Don't fly overseas. Don't get salad from the grocery store; it might have E. coli.*

She'd learned a long time ago that she was better off ignoring the voice.

Ironically, she locked her car, then stopped and deliberately turned back to unlock it. If she was going to take a chance on being here alone at this hour, her car could, too, damn it.

Besides, if she had to run for it, it would be better to leap into an unlocked car than to have to stop and fumble with the electronic fob, probably locking it over and over instead of unlocking it.

See, she was cautious enough to think of *that*. She wasn't completely without common sense.

She walked through the Bishop's Garden, a maze of boxwoods that smelled of a hundred years of earth, and green, and beauty. It was a pathway filled with large flagstones, winding around through the foliage. There were little coves along the way — a garden bench here, a wrought-iron chair there — but she was on her way to the prize: the small, wooden gazebo, called the Shadow House, in the center of the maze.

When she was little, it had seemed almost impossible to wind through and finally get to the gazebo, but now she wondered how she could ever have gotten lost. Anyone who could see over the bushes could see exactly where it was and how to get there, though it required a bit of dodging through the low tree boughs.

Maybe that was the key right there. When she was little, her grandfather had delighted in taking her hand and winding her this way and that, pointing out all the little flowers, creatures, and bugs along the way.

Now, even though he had gone on to be God's own gardener, she almost felt he was with her, guiding her through the earthy, dark path to the best thinking spot in the world.

She climbed into the gazebo, her feet thudding dully on the wet wood, and sat down.

Peace took over. The artificial environment of the hotel melted away, along with the sequins and the makeup and the falsely smiling faces and their pretense at recognition, and finally Allie was alone with her own feelings.

It was strange how little she'd thought of Kevin tonight. That was the first thing that struck her. After two years with him, she might have imagined she'd feel something more than anger at his betrayal and annoyance that his timing had left her to go to her reunion alone.

But that was pretty much all she'd felt. No heartache, no regret at lost opportunities, no wish that he'd stepped up to the plate.

It wasn't that she was heartless. Heaven knew she'd been faithful and loyal to Kevin. She'd never treated him with anything less than the utmost respect, and as long as he did the same, she could see spending forever with him.

Happily(ish) ever after.

It was that *ish* that got to her.

She sighed and leaned back against the hardwood arm rail of the gazebo. The sky was in plain and glorious view. The clouds were beginning to part and the moon was touching their edges, lighting them up like the opening scene after the credits from some impossibly romantic 1940s movie.

Kevin would have thought that was a weird analogy.

And there it was. He didn't get her. And she, to be fair, must not have gotten him, because *something* had made him turn to Charlotte even though he had a perfectly faithful, intelligent, kind girlfriend of child-bearing age (barely) who was, on the surface, perfect for him.

Maybe her incessant Cary Grant references had annoyed him, as much as his lack of comprehension had annoyed her. Maybe he hated her Cheesy Beef Macaroni Dinner as much as she hated the rare tuna steaks he loved so much. Maybe just the sound of the opening strains of the Beatles' "I Feel Fine" made him want to tear his hair out the way the endless jams of anything Dave Matthews made her want to.

In short, maybe they were just wrong for each other and there wasn't much more to it than that.

Why *should* she feel remorse for losing

something she hadn't actually *really* wanted?

So what *did* she want?

Now *that* was the question. She wanted to be happy, and she wasn't. She wished she'd stayed thin and pretty, like she used to be, but she hadn't. She wanted to go back in time and wow everyone at the reunion, the way Olivia had, but she couldn't.

And she wanted to tell Noah that Vickie was a nasty piece of work who hadn't changed since high school, but she wouldn't.

Hell, if he'd tried to tell her the same about Kevin, she wouldn't have believed him, either. Or, to be more realistic, if he'd tried to tell her that Kevin was sleeping with Charlotte while Allie was out working, she would have said he was crazy.

Even though, as it turned out, he would have been right.

No one could have made her believe it beforehand.

So this was like one of those bad time-travel movies, where you just *know* what's going to happen, it's predestined, but there's no way to stop the stupid guy from running (or driving or skateboarding or surfing) straight into his misfortune.

Clouds moved across the moon again and Allie heard a few fat raindrops hit the wooden roof of the gazebo.

She didn't mind. A long time ago she'd heard that spring rains brought negative ions with them, and that negative ions were capable of improving moods.

She could use that right now.

She took a long, cleansing breath and studied the intricate architecture of the cathedral reaching into the sky. The base lights illuminated the structure, casting shadows, lighting carved angels, making menacing the expressions of the gargoyles on the first roof tier. It was so beautiful it made something inside of her ache. Even while she sat here, feeling unafraid, she also felt painfully alone.

The idea of "soul mates" was something that Allie had rejected for a long time. Sure, once she and Olivia thought *they* were soul mates, but they were kids then, and spent so much time together that it wasn't surprising when they finished each other's sentences. But they weren't — they were friends.

Then again, she and Noah could finish each other's sentences, too. Would she have said they were soul mates?

She thought about it. Really thought about it. Because the first answer that came to her — fast and sure — was *yes*. They'd known each other forever, they could trust each other *completely,* and they had that same kind of shorthand she and Olivia had had once — the kind of understanding that didn't require explanation all the time.

Now Vickie was going to ruin all of that.

It wasn't as if Allie had been unaware *someone* would come along someday. And it wasn't as if she had been unaware that that *someone* wouldn't be her — the cliché of friendships being ruined by sex was so common that just about every sitcom had used it by this point.

It was just that, even though she'd known it in the back of her mind, she'd never fully *believed* there would be someone in her relationship with Noah other than her and Noah.

It was stupid, really. She'd banked on him being a serial dater forever, and no one — not even Warren Beatty — kept that up.

That it was Vickie Freedman — of *all* people — who entered the picture was just the icing on the cake. Anyone else and Allie would have been sad for herself, but the fact that it was Vickie made her worry about Noah in addition to feeling sorry for herself.

And there was no way she could save him.

But there was nothing she could do about it. One thing she had learned in her thirty-eight years was that no one ever believed anyone else about the person they were sleeping with. That was something that *always* needed to be found out for oneself.

And sitting here, or at home, or anywhere, moaning about how unfair it was and how *stupid* Noah was wasn't going to change things for Allie *or* Noah one iota.

If things went as they should, Noah would realize Vickie was a bitch before too long, and the world would spin right on its axis again.

Until then . . . she needed to move on.

The fact that she didn't have a fulfilling job to throw herself into just made it worse.

And the fact that she was *completely* jealous of Olivia for coming to the reunion all gorgeous and youthful-looking, and polished and, on top of all that, having Allie's own dream job was also just a symptom of how bad things were in her own life.

So, instead of putting so much energy into being jealous of, and overprotective of, others, she needed to restructure her life. Or at least the way she thought about her life.

She needed a life makeover. She needed to get control of the things that had troubled her for so long and she needed to turn them around.

It would start tomorrow.

■ ■ ■ ■

Had there been a car rental office open nearby, Olivia would have rented something — anything — and gotten out of town that night. A pickup truck, a bike, a camel — anything.

As it was, she stopped at the business center of the Wardman Park and tried in vain to find a late flight out, but the last one had left ten minutes before she got there.

It was silly to be so desperate, she knew that. She *was,* after all, in one of the most beautiful hotels in one of the most beautiful cities in the world.

And she'd been to almost all of them at this point.

But it was hard to argue logic with emotions. It didn't matter how great the hotel was, or how innocuous the reunion had been (once all was said and done), or even how far in the past her unpleasant memories were of a place a good ten miles from here.

In a way, it all felt like it was right here, right now.

It was hot. Her room was stuffy. She turned on the air conditioner but ended up with a blast of cold air pounding against her. No matter how she shifted in bed, the air felt like it went right to her bones.

So finally she turned the whole system off and opened the windows. That was one advantage of staying in an older hotel — the windows still opened.

She turned out the light and returned to her bed, breathing in the gentle breeze that lifted the curtains as it passed. It carried the mingled scents of rain, boxwoods, and exhaust, and reminded her that she once loved this town and never more than when the weather started to get warm and two hundred years' worth of landscaping came to life again.

The clock said it was ten minutes until midnight. She was wide-awake.

This promised to be a very, *very* long night.

Ten

You'll be glowing tonight.
— ad for Sun-In

Despite a lifetime that suggested this was exactly what would happen, Olivia was, nevertheless, surprised to return to her apartment Sunday morning to find that her mother had had an overnight gentleman caller.

"Olivia, this is Bob," her mother said, scooping pancakes onto Olivia's Fiesta ware plates.

"Rob," he corrected, keeping his eyes on Olivia. He was short and compact, with a ruddy face and eyes like those of a small, twitchy animal. "And I have to say, I would have known you anywhere." He wagged a stubby finger. "I know where you get your looks, young lady."

Olivia was speechless for a moment, then looked from Rob to her mother and said,

"Thank you." To her mother, it was, "Mom, could I have a word with you in the other room?"

"Uh-oh, am I in trouble?" Caroline trilled.

"*Now,* Mom." She pushed through the swinging kitchen door and paced in the living room until her mother joined her.

"That was very rude," Caroline rasped in a stage whisper. "You're going to make our guest feel unwelcome!"

"*Our* guest? Are you kidding? He's *your* guest. In *my* apartment. Where did you meet this guy anyway?"

"Olivia! He'll hear you!"

"I don't give a damn." Olivia was exasperated. "Just tell me you didn't marry him yet."

Caroline's jaw dropped. "Olivia Rose Pelham, you take that back this instant."

She wouldn't. "Who is he, Mom?"

"He's a nice man."

"Who *is* he?"

"He's my cousin."

It took Olivia a moment. Of all the comebacks her mother could have conjured, this was one of the better ones. "He's your *what?*"

"Cousin. I think." Caroline looked off into space, tapping her fingertips against her face as she spoke. "He was married to Aunt Cas-

174

sandra's niece, who was my cousin-in-law, so" — she looked at Olivia — "well, technically perhaps he's my cousin-in-law once removed. I'm not sure. What are your cousin-in-law's spouses?"

"Strangers," Olivia said. "But they're usually *not* strangers sleeping in my apartment."

"Yes, I can see how that was surprising, but he was at Aunt Cassandra's yesterday, dropping off her groceries, which was so sweet, then he offered to give me a ride back into the city so I didn't have to rely on public transportation."

"Then he stayed overnight." Olivia felt weary. "So where's his wife?"

"They're divorced."

"Mom!"

"What?"

"So this guy isn't your cousin-in-whatever or anything like it anymore. He's just some guy, sitting in my kitchen, drinking my coffee, who used to be married to some distant relative at some point who-knows-when. He could have been a psychopath!" She lowered her voice. "Jesus, Mom, he still could be. *Why* is he *here?*"

"Well, if you *must* know, it's because he had a *friend* he thought I should meet. Someone who lives here, up in the East Side somewhere."

Olivia sat down and dropped her head into her hands. How many times in her life would her mother behave like a fool in the name of finding romance? When would it stop? Seventy? Eighty? A hundred? Would it stop at death, even? "And did you meet this mystery man?"

"As it happened, he was out of town."

"And Rob —"

"Bob."

"— is staying here until his friend gets back?"

"Of course not, don't be silly. He lives right across the river, in Harrison."

It was hard to be patient with this, it really was. Olivia could have come home to some horrendous bloody scene in her apartment and never known exactly what had happened. If this guy was normal — and the jury was still way out on that — it was just lucky.

But why would a normal sixtysomething man have driven her mother here and stayed over instead of driving home when it was just twenty minutes away? Even if he really *did* want to introduce her to his friend, which in itself was really weird, why stick around after it's become evident that the friend is out of town?

Whatever the answer, Olivia didn't trust

her mother to handle it from here. "I'm getting rid of him," she said, moving toward the kitchen door.

"Wait! What about his friend?"

"At this point, I'm just glad his friend isn't here, too." She pushed through the door back to the kitchen, nearly clipping Rob in the face as she did so. He must have been listening.

She didn't care.

"Rob, I appreciate your bringing my mom home last night, I really do, but I'm afraid we're going to be very busy today, packing up, so I'm going to have to ask you to leave."

"Packing up?" Rob asked, shooting a puzzled look at Caroline.

In her peripheral vision, Olivia saw her mother shrug.

"Lease is up next week," Olivia said. "Fortunately the place came furnished, but Mother and I are going to have our hands full still packing clothes and books and so on. So" — she tried to look rueful — "if you don't mind . . . ? Unless you want to help move boxes."

"No, no!" Rob sprang back, his small, wiry body like a coil. "I need to get home myself. Leanne is waiting."

"Leanne?" Caroline asked.

"My wife."

"I thought you were divorced," Olivia said, flashing A Look in her mother's direction.

"*Audrey* and I are divorced. Leanne and I have been married for two years."

What was with her family? For all of them life was just one big game of Marital Chairs.

"Audrey," her mother said to her, triumphant. "You remember cousin Audrey."

Olivia shook her head. "No."

"She went by the name Mary Pat when you knew her," Rob clarified.

"You remember cousin Mary Pat, don't you?" Olivia said pointedly to her mother.

"She's not your cousin, strictly speaking," Rob began. "But she's an old friend of the family. Close enough to be a relative. Almost."

Caroline finally looked like she got it. "Thank you again for the ride home, Bob, but as my daughter said, we really do need to get packing."

"Would you like to have dinner sometime?" He switched his gaze to Olivia. "Either of you?"

Olivia rolled her eyes and left the room. Behind her, she heard her mother declining but adding, "Do keep in touch. Let me write down my e-mail address for you . . ."

"You could have been killed."

"He's family. I hardly think he'd kill me."

"Family? You don't even know who he was married to."

"Of course I do, it was Mary Ruth."

"Pat, Mom, it was Mary Pat, and *she's* not the one Dad was related to. *You* weren't related to any of them, and don't think for a moment he wasn't aware of that."

"Now, Olivia —"

"And anyway, you don't know who she is any more than you know who Mary Ruth or Audrey or Peewee Picklepooch is."

"There is no Peewee —"

"Bringing a strange man here was dangerous, both for you and for me. And, for God's sake, for my *stuff.* My jewelry, my clothes, my electronics. He could have robbed me blind!"

"Not with me here!"

"Mom." Olivia tried to be patient, but she felt anything but. "It's been a hell of a long time since I had a roommate, but even then we both knew better than to bring a stranger into our apartment. That's something you need to learn *now,* not just for me but for you, too. In fact, more for you than for me, because you won't be living here forever and you need to learn to take care of yourself."

Caroline looked wounded. "Are you kicking me out?"

Damn it. How did this get to Olivia still, after all these years? "No, Mom, I'm not kicking you out." What would it take? "I'm saying you need to be a lot more careful, no matter what. Regardless of where you are."

Her mother gave a nod. "I see. And while I still think you're wrong to be that paranoid about family members, I will respect your wishes while I am staying in your home."

Good old Caroline. She wasn't going to admit to being wrong. Even when it was patently obvious and she was changing her own behavior to reflect it, it still had to be presented as a choice of consideration for others, not as the necessity it was.

For Olivia, stuck in her role as Dutiful Daughter, it was easier to let it pass than to try to get her mother to concede the point.

They both knew who was right.

But only one of them would admit it.

"So no more strange men here," Olivia clarified. Her mother had a way of slipping things in under vague technicalities.

"Not overnight, no."

"I'm sorry?"

Caroline gave a little bell of a laugh. "I do plan to date, of course."

"But you said your whole point in coming here was to *stop* looking for romance and start accepting yourself for who you are. Alone."

"Well . . . yes. I'm working on that right now. And feeling better, as a matter of fact." Olivia straightened righteously. "But I'm still in my prime, you know. I'm hardly an old horse that needs to be put out to pasture."

Whether or not she was still in her prime, as far as dating was concerned . . . well, Olivia didn't want to have that argument. She didn't want to be the meanie who called attention to everything Caroline undoubtedly already knew about the market for mature men.

Specifically the fact that mature men with any means and looks at all were probably more likely to go for Olivia or perhaps even someone younger.

Now *that* was a depressing thought. Somewhere along the way Olivia and her mother had both gone over the hill.

"No men here at all," Olivia corrected.

"You're not saying I'm too old for love, surely?" Caroline asked, her voice trembling slightly.

God, it was tempting. There was so much Olivia wanted to say and now would be the perfect moment, in a way, to lay it all on her mother. The truth, with no varnishing.

But the truth was too harsh.

"No, Mom," Olivia lied at last. "I'm not saying that at all. I just want you to be careful. It's a jungle out there. You may have heard. You need to have a few basic rules down before you do anything else."

"Basic rules of dating?" Caroline repeated, as if she couldn't believe Olivia would presume to know more about it than she did.

Olivia didn't. "Of safety, Mom. *Safety.* First, dial star and then six and seven before you call a blind date so he can't trace the call back and find out where you live. Second, don't have him pick you up or drop you off here because that will probably give him an idea of where you live."

"Oh." Caroline looked relieved. "Those are good suggestions. And I'm glad we're not really moving. This is a lovely apartment you have, truly."

Olivia nodded. "That was just to throw old Rob off the track."

"Bob."

"No, Rob. His name was Rob."

Caroline shook her head. "No, dear, his name is *Bob.* As in short for Robert."

"Rob is short for Robert, too."

"But it's not his name."

Olivia threw her hands in the air. *"Third,"*

she said pointedly, "get his name right off the bat. It will help us when we're filing the police report . . ."

ELEVEN

More where you need it,
less where you don't.
> — ad for Silkience Shampoo

It didn't matter that half the people milling around the room were bigger than Allie, she did *not* want to get on a scale in front of *anyone,* much less a crowd.

Yes, they made it private.

Somewhat.

But weighing in, it seemed to her, was the kind of thing one should only do in the privacy of one's home, with a large glass of vodka on hand in order to ease the bad news.

The pools had opened a couple of weeks ago, over Memorial Day weekend, so chances were that most of the people here had experienced the same shock and pain she had — that of putting on a bathing suit for the first time in a year and going out in public.

Somehow, going to the pool didn't hold the same excitement as it used to, back when she was eight.

She stood in line for the scale at the Weight Watchers meeting, feeling like a doe in hunting season, looking left and right for the perfect escape. Because she was *not* going to go up there and have a stranger record her weight, maybe even say it out loud for others to hear.

At best, it would amount to a single night of humiliation, and at worst, it would be week after week of coming and being shamed into losing weight.

Most people were getting hearty congratulations, even for a quarter of a pound down. What happened if you *didn't* lose weight one week? What if you *gained?* Were you flogged publicly?

She could see how that could conceivably be motivating, if not actually *fun.*

"Next."

Could a person get kicked out of Weight Watchers? If you just flat-out failed, couldn't do it, didn't do it, gained a pound a week, or even if you just stayed steady and didn't lose anything — what happened then?

"Excuse me, Miss . . . ?"

185

Maybe they put your picture up behind the counter, like businesses did with bad checks.

Someone poked her back and she whipped around, startled.

"You're up," a large man said in a faint Jersey accent. He pointed a sausagelike finger in front of her.

"What?" She turned around and saw the scale was empty and there was a woman with a clipboard next to it, looking at her expectantly. "Oh." She moved forward, like she was going before a firing squad.

This was seriously uncomfortable.

She hadn't even been to the doctor in years because she didn't want to get weighed; why would she do it here, and now, and under these circumstances?

Because she wanted to look good, that was why. And be healthy and blah blah blah, but really it was about looking good. She wanted to be hot again. She wanted to be annoyed with construction workers who yelled foul things when she walked past, because their current silence was far more upsetting.

Then there was that one guy in Georgetown who'd turned off the jackhammer and watched her cross the street before starting to sing "Baby Got Back." *I like big butts and I can not lie . . ."*

She took another step toward the scale. "Can I get on backward?" she asked.

"Why?" the woman asked.

"I don't really want to know the number. Maybe you can just write it down for my file, but not tell me. Oh, and don't gasp or otherwise indicate it, either."

The woman smiled, revealing a gap between her front teeth. Allie's brother, Ross, had had a poster of the model Lauren Hutton on his wall a thousand years ago and she had the same gap.

Beauty had all kinds of definitions.

"Like at the doctor's office?" the woman asked.

"Exactly!"

"Sorry, we're not here to administer the correct dosage of antibiotics. You're going to have to face it, own it, and take *tremendous* pleasure in watching that number go down."

What if it doesn't? Allie ignored the pitiful voice in the back of her mind and instead asked, "Is it not possible for you to just record it in silence for a few weeks until my pants maybe get a little looser and I feel like I can handle it?"

The woman shook her head. "It only hurts for a minute."

"The first time's always the hardest," the man behind Allie said. She turned to see him and he stuck out his hand. "Glenn Steckman. Lifetime member." He was tall and broad even apart from being a little heavy in the middle. With his shock of white hair and smiling visage, he looked a little like Santa Claus's older, taller, slimmer brother.

"Allie Denty."

"Yeah, Allie, like I was saying, the first time is the hardest. Everyone says it. But like Arlene said, as soon as you lose even half a pound and you see you can do it, you feel a whole lot better 'bout yourself."

At this point it didn't matter what Allie thought about staying or coming back, she couldn't spit in the eye of all this goodwill. "You're probably right. Okay." She took off her shoes. "I'll do it."

"Good for you!"

"I'm not sure about *that*." She took off her bracelet and laid it on the counter. "But I'm going for it." She took off her watch and caught Arlene's eye. "Hey, I'm not taking credit for one gram more than I have to." She reached up and looped her earrings out.

"I'm afraid we don't have any place private enough for you to actually strip," Arlene said, looking a little concerned.

"I've already thought of that," Allie said, taking a rather heavy barrette out of her hair and wondering, for a moment, how much her hair weighed and if she should get it cut. "I'm adding four pounds for my clothes."

Arlene looked dubious.

"Okay," Allie said, anticipating the argument, "but consider this: These are heavy sweatpants. I chose them specifically because I plan to wear the exact same thing for every weigh-in, and since I don't want to freeze to death in the winter, I picked something heavy. Besides, even if they don't weigh four pounds, I'm taking that window with me to every weigh-in."

"All right." Arlene smiled. "Everyone seems to have a system of one sort or the other."

"That's mine." Allie moved onto the scale, closed her eyes tightly, and said, "Give it to me."

Arlene said a number that was a good ten pounds higher than Allie had feared, even *with* the four pounds for clothes.

She felt like she was going to faint.

"Are you sure?" she asked, hearing the tinge of hysteria in her voice.

"It's not so bad," Glenn said behind her.

He'd heard! Everyone had probably heard! Allie could feel the color draining from her face.

"I'm lookin' at you," Glenn said, splaying his arms. "It *can't* be that bad."

So he hadn't heard. He'd only heard her reaction.

"Are you okay?" Arlene asked, looking alarmed. She set her clipboard down. "I'll get you some water."

"No, I'm fine." Allie tried to collect herself but she felt like she couldn't breathe. This was horrible. How had she let things get so bad? How had she put on pound after pound after pound after pound without realizing she was out of control? If she'd known sooner, she might have been able to stop it, get back to her real weight sooner.

Except that this was her real weight.

For others it might have been a joke weight. The Thanksgiving night punch line to *Oh, my God, I am so full, I feel like I've gained twenty-five pounds.*

Allie weighed twenty-five pounds more than she should.

Five bags of flour. Twenty-five packages of butter. The grocery store checker would have to put those in multiple bags and she'd have to make multiple trips to the car to put it in, but here it all was, on her stomach, her hips, her butt . . .

"I can't believe it," she breathed.

"Don't worry, kid," Arlene said, putting a reassuring hand on her. "You're in the right place. And you've taken the first step. The weight will be gone before you know it."

There was a certain amount of truth to the contention that the pain of the weigh-in was worst at first.

A couple of days after the hell of her first Weight Watchers meeting — and the truth had been hell — Allie was still determined to lose the excess weight no matter what.

So she went to Target and purchased a digital scale (one that had fractions included, so if she lost .01 pound she could celebrate it), some resistance bands (since the talk of the meeting had been about them and how great they were for building muscle, which in turn burned fat), a case of bottled water, and some of the various emergency snack foods that had other members' seal of approval, and if there was one thing fat people knew, it was what tasted good.

Getting the snack foods was key. Allie was nothing if not realistic about her appetite: There would come a time when she wanted benefit-free tasty junk food, so she had to have a reasonable facsimile at the ready or else she was in danger of eating the real (and good) thing.

She did not want any huge remorse from a middle-of-the-night trip to Giant or Safeway.

When she got back to her apartment, the answering machine was blinking. For one crazy moment, she hoped Kevin had called to apologize and grovel and beg to somehow make life the way it had been a year ago, a month ago even, before she had known that Noah was dating the Worst Person in the World and that she, herself, was a big fat pig.

But it wasn't Kevin. The first two messages were from Temporaries, Inc. In the first, they offered her a job starting tomorrow and lasting a week that paid almost twice what she normally got. Pam, over at the Temporaries office, liked Allie and usually gave her first dibs on the really sweet jobs.

Unfortunately, when Allie hadn't gotten back to her quickly enough, she'd left another message, bemoaning the fact that Allie's cell phone was off — she'd turned it off for the Weight Watchers meeting — and that she'd had to give the job to someone else.

Probably Vickie Freedman.

The third message was the clipped end of a recording imploring her to hold for an "important message." Apparently unmoved, her answering machine had opted *not* to hold past thirty seconds so she'd have to either guess at which bill was late or unpaid or wait for them to call back.

The fourth message was from her mother.

"Hello there, I'm calling to let you know there's a wine and cheese event at the Kennedy Center next Thursday at seven. There's a concert on the Millennium stage first. A woman playing toy pianos, I hear it's marvelous. Anyway, it's all in the evening, that is, don't worry. Let me know if you're interested!"

She'd been to one of those wine and cheese tastings at the Kennedy Center before, it was wonderful! But — oh, no — she'd have to look up the points value of wine. And cheese. And she'd have to decide from there if she had the willpower to go.

Old Allie would have decided to go and just "forget the diet and enjoy life for one night" but New Allie was smarter than that. And hopefully New Allie was, or would be, *thinner* than that.

In fact, New Allie didn't even need to look up the points values to know that a little wine would beget a lot of cheese, which she would, in turn, need to wash down with a lot of wine, and . . . ultimately a lot of guilt and self-loathing.

She made a sad mental note to decline the invitation.

She started to pick up the phone when the machine played a fifth message, this one from Noah.

"Hey, it's like, I don't know" — there was the sound of him fumbling a little — "six-thirty. Between six-thirty and seven. I'm out. Thought I could run by and talk to you. Well, that's the point. I sort of need to talk to you. Give me a call."

That was weird. He sounded upset. Or something. She looked at the wall clock. It was five after eight. She dialed his number and pushed *talk,* wondering if the moment had passed or if she'd even be able to get ahold of him.

"Allie."

"Noah, is everything okay?"

"Sure! Great! Why? What have you heard?"

"Your message on my answering machine. It sounded . . . well, never mind how it sounded. Is everything okay?"

"Fine. Why? What have you heard?"

She laughed and sighed at the same time. "Joke's getting old, Noah."

"Sorry. I have another one. These three nuns walk into a bar and one of them says —"

"Have you been drinking?" She carried the phone into the kitchen and opened the fridge to look for some Diet Coke. One of them needed to be awake and sober for this conversation.

"I don't think that's how it goes."

"It isn't. The nun was drinking. I'm asking if *you* are drinking."

"Depends what you mean by *drinking.*"

Oh, he'd been drinking, all right. Was it too much to hope it was a postmortem blast because he'd dumped stupid Vickie? "Opening your mouth and imbibing liquid. Alcoholic liquid."

"Then yes." She imagined him nodding. "By that definition, I have been drinking. Yes."

"Then I'll ask again, and if you give me the same stupid answer, I'll be pissed. Seriously. What's wrong?"

"Nothing!"

"You don't call me, drunk, from a bar, denying anything's wrong unless *something* is wrong, Noah. Please. Now tell me what it is."

"It's complicated."

"Are you alone?"

There was a pause. "Nah, the place is full of people."

"What place?"

"Durty Nellies."

He hated that place. Ever since the fire that had stopped it from being good old Durty Nellies and turned it into some slick yuppie bar with a new name. "Are any of the people there actually *with* you?"

"Not actually, no." He sighed, his breath making a loud hiss on the phone. "Listen, we need to talk."

"Okay. Let me come down there."

"No, no! I'll go up to your place."

"How?"

"I have my car."

No way. She wasn't going to let him drive like this. If she had to physically block his car in, she would. "Are you parked in the Hyatt lot across the street?"

"Yup. Give me ten, no, give me twenty minutes and —"

"I'll be there. You are *not* driving in this condition."

"I'm fine!"

Tomorrow, or next week, or in a month, she'd lord that absurdity over his head, but at the moment, she needed to keep him from getting defensive so she could get to him before he got behind the wheel.

"You're also in the place with the best chicken wings in D.C.," she improvised. She hated chicken wings, stringy little bony things, so they'd be easy to resist. "Order me some extra hot ones for carryout and I'll come get you *and* the wings."

"You hate chicken wings."

"I do not!"

"Yes you do. You're just trying to keep me from driving."

Drunk, maybe. Stupid, no. "You got me, Noah. I don't want you to drive and in the morning you'll be glad I felt that way. So will you just wait for me to get there? It'll be ten minutes."

"Okay."

"That was easy."

"I'm a little buzzed, Al. I'm not dumb. Not completely dumb. No, wait, I might be *somewhat . . .*"

Thirty-five minutes later he was sitting on her sofa drinking coffee that he desperately needed.

"Remember that time we went cow tipping?" he asked after his second cup.

Cow tipping was legendary in northwest Maryland — drunk teenagers allegedly liked to run into pastures where cows were sleeping standing up and tip them over.

Neither Allie nor, to her knowledge, Noah had ever done it.

"We didn't go cow tipping," she said. "But we talked about it a lot."

"Yeah, we did, remember? We went? And we . . . tipped them over?"

"No, Noah. We didn't."

He contemplated that. "We should have, then. It sounds fun."

"It really doesn't. I mean, think about it. If nothing else, it's mean. *And* it has the potential for real danger. Who knows how fast those cows can stand up again?"

"They could be fast," he agreed.

"They could be *really* fast."

"Here's the thing," he said, holding the coffee mug in two hands and staring into it.

She was ready for more cow-tipping philosophy, so when he said, "I have a situation I need to talk to you about and it's not going to be easy," it threw her for a major loop.

"You know you can talk to me about anything," she said, hoping she wasn't about to find out the one thing he *couldn't* talk to her about.

He met her eyes and nodded. "Usually."

"But this is different?"

He gave a humorless laugh. "Oh, yeah."

"Noah, you're kind of scaring me. Out with it."

He inhaled deeply, held his breath for a moment, then expelled with the words "Do you have a beer?"

She eyed him for a moment, considering the options of playing Mom versus being a friend. "Are you staying over?"

"I can get a cab."

She held out her hand. "Give me your keys."

"I'd have to walk forty minutes just to get to my car!"

"Whereupon you might still be drunk. *Or,* knowing you, when I'm not looking you might whip a twenty out of your wallet and take a cab there so you could arrive both sooner and drunker." She shook her head. "Give me your keys."

"But I need to get my car tomorrow."

"Then I'll take you to it tomorrow. After some coffee."

He reached into his pocket and took out a key chain containing three keys and an electronic fob. "Here." He tossed them to her. "Satisfied?"

"I am, actually." She took them with her into the kitchen, hid them out of sight in a drawer, and took two Corona Lights out of the fridge, opened them, squirted lime juice from a plastic lime into each, and took them back into the living room. "Sorry, I don't

199

have any real lime slices." She handed him one.

"Last time I come here."

"Who could blame you? Now" — she sat down on the chair opposite him and looked into his eyes — "what the fuck is going on?"

"You look really pretty tonight."

Completely scrubbed of makeup and wearing a very old pair of sweats from Rutgers with an equally faded MARY IS MY HOMEGIRL T-shirt, she knew, without a doubt, that he was full of shit.

"Okay, are you trying to charm me into doing something? Is that what this is all about?"

"I wish." He rubbed his bleary eyes. "That would be so easy."

"I'm such a soft touch."

He looked over at her. It was only for a moment, but something about the way he raked his gaze across her quickened her pulse.

"So," she said, erasing the moment even while she wanted to examine it. "Are you going to talk or do I have to keep guessing?"

"Have a drink." He raised his bottle to her, and took a long swig himself. "Really, Al." He nodded in her direction and looked sober for the first time in almost an hour.

"You're gonna need it."

Her chest tightened. "You're not sick, right? Because all this lead-up sounds like one of those movies where the guy with a heart of gold is dying, and if something bad like terminal illness is coming I wish you'd just —"

"I'm getting married."

"— tell me." She stopped.

Rewound the words in her head.

Couldn't believe them.

"You're kidding."

He shook his head. "I'm getting married," he said again, like he was just trying on the words himself and they didn't quite fit.

How long was it? Five seconds? Five minutes? It felt like five hours before she could wrap her mouth around the question to which she already knew the horrible answer. "To whom?"

"Tori," he said, and again he raised his beer. "Tori and I are getting married. So . . . how about a toast?"

She drank.

Twelve
TENTH GRADE

Sensual, but not too far from
innocence . . .
— ad for Jontue perfume

"Sit still."

"It stings!"

Allie kept going, impatient. "You have to
go through a little pain to get gorgeous."

"That's stupid. And it's not true."

"It *is* true. There's a reason people use
that cliché, you know. Clichés have to come
from some truth."

"Let me wash it off."

"I haven't even finished putting it *on*." Allie scooped her fingers into the pot of
Queen Helene Mint Julep face mask and
patted it onto Olivia's forehead. "There.
Now you just have to wait for like ten
minutes. Honestly, Liv, this stuff has done
wonders for my skin."

It was true that Allie's skin had cleared up
quite a bit, but Olivia also knew she'd been

202

to a dermatologist who had put her on tetracycline and that was probably what had helped more than anything.

Olivia raised a hand to her face, then drew it back and looked at the green sludge on her fingertips. It wasn't like any color she'd ever seen in nature. She almost couldn't call it green. "I don't think I can stand it."

"It gets better," Allie assured her. "Not worse. Well, it gets better, then it dries and you can't talk or laugh or your face will crack and *that* is excruciating. But it won't sting anymore."

How was this green crap going to give her skin the dewy glow Allie had promised? It seemed like all it was going to do was make her blotchy and red from the sting.

But Allie had been so confident, so *enthusiastic,* about this makeover day she was having for Olivia that Olivia didn't want to hurt her feelings.

Besides, it had been fun having someone devote an entire afternoon to her. Everything they did tonight was for her. Allie had even made sure they had her favorite frozen pepperoni pizza for dinner before they went to the school's December Teen Club dance at eight.

From Allie's brother's room, they could

hear Foreigner on the stereo, singing "Cold as Ice."

They were going stag to the dance, together, and they'd decided to act like they were confident with that.

But they had to keep reminding each other that they were confident with that.

The truth was they'd just started high school in the fall, and suddenly they were mixed in with kids from other schools, kids who were older and some who were even about to go to college. There was a lot to feel insecure about, and though Allie was beginning to adapt, when Olivia finally admitted to her that she *was* insecure — about her looks, about her wardrobe, about the fact that no guy had ever asked her out — Allie had taken matters in hand.

She'd decided to fix Olivia.

It was easy for her to be charitable, she'd already had three boyfriends and she'd broken up with Chris McClure two or three weeks ago without any concern at all that the holiday dance was coming — that the holidays in general were coming — and she would be boyfriendless for it.

"Is the sting going away?" Allie asked, turning on her radio. The Carpenters were singing about Christmas cards and lights on the tree.

"Kind of." It was better than the Miracle Whip mask Allie had made her use first with the idea that it would "roll off the dead skin," which was a completely gross thought.

And even grosser when it worked.

"Now use this. The cotton balls are in the drawer." She handed Olivia a bottle of Bonne Bell Ten-O-Six lotion. There was no point in warning her it would sting, too — it would just stop her from using it and everyone knew it did awesome things to your skin.

"Ouch!" Olivia cried as soon as it hit her skin.

"It feels better in a second."

"It better." Olivia waved her hands in front of her face.

"See?" Allie hummed along with the song as she opened her closet doors and took out several shirts, including the dark emerald wrap top that had been her favorite throughout ninth grade. "I told you it wouldn't hurt for long."

Olivia thought Allie was probably too big in the chest to wear it now, but she decided not to say anything unless it was so bad she had to stop Allie from flat-out embarrassing herself.

Allie came over and stood in front of where Olivia was sitting at her vanity. "Now.

I have another suggestion. And I really, really want you to trust me."

Olivia tried to frown but her skin pulled under what remained of the mask and it hurt. "With what?" she asked through barely parted lips.

"I think you should let me cut your hair."

"What?" Ouch!

"Calm down, you're cracking. But listen, I'm serious. You haven't had your hair cut into a style in, like, forever. You've never had it styled. I think you'd look really good with bangs and my mom's friend is a hairdresser and she told me how to do it."

It was a coincidence, because Olivia had seen a picture of Cindy Harrell on the cover of *Seventeen* with stick-straight hair, just like Olivia's, cut into nice, even bangs. But what if Allie screwed up? What if she cut them too short and she looked like a second-grader?

"One minute," she tried to say, holding up her finger. She got up and went to the bathroom to rinse her face.

This was a conversation that required facial mobility.

She splashed and rubbed and rinsed and when she was through, sure enough, her skin had taken on a nice, pink bloom.

"Put some of this on," Allie said, seemingly having come out of nowhere. She handed Olivia a bottle of Milk+6 lotion.

Obediently, Olivia smoothed the lotion on. Where this kind of thing was concerned, Allie was, by far, the expert. There was no denying it.

The lotion disappeared into her skin and she still looked good.

It felt kind of like a miracle.

Except, that is, for the plastic bag she had on her head to cover the Clairol Condition cream Allie had also made her slather on. It smelled great but felt like slime.

"Looks good," Allie commented expectantly.

"It does." Still looking in the mirror, Olivia touched her cheek. It felt soft. Not dry, like paper, the way it usually did.

"So what do you say? About the bangs?"

She'd trusted Allie this far, she might as well trust her the rest of the way.

"Okay." She swallowed. "Just make *sure* you don't cut them too short."

"I won't. Come on, I'm not stupid." She went to the tub and turned on the shower. "Rinse and I'll go get the scissors."

Olivia got into the shower, closed the jungle-themed shower curtain, and tipped her head back in the hot water. It felt great. It *smelled* great. This was turning out to be

207

a really fun day. She'd been nervous for a week about the dance, changing her mind about going over and over again, but today for the first time she felt hopeful.

When the water ran clear and there were no more soapy bubbles collecting at the drain, Olivia turned the shower off, reached for the plush towel hanging on the wall, and wrapped it around herself before stepping out.

Allie wasn't back yet, so Olivia rubbed the fog off the mirror and brushed the tangles from her wet hair, trying to look objectively at the reflection that looked back at her.

She wasn't pretty. She wasn't ugly, either, but she wasn't pretty. She was just plain. Plain pale eyes, plain pale skin, an ugly sprinkling of freckles, and bony shoulders. She couldn't see the rest of her body, but it was bony, too. Not in a good way. Not in a *I just eat and eat but I can't gain weight* way, but in a gangly, coltish way that made her look like a twelve-year-old boy.

So there was nothing to lose, if she thought about it. Maybe Allie's haircutting skills would turn out to be pretty good and it would work after all. But if they weren't . . . well . . . would she really be any worse off?

"Sorry," Allie said, coming in the door

with a shocking blast of cold air from the hall. "I couldn't find them. My mother was using them to wrap presents." She rolled her eyes. "I paid a lot of money for these."

She probably had. Allie seemed to spend all of her allowance on beauty-related products.

Maybe Olivia should do the same. Allie was definitely prettier than she was.

She was also happier.

To say nothing of bossier.

"Sit." Allie pointed at the toilet.

Olivia put the seat down and sat.

"You're going to have to be perfectly still while I do this." Allie took a comb from the drawer and carefully started combing Olivia's hair into its usual center part. "No flinching or freaking out unexpectedly. I am *not* responsible if you do that and the scissors hit your eye."

"I'll try not to." But privately Olivia knew she wasn't going to freak out. Deep in her chest, an excitement was building, thrumming away like the drums on Men at Work's "Down Under."

Which, at the moment, would have been way better than the Carpenters.

Allie combed her hair forward over Olivia's face. It was longer than her chin. In fact, it almost hit her chest. It had probably been growing since the last time she'd had bangs, in elementary school.

With great care, Allie combed the section so it was perfectly even on each side. She knelt in front of Olivia, looking at her hair with tremendous concentration, her pool-blue eyes shifting from one side to the other. Then she held the hair between the index and middle finger of her left hand, drew it down to the middle of Olivia's nose, and put the scissors up.

"Count to three," she instructed.

Olivia took a deep breath. "One . . . two —"

Snip!

"Hey!" Olivia drew back sharply. "You said to count to three!"

"I know, but you would have freaked if you'd known it was coming. This had to be done like pulling a tooth. Fast and unexpected." She held up the hair she'd just cut off. "Kiss it good-bye." She dropped it into the trash can.

"Are you sure this is a good idea?" Olivia asked, although *obviously* she knew it was too late to do anything about it.

Allie began brushing her new haircut into place, and smiled. "Oh, yeah. It's a good idea." She made a few more snips here and there, always drawing back to look and make sure it was even.

"Let me see." Olivia started to stand, but Allie pushed her back down.

"No, you have to wait. Let me blow-dry it and do your makeup so you can get the whole effect at once."

"I don't think I can wait."

"Sure you can." With one hand on Olivia's shoulder, holding her down, Allie reached for the blow-dryer that was always plugged in and ready to go on her bathroom counter. She turned it on and began drying Olivia's new bangs. "I bet Mark Grudberg asks you to dance tonight."

"Give me a break."

"I'm serious, you're going to go in there with so much confidence. In fact, maybe *you* should ask *him* to dance."

"There is no way."

"I dare you."

"I don't care, there's no way I'm going to ask him to dance. He'd think I was a total freak."

Allie smiled and shook her head. "I don't think so. But you just wait and see, okay?" She looked so giddy as she worked on Olivia that Olivia couldn't help starting to get really excited herself.

What if this worked?

Once the blow-drying was done, Allie got

out her makeup box, which consisted of a bunch of plastic and glass containers jumbled together in a Thom McAn shoe box.

"You just won't even believe how great you look," Allie trilled, shaking a bottle of Cover Girl foundation, then unscrewing the top. "Jeez, Louise." She got out a small, triangular makeup sponge — she said all the professional makeup artists were using them — and dabbed the medicinal-smelling liquid onto Olivia's skin.

"Don't make me look like a clown."

"I'm not even going to dignify that with a response."

Olivia waited a moment before saying, "I really do appreciate this, you know."

"Not half as much as you're about to."

There was powder blush, liquid eyeliner, a big puff-powder finish, and, last of all, Cover Girl Professional Mascara, with the new curved application brush.

"No way," Olivia said as soon as she saw it. "I can't stand having stuff on my eyes."

"It's going to look amazing," Allie assured her. "Look at the wall behind me. And up. Higher. Look behind me at where the wall meets the ceiling."

Olivia did, making a tremendous effort not to blink while Allie brought the brush in close to her eyes, one at a time, and lightly feathered it onto her lashes.

"Oh, my God." Allie took a sharp breath in. "Oh, my God, you look so amazing."

"Let me *see*." Olivia tried to get up again, and, again, Allie pushed her back down.

"*One* more thing. Then you can look. Okay?"

"What is it?"

"I have to go get it. Promise me you won't peek while I'm gone."

"No."

"Come on, Liv. *Please?* Just play along a little bit more." She was genuinely pleading. "I'll be back in ten seconds."

Olivia grimaced. "Okay, I'm counting. One . . ."

Allie jumped up and thundered into the hallway.

"Two . . ."

She wanted to look but she knew Allie would be crushed if she cheated, so instead she reached up to feel her hair.

It felt short.

"Three . . ."

What if Allie ended up with some guy tonight and Olivia ended up alone?

"Four . . ."

There was that possibility. Allie had gotten really popular with guys this year. All the kids from Herbert Hoover Junior High and Potomac Junior High were strangers and so when they saw Allie they saw blond hair, big boobs, pretty blue eyes . . .

"Five . . ."

There was no point in thinking about that. A moment ago she'd been feeling optimistic. She needed to regain that.

"Six . . ."

Mark Grudberg. He'd probably be there. What if he noticed her? What if there was a miracle and suddenly he noticed her? Maybe he wouldn't ask her to dance, but a word or two would be enough.

"Seven . . ."

Actually eye contact would be enough. She'd stared a hole through him a couple of times when they'd passed each other in the hall but he didn't notice her at all. Maybe — just *maybe* — things would change to-night.

"Eight . . ."

Her heart began to pound. It was almost time to go.

"Nine!" she shouted, just as Allie rounded the corner and hopped back into the bath-room, holding the emerald wrap top.

"I'm here, I'm here. You didn't look, did you?"

"I wanted to, but I didn't."

"Good." Allie held the shirt out to Olivia. "I think this would look really good on you. I want you to have it."

Olivia was speechless.

"I mean, unless you don't want hand-me-downs. I'm not, like, saying you should only have seconds." She drew the shirt back, uncertainty painting her features into regret.

"Do you mean it?" Olivia said. "I can *have* it? But it's your favorite shirt."

"I seriously doubt it would even fit anymore. But besides that, I think this color would look really pretty on you. And you haven't ever worn anything like this. You know, with a little bit of a v-neck. You've got to be tired of plain old T-shirts and polo shirts."

"I am." Olivia took the shirt in her hands. It was soft, like silk. It was probably polyester, but still it was really nice quality. She could already picture herself wearing it, like, every day this week.

She dropped the towel she was wearing down to her waist and slipped the shirt over her head.

Allie's face broke into a wide, appreciative smile. "It's *perfect!*"

"Is it?"

"See for yourself." Allie grabbed her wrist and pulled her in front of the mirror.

The girl that looked back at Olivia was, for a moment, literally unfamiliar. With her coppery hair (*"Not red,"* Allie had corrected) framing her face, her eyes looked huge. And, somehow, not so bland, but a bright, vivid blue. The dark lashes were a huge improvement, she had to admit with awe, over the strawberry-blond lashes that came naturally to her.

She looked like a completely different person.

She was pretty.

Wow, for the first time in her life, she really honestly and truly felt *pretty.*

"Thank you," she breathed to Allie, fighting the sting of tears in her eyes.

"It's not *me,*" Allie said, unsentimental. "It's *you.* This has been you all the time, you just didn't know it!"

It was on the tip of Olivia's tongue to object, to say it wasn't real, it wasn't there yesterday, it probably wouldn't be there tomorrow, except that she knew Allie wasn't a magical fairy godmother and there was nothing supernatural about this.

All it took was just a little bit of effort.

"Come on," Allie said, eager to show her work off to the rest of the world. "Let's go. You're going to have to borrow my white rabbit coat, too." It was fake but no one knew it. "That thing you have isn't glamorous enough for you tonight."

"Thanks."

They went to the dance, walking through the crisp December air — past the suburban houses encrusted with lights and animated snowmen and moving reindeer, and, in one unfortunate case, the bottom half of a Santa on a roof — singing Christmas carols at the tops of their lungs until they got close enough to the school that someone they knew might hear them.

They handed over the two-dollar fee at the cafeteria, which still had the smell of spaghetti under tinfoil hanging in the air, but soon all associations with the day would disappear.

It was a magical night, before, during, and after the dance, remembered later as a blur of lights, music, smiles, laughter, anticipation, and reward.

It was an extremely significant night in Olivia's life and she would point to it many times in subsequent years, and not because Mark Grudberg *had* asked her out and become her first boyfriend (though at the time that had been awesome).

No, it was significant because it was the first time she truly saw — and, more important, *felt* — how transforming the beauty

217

game could be.

It was something she'd never forget.

THIRTEEN

Maybe she's born with it.
— ad for Maybelline

"The way this works is that it has actual snake venom in it to sort of freeze your muscles —"

Caroline drew her hand back from the gel Olivia was squeezing out of a tube, and shrieked. "*Snake venom?* I asked you to help me freshen up my look, not kill me!"

"It's safe, Mom."

"How could it be?"

Olivia held up the bottle. "Look at this packaging. For one thing, the marketing alone cost a fortune. And for another, it's Peter Thomas Roth. They make some of the best skin products you can buy. *It's not going to poison you.* For God's sake, Nicole Kidman uses it! She *loves* it!"

Her mother reacted as if this were the proof she'd needed that the whole thing was

219

crazy witchcraft. "I always thought there was something about her that was not right."

"Oh, Mom."

"Well, there was that weird marriage to —"

"Do you really want to talk bad marriages?" Olivia asked, as if she and Nicole were the best of friends and she had to defend her.

They weren't, of course, and she didn't. But at the same time she sure as hell didn't want to listen to her mother spitting out platitudes about what made a good marriage.

"I take your point," Caroline said crisply. "But I don't know about putting snake poison on my face." She reached up to wipe it away.

Olivia grabbed her mother's hand and held it while she put some of the gel onto her knuckles. "There. See? You're still alive. Now smooth it onto your forehead."

Caroline looked dubious. "The skin on your face is very thin, you know. Something like poison could sink right in."

"Yes, I know. That's why it wrinkles." Olivia dabbed her fingers into the gel to put it on her mother's forehead herself. Then she stepped back. "Can you feel it?"

Caroline wiggled her eyebrows. "I'm not sure . . . It's tingling a little."

"That's as bad as it gets. Just a little tingle." She took the extra and dabbed it onto her own forehead. "But do you notice how your forehead feels a little stiffer?"

Caroline wiggled some more. "I guess it does."

"Good. That will help you from deepening your frown lines."

"Who says I have frown lines?" Caroline objected, drawing back.

"I do, Mom. You've got frown lines." Olivia looked on the shelves and picked up another tube. "Now dab this on around your eyes *very* gently."

"What is that? Cyanide?"

Not bad. Olivia almost laughed, but she wasn't going to hand it to her mom on that one. It would just encourage Caroline to pooh-pooh everything else Olivia suggested.

"It's a mushroom complex that helps erase those fine lines. And look." She held it up so her mother could see Dr. Weil's name on the Origins label. "It's made by a *doctor,* Mom. That means it won't *kill* you."

"It's amazing what we'll do for youth and beauty. But I'm tired of feeling like an old hag. If I'm starting a new life, I need a new look." Caroline dabbed the cream around her eyes, while Olivia looked at her. Really looked at her.

The once copper hair — which Olivia had to admit had been stunning in the sunlight — was now a dull electric red, the result of too much home-coloring on dull, aging hair. Her face was still quite lovely — the routine of Pond's cold cream that had served her grandmother and great-grandmother so beautifully was also treating Olivia's mother very well. The new products Olivia had given her would only help. And her teeth were a nice, natural light shade, unlike the dull gray so many women her age sported.

But she was thin. Perhaps twenty pounds too thin. Knowing Caroline, as Olivia absolutely did, she probably thought it was a better look than a healthy weight would give her, but to Olivia she looked like a frail little bird.

"You'll be amazed how well it works," Olivia said, giving her the cream.

"I hope so. Though I don't know how I'll keep it up at these prices."

Olivia smiled. "I'll hook you up."

"I can't let you get it for me."

"It's no big deal. All of this" — she gestured at the shelves upon shelves of bottles, jars, tubes, and dispensers — "is sent to me for free."

"Why would they do that?"

"Because the companies want me to try their stuff and love it and put it in the magazine." She handed a jar of Elizabeth Arden's Visible Difference moisturizer to her mother. That was one product she could only use in the dead of winter, when the indoor heat had blasted the life out of her skin. But for her mother's aging skin, it would be perfect year-round. "Take this. Use it twice a day. You'll love it."

Her mother held the jar up and looked at it. "Oh, yes, I have this already."

"Do you use it?"

Her mother shook her head. "I save it for special occasions because it's expensive."

"Mom, it's moisturizer, not Chanel No. 5. Put it on when you get out of the shower or after you wash your face and a tiny bit will go a long way."

"I'll give it a try." Caroline looked at her. "Heaven knows you look better than I did at your age."

"If that's true, I'm sure it's because I'm not married." Olivia looked at her watch. It was one-thirty. She had a meeting in an hour and her mother had a hair appointment in half an hour. "You need to go, they're expecting you at the salon."

"Oh, yes. Now, where is this place? Saks?"

"Bergdorf Goodman. It's on the seven-hundred block of Fifth Avenue, you can't miss it."

"And the name of the stylist?"

"John Barrett." Most people would kill for an appointment with John Barrett but if Olivia told her that, she'd probably decide it was too extravagant and go to Express Cuts for an appointment with the first available cosmetology student. "His name's on the salon."

"Are you sure he's experienced styling women of a certain age? I don't want to come out looking like some young punk."

Olivia laughed. "There is no way, Mom. No way."

There was a moment of silence before Caroline said, "I appreciate all of this you're doing. It's been a long time since I felt good about my appearance."

"Then you're about to be really happy. Now go. I've got work to do." She watched her mother retreat, then called, "And stop at the café after your cut. You need to eat!"

Their roles — or at least the roles they were supposed to play — had been reversed.

". . . so now he's going to marry her," Allie huffed. "*Marry* her. As in *till death do us part*. God. I might just have to kill him myself.

Or her."

She and her mother were on a brisk walk along the C & O Canal, just north of Georgetown. Her mother seemed to be going strong, a geriatric Denise Austin, but Allie was breathlessly aware of the fact that every step they took put them one more step away from the car.

The treadmill would have been better, she decided. On a treadmill she could measure her progress daily, push herself, but stop when she wanted to.

Or when she *needed* to.

"Noah marrying Victoria Freedman." Her mother clicked her tongue against her teeth. "Now, I have to say, you and I don't always agree about Noah's girlfriends, but that is one pair I would not have seen coming."

"It's crazy, right?"

"Well, I haven't seen Victoria for years." She made a small wince. "But if she's anything like her mother . . ."

"Exactly! *Exactly.* And why *wouldn't* she be like her mother? The apple doesn't fall far from the tree."

Her mother eyed her.

"Anyway," Allie went on. "She's a horrible person and I freaked out so badly when he told me that now he doesn't even want to talk to me."

"What happened?"

"We'd had some beers and he was going to stay over on my sofa, but the conversation went so badly that he took a cab home. It was ugly."

"Have you talked to him since then?"

"We've had a couple of awkward, chilly calls." Allie started walking faster, her feet stomping her anger as she went. "You'd think he'd be back to normal by now."

"Slow down," her mother said.

Allie immediately lessened her pace.

"I meant that figuratively," her mother said. She was being kind, because that was her default mode, but she was also making it clear that her daughter was being kind of a jerk. "Slow down with your judgment of Noah. This is a big move for him. Arguably, my dear, it's bigger for him than for you."

Allie scoffed. "Arguably."

Her mother ignored her petulance. "Did he tell you anything about why he's made this decision?"

"No, but it's a snap decision, isn't it? You noticed it, too!" There. Allie wasn't just being shrewish or petty about past grudges. Her mother also thought this was awfully quick. "All he'd say was that it was right and that these things couldn't always be explained and a bunch of that kind of bull.

226

If you ask me, it's weirdly fast."

"Do you suppose Victoria is in trouble?"

"I can't imagine that she's not." Allie stopped. "Wait, you mean *in trouble?* Like, pregnant?"

Her mother nodded. "That's one reason young people get married quickly."

"Oh, Mom." Allie put an arm around her mother's shoulder, and they walked forward, slower now. "That is so sweet, but we're not *young people* anymore. And we don't get in that kind of trouble. Unless we're morons. And I can't speak for Vickie, but Noah's not a moron."

Or was he? She didn't know for sure what his sexual habits were. Apart from the fact that he was a great kisser. *That* she knew.

That she remembered.

But it had been so long ago . . . one night that he'd undoubtedly long since forgotten. She didn't know anything about what he was like romantically now. If he was the kind of guy who didn't make sure everything was in order, so to speak, before, well, doing the Deed.

He would probably be shocked to know she was giving this any thought at all. But she couldn't help it.

When he first came to school, she'd thought he was cute. And he *had* been, in a

227

very cute-boy way. But somewhere along the line, instead of taking that turn into weird Man-Boy that so many cute boys took (see Jerry Mathers of *Leave It to Beaver*), he'd instead become a really *really* attractive man. His once-softer features had etched into masculine contours; his mouth had a curve to it that was sexy without being too soft; his teeth, straightened by several unfortunate years of braces, were now worthy of a movie star close-up; and there were small lines around his eyes that Allie knew were both from smiling and from the way he'd squint when he was concentrating on something

Then there was the blue of his eyes. Not startling, not washed-out, just . . . warm. If blue could be warm. Allie had contemplated that blue many times in her life, trying to figure out what exact color it was, but all she could come up with was Noah.

Noah blue.

It could be a crayon color.

On top of all that, Noah was quite possibly the smartest person Allie had ever met, able to understand complicated tax forms and political issues and yet explain them to Allie as if she were a six-year-old, yet without talking down to her.

She liked that.

He was really damn near the perfect guy.

It was no wonder Vickie wanted him.

Suddenly Allie was picturing him with Vickie. Kissing her. Touching her. It was a stomach-twisting thought.

"Allison, I did not call anyone a moron."

Allie returned her attention to the conversation. Moron. Right. "All right, well, as long as we're clear that Noah isn't one." She frowned, still disconcerted. "Except as far as his choice of girlfriends goes."

"Unless it was you?"

"What?" How did she do that? "Me? With Noah?"

Her mother nodded.

"We're friends!" But her objection sounded weak.

"Good relationships have been built on less than that." Peggy Denty stopped. "Let's turn around. If we keep going we're going to end up in Georgia."

Oh, thank God. Allie needed to change the subject. She needed to change the direction of her thoughts. "Sure, whatever you want," she said, and they turned around. She faced the path they'd just walked with gratitude.

"You were saying?" her mother prodded.

"That there's nothing more to Noah and me besides friendship, so if you're gearing up to accuse me of being jealous, you can stop right there."

"I didn't say anything like that!" Her mother looked so genuinely surprised that Allie was immediately embarrassed.

"Good."

"But now that you mention it —"

"I didn't. Forget I said anything. That will take us down the wrong road." She was trying to make that U-turn right now. "The thing here is that Noah's planning to marry the Wicked Witch of the West and I have to stop him."

"But honey, don't you know this by now? You can't. People need to make this kind of decision for themselves, and it sounds like Noah has. You need to just accept that and be his friend anyway."

Allie thought about that. Gave it sincere consideration. She just couldn't imagine standing by and watching Noah marry that woman. She couldn't imagine calling his home and politely asking Vickie if Noah was available.

She couldn't imagine going to their children's birthday parties and graduations.

Actually she could imagine that, and it was gruesome. There were ponies and clowns and Freedmans all over the place. Little children with good Haller blood running around like Freedmans.

The thought was too much to bear.

"I'm not sure I can, Mom," Allie heard herself say. Then she knew it was God's honest, too-horrible-to-admit truth. She wasn't sure she could stand by as his friend and watch him make such a terrible mistake. Maybe it would be better for her to back off altogether. "What do you do when someone you love is doing something you're absolutely sure is a horrific mistake?"

Her mother slipped her hand through her arm and gave her a squeeze. "You stand by their side anyway," she said. "And hope they figure it out for themselves."

FOURTEEN

As individual as you are.
— ad for Cachet perfume

When she got to the office Monday morning, a week after the reunion, Olivia's administrative assistant, Tim, was ready with the gossip.

"You have a message," he said, holding the little yellow slip of paper up and swinging it from side to side.

"Okay, I'll bite. What is it?"

"It's from an old friend."

"Of mine or yours?"

"Yours, of course. It's someone you saw at the reunion." He put the message down and put his hands on his hips, even though he was sitting. "I cannot *believe* you didn't tell me you were going to a class reunion!"

Olivia rolled her eyes. "I didn't even know I was going until after you'd left for the day on Friday or, believe me, you would have pried it out of me somehow."

"Friday a week ago," he said, looking at her expectantly.

"Once I'd gone, what was the point in bringing it up? It certainly wasn't interesting."

"I'll be the judge of that."

"Later. I've got work to do. What have you got?"

Tim sighed. "Okay." He picked up the message again. "So your friend *Allison,* do you know her?"

Olivia frowned. "Yes. Is something wrong?"

"She didn't say, but she sounded upset. Or maybe she had a cold. Actually" — he handed the message over — "she could have been drunk. Some people's voices get that nasally quality when they've been drinking —"

"When did she call?"

"It was in the voice mail system. The call came in at two A.M."

"Is it still there?"

Tim nodded. "Saved."

"Thanks." Still holding the yellow slip, she went into her office, closed the door, and sat down at her desk — where Tim had left a stack of apparently less interesting messages for her — to check voice mail.

Allie's was the first one on there. *"Hi, Olivia, this is Allie. Allison Denty. From the reunion. Which you probably figured out. Duh."* She talked fast, like she did when she was nervous. *"Anyway, I'm calling in the middle of the night with the hope that you'll get this message first thing in the morning. Call me back. I have . . . well, there's just a situation I wanted to talk to you about. So, call me. Thanks. Bye. Oh! My number is 301–555–1593. Thanks."* She hung up.

That was an upset call. Not a cold. Not drunk, though there might have been some alcohol giving her speech that lazy slip from consonant to consonant.

Olivia hesitated. She didn't want to get caught up in any drama. God knows she'd had more than enough of it in her lifetime.

She'd had more than enough of it this month.

Then again, Allie hadn't exactly been calling obsessively these past twenty years, so if something had happened that she thought she needed to talk to Olivia about, Olivia should probably take it seriously. She wasn't completely cold to her past friendship with Allie.

She dialed the number and waited for it to ring.

"Hello?"

"Allie?"

"Olivia?"

"Yes. I got your message." Olivia started dividing her messages into piles, according to their level of importance. Three of them were from Vickie Freedman, wanting to come to town for lunch, and clearly angling for some sort of celebrity encounter that she thought Olivia could provide. "What's up?"

"Well . . . I . . . I probably shouldn't have bothered you. I know it was sort of alarmist and shrill, and in the middle of the night like that, it probably sounded like something was really wrong."

Olivia was relieved. "So it's not?"

"No." The way she said it sounded like a question. "I was just wondering . . . I had an incident with a lip plumper. It over-plumped my lips. So I was just wondering if that was a problem with all of them or what."

"I don't know, Allie, I've never heard that one. Most people think they don't work at all. But you don't need that anyway. Just get a great, neutral pencil, like MAC's Spice, and —"

"Olivia."

"What?"

"I'm sorry." Allie was really sounding fret-

235

ful now. "I didn't call about that. I called because something awful has happened and I didn't know who else to call, and by the time the sun came up I realized that it was completely inappropriate to bother you."

But Olivia had been *glad* Allie had called. Hearing her regret it now was a little . . . disappointing. "It's not inappropriate, Allie. What the hell is going on?"

Allie sniffled. "Oh, my God, he's going to marry her!"

Olivia was taken aback. "What?"

"Noah. Vickie." Allie sniffed again. "See? It's not really even my business, so I shouldn't be dragging you into it."

"Wait a minute." The brief conversation replayed in Olivia's head. "He's going to *marry* her?" She couldn't believe it. *"Vickie?"*

The messages from Vickie suddenly seemed to glow, like they were on fire or something.

She was everywhere.

"He can't. I mean, yes, that's what he said, but he *can't.* Seriously, I have such a bad feeling about her and it's *not* just some carryover grudge from adolescence."

"Is that what Noah said?"

"Word for word."

Olivia could imagine him saying it. "That must have stung."

236

"Yeah, well, I don't care if he thinks I'm a big, immature baby. Which he does, by the way. He said that, too. This time I'm *not* being selfish. I just don't want him to ruin his life."

"No, neither do I."

Allie drew in a quick breath. "Then talk to him. You might be the only one he'd take seriously. Certainly the only one out of the two of us."

She was right, but it was only because Noah and Olivia had the slightly stiff friendship that distance and time carved out. They didn't talk every day or every week. They didn't have the shorthand he and Allie seemed to have, the inside jokes, the familiarity and ease of communication that would let him say *this is just a carryover grudge from your adolescence* without fear of crossing a line.

So, to that extent, Allie was right. And Olivia was glad, because she cared about Noah as much as Allie did, and if he would take what she said with a little more consideration then maybe this could work.

"Did he say why?" It was a funny question, she thought later. Usually when someone says they're getting married it's a pretty sure bet that they're in love, but when talking about Vickie Freedman and Noah it

237

wasn't even one of her first thoughts.

"Um, not really." Allie sniffled. "He didn't give any grand speeches about love, though the truth is, I think I was so whiny and hysterical about it all that it came off sounding like I thought it was all about me. Which I totally *don't* think, but all I could ramble on and on about was how big a bitch she was to me, because — am I right? — that's all I really *know*. But from that, I *know* she's a deeply mean person." She took a breath. "And I don't think that kind of fundamental personality really changes with time, do you?"

Anyone else might have been left breathless by Allie's rapid-fire delivery, but Olivia had grown up with it and the instinct to pull out the salient facts was still strong. "I don't know." But she was inclined to agree. "So basically instead of getting his side of things, you just got his defense of Vickie."

"Exactly. And I know it's my fault, but . . . that's where we are. I don't know what the hell this is about."

"Maybe I should call him."

"I think you should." Allie sounded relieved.

"But I don't want him to feel ganged up on by the two of us."

"Don't tell him you talked to me. There's

no way he'd leap to that conclusion. Just call and act like you're seeing what's up, how it's going" — Allie took a shuddering breath — "how he's going to blow his entire future. That kind of thing."

Olivia considered. She had a lot of things to do — her desk was evidence of that — but if there was something she could do to help Noah, she could certainly fit it in. And though she and Allie hadn't always agreed on everything, obviously, they did agree on this point. And Olivia believed, absolutely, that Allie's concern was for Noah and not for herself. If her only reference point was her experience, Olivia could see why, but she could also see why Noah *didn't* get it.

It wasn't anybody's fault.

Maybe Olivia could help, maybe she couldn't, but she had to try. She really did, she had to try.

"I'll give him a call, Allie."

"Soon?" She tried to disguise it but there was no mistaking the frantic edge to her voice.

"Today. Now. Don't worry."

"Will you call me back and let me know what he says?"

"Sure. As soon as I know anything."

"Thank you." Allie let out a long breath. "Really, thank you from the bottom of my heart. Maybe between the two of us we can save Noah from making a terrible mistake."

"Let's hope so," Olivia said, and set down the phone.

The days before the hard deadline for production were always busy so Olivia wasn't able to call Noah until that evening and when she finally got through to him he was with Vickie and he couldn't talk.

So it wasn't until the next afternoon that she finally got to talk to Noah.

And his mood was not great.

"Allie called you?"

"She was concerned," Olivia said. There was no point in denying it — he knew. "And honestly, Noah, so am I. This seems awfully fast."

"Yes."

That was it? *Yes?* "So you can see where your friends might be worried."

"Okay, well, thanks, but I didn't realize I needed to run it by everyone first."

Olivia was surprised by his tone. "You don't. Of course. But your friends —"

He let out a short, tight breath. "Look, I'm in the middle of a crunch here. Can I give you a call later?"

"Yes. Call me back whenever you can. And Noah?"

"What?"

"I'm sorry if I'm butting in where I don't belong. It's just that I care about you. Allie does, too."

He made a scoffing sound, then said, "Got to go."

Olivia called Allie back and it was obvious that Allie had been getting antsy waiting for the call. Olivia hated feeling like a gossip but in this case she and Allie were the closest people Noah had and it was clear that something about his engagement was making him less than thrilled. As his friends, they needed to at least be on the same page as far as supporting him went.

Olivia told Allie about the conversation, such as it was. "I don't know what's going on," she concluded. "But maybe the problem is that from the moment we found out he was seeing Vickie, we've done little more than tell him what a bitch she is."

"You didn't do that," Allie said. "I did. He's mad at me."

"I haven't been warm about her, either."

"Maybe, but if that's what he's pissed about, why wait until now to express it?" Allie asked. "Two weeks ago he was still acting normal."

"This is the first I've talked to him since the reunion." Tim came in and handed Olivia a handful of yellow message slips.

"So maybe he's been mad at me ever since then and I just didn't know it."

Allie made a dismissive noise. "This isn't like him. Noah doesn't get mad."

Olivia put the messages into piles according to importance, keeping an eye out for something from Noah. "Maybe he was just busy. I might have misinterpreted his tone."

"I've left him three messages and he hasn't called me back."

"Like I said, maybe he's busy."

"No, he *always* calls me back. This is weird."

"Allie." Olivia set the papers down and tapped a newly manicured finger on her desktop. She shouldn't say this. She should just mind her own business and keep out of it. "Has it ever occurred to you that maybe Noah has feelings for you that are more than platonic?"

"No!" Allie's answer was immediate and explosive. "That's crazy."

"I don't think it is."

"It is, Olivia, believe me. He had his chance but never took it, and if I had a chance, I didn't take it, either."

"Recently?"

"On and off for years. You know, he'd be dating someone or I'd be dating someone but then there would be those times when neither of us were dating anyone and he *could* have made a move but he never did."

"Did you?"

There was a long silence. "No. Even if I'd been desperate to, I couldn't have. It's really hard for me to be forward about that kind of thing."

Because she'd never had to be.

"I think it's hard for Noah, too. Especially where you're concerned."

"I just don't believe that."

What should she do? Tell Allie about ancient history, or keep the confidence she'd kept for all these years? "Think about it. If he *had* wanted to make a move, how would he have done it? When you're friends with someone for a long time you develop a rapport that's hard to break. How do you tell your best friend you're in love with them?"

Allie gasped. "Did he tell you that?"

Not in ages. "No, he didn't. But then, he wouldn't, would he? But that doesn't mean it isn't true."

FIFTEEN

Raise your hand if you're sure.
— ad for Sure antiperspirant

In her first week of dieting — or *lifestyle change* as she was supposed to think of it, although who was she kidding? As soon as she reached her goal she was going to go out for a huge, fattening dinner — Allie lost four pounds.

She'd seen people on *Oprah* before who had lost more than that in their first week, spectacular stories of eight pounds in one week, but as soon as she expressed disappointment at the meeting everyone told her she was crazy and that four pounds was a great achievement.

It would have been nice to have lost all twenty-seven (as they'd determined her final goal to be) but clearly not realistic.

Week two, with more realistic expectations, she'd lost two. Week three it had been two and a half. This week she was down half a pound, but with a total of nine pounds off — nearly two bags of flour in weight — she was satisfied.

That, in and of itself, was a real difference for her.

It was progress. She hadn't made progress in *anything* in a very, very long time.

"You've done a wonderful job," Arlene told her after the weigh-in.

"Thanks," Allie said, putting her watch back on. "It's funny how good it feels to lose even a little bit."

"It's as addictive as Twinkies after a while," Arlene said, then smiled. "Or whatever your particular weakness is. Mine was Twinkies. And Ho Hos."

"Pizza." Allie wasn't over that yet. "And bread. All kinds of bread. Especially those Parker House dinner rolls when they're hot with butter melting into them."

"Nothing tastes as good as being thin feels," Arlene parroted, then winked. "I know what you mean about the rolls, though."

Allie finished putting her earrings on and went in to the meeting. Even after this short time, she had come to feel like the other people here were family, so when Marianne got up to speak to the group, Allie was really pulling for her and hoping she had lost this week after two weeks of gaining.

"I lost two point three pounds this week," Marianne said, and everyone clapped.

Her apple cheeks went red but she smiled. Marianne was pretty, but she had told Allie she had a hundred and twenty pounds to lose and there was no convincing her that she was.

"I had an important revelation this week." Marianne went on, clasping and unclasping her hands in front of her. "I started to gain weight after my father died ten years ago. You may remember me telling you that my mother died when I was little. Well, Dad was a mother and a father to me, and even though he didn't always have the answers, especially during those stormy adolescent years, he never stopped trying." Tears started to roll down Marianne's cheeks and she swiped at them with the back of her hand. "I promised myself I wasn't going to cry."

"It's okay," Heather, the group leader, said, urging Marianne on. "We want to hear what you have to say. Don't let a few tears get in the way of that."

"Thanks, Heather. Well, anyway, it's pretty simple. Dad always used to tell me how pretty I was, especially when he was at a loss dealing with my youthful insecurities and so forth, and I think when he died I felt like he should take that with him. I think, on some deep level, I got fat on purpose. Like it was a tribute to him." She wiped her tears again and sniffled. "But it's not a tribute. I'm killing myself and he'd hate that and now I'm more motivated than ever to get healthy." She gave another embarrassed smile. "I just wanted to share."

"That's an incredible story," Heather said. "You are truly an inspiration."

Gilda raised her hand and spoke. "Marianne, maybe you could think of your good health as a tribute to your father. Because you're living on *for* him and I know he'd want you to live a long and healthy life."

Again the group clapped, and for the rest of the meeting they kept going back to Marianne's turnaround.

On her way home, Allie asked herself if she had been overeating for some reason, too.

At first she scoffed the idea away. She'd put on weight because she loved to eat. She didn't buy that Dr. Phil crap about eating in order to make up for something lacking. Allie ate because she loved to eat and she always had. In her teens she could get away with it because her metabolism was so good but now she couldn't.

It was that simple. Not easy but simple.

She was addicted.

Now she just needed to get addicted to healthier stuff.

The doorbell buzzed shortly after seven P.M.

Allie paused the DVR and went to the door in her tattered robe and with her hair in a towel, expecting to see Sing Yee, for Café Hong Kong, there to deliver her steamed veggies on steamed brown rice. She secretly hoped he'd accidentally bring someone's General Tso.

But it wasn't Sing.

"Noah!" Her breath caught in her chest. "What are you doing here?"

"We need to talk." He brushed in past her, looking like he hadn't slept in a week. "Now."

"Okay." She glanced out in the hall to see if Yee was coming, but it was empty. She closed the door. "Let me change my clothes, and I'll be —"

"Why did you call Olivia?"

"What?"

"You heard me. Why did you call Olivia about Vickie and me?"

"I'm sorry, was it supposed to be a secret?"

His face was pale and drawn. There were dark circles under his eyes. "Why can't you just, for once, mind your own fucking business?"

She was defensive immediately, because inside she was hurt. "Because when my best friend won't talk to me, won't return my calls, that *is* my business!"

"Best friend?" He shook his head. His hair was rumpled. Yet somehow he looked . . . good. "Are we *friends,* Allie? I can't keep up. Are we friends this week or not?"

She felt as if he'd slapped her. What was going on? "We're always friends."

He shook his head. "Then why didn't you talk to *me* about this, if you have such a huge problem with it? Why the hell did you call Olivia?"

She gaped at him, pulling her robe tightly shut. The towel on her head suddenly felt heavy and stupid-looking. "Because, as I *just* said, *you* wouldn't call me back. You could have been dead, for all I knew, or pinned under something really heavy in your apartment."

He sat down heavily and steepled his hands in front of him. "Then it's a good thing you called Olivia. In fucking *New York.*"

"Noah, what is *wrong* with you?"

He looked at her. "What do you think is wrong with me?"

She thought what was wrong with him was that he was about to marry one of the nastiest people she had ever met in her life, but he'd just made it clear that that particular brand of honesty wasn't welcome right now.

"I don't know," she said, pulling the towel off her head so she looked at least a little less ridiculous. This was not the kind of conversation one should have in a ratty robe and a towel turban. "I honestly don't. You're supposed to be happy right now."

"Yes. I am." He straightened up and gripped his hands on his knees and met her eyes. "I'm supposed to be over the goddamn moon."

There was trouble.

Hope surged.

Followed quickly by guilt.

She sat down next to him. Her wet hair fell in front of her eyes and she raked it back with her hand. "Aren't you?" she asked quietly, putting a hand on his.

"Don't do that." He shook off her hand.

"Don't do what?"

He shook his head.

"Noah?"

He sighed heavily and looked down at his feet. "You should get dressed."

This was giving her whiplash. "You should tell me what the hell's going on."

"You *know* what's going on. Tori and I are getting married."

"And that's why you're yelling at me?"

"I'm not yelling at you."

"Then your normal speaking voice has gotten really loud and kind of mean."

A small smile played at his lips for a moment, but then he sobered and said, "The wedding is next month."

"Next *month?*" Allie felt like she'd been sucker punched. "No!"

"Yes."

"But that's so soon."

"Why wait?"

"Because . . . you should. People do. Why don't you have a nice, long engagement? Time to" — *think about this, come to your senses, change your mind, call it off* — "prepare."

For a long moment, he didn't say anything. He just stared at the floor while she stared at him.

Eventually he looked up again. "Do you remember when you met Kevin?"

That was out of left field. "Kevin?"

"Yes, Kevin. Do you remember when you met him?"

She thought a moment. "We were at

251

Windsor McKay's. You and I were there and I was coming out of the bathroom and I knocked into him and he spilled his wine on me."

"Right. First of all, what kind of guy drinks *merlot* in a place like Windsor McKay's —"

True. It was a peanuts-on-the-floor, drink-your-beer-from-the-bottle sort of place.

"— and second, I was trying to tell you something that night before that happened."

"Really? What?"

He clenched his teeth and the muscle in his jaw twitched. "That I —"

Her phone rang. It *never* rang.

"What?" she prodded.

"Go ahead and get it."

"Ignore it. What were you going to say?"

The answering machine kicked on. She had the volume turned too high. First there was her voice, bellowing to leave a message, then her temp agency, reporting that there was a job available for the next week and a half.

There was really no talking over the noise, and once it had finally stopped the momentum was lost.

"You were saying?" she asked.

He shook his head. "It doesn't matter. I don't even know why I brought it up."

"Don't be so cryptic!"

"I'm not being cryptic. I just don't want to talk anymore. I'm sick of talking."

She was astonished. "We've barely spoken for weeks!"

"That's because we don't always connect, Allie. We don't always get each other." He paused. "It's not fair for you to make this harder on me just because you don't understand it."

Harder?

"Funny, that's the same reason I can't make it easier on you."

He turned to her and took a short breath. "Allie."

"Yes?"

He looked pained. He started to speak, then stopped.

"Noah!"

"I can't do this." He started to get up, but she pulled him back down.

"You can't do what?"

"This." He gestured at her, then around the room. "Any of this."

"Noah." She moved closer and put her hand on his shoulder. "Come on. We've been friends most of our lives. You can talk to me about anything."

He looked back at her and reached up to touch her face, her hair. "Not this time."

She felt a shiver come over her. When they were kids they'd said *someone's walking over your grave* but that was definitely not the case right now.

Right now Allie looked into his eyes and suddenly wanted nothing more than for him to kiss her.

"I can't . . . we can't . . ."

Fear struck her. "Can't what?" she asked quietly, trying to brace herself for his response, whatever it was.

He stood up and walked over to the window. "Do you really believe in love, Allie? Do you think there's a *one* for everyone?" He turned back to face her. "Or do you think that's all just a bunch of horseshit?"

"I . . . don't know." Which answer would make him prolong his engagement or, better still, end it? She opted for the truth. "I think I believe in love."

"Have you ever been in love?"

She hadn't been in love with Kevin. She hadn't even thought she was. What about Joey Chapman?

No.

Chris Rescott?

Nope.

Actually, the only guy she'd really loved unconditionally for any great length of time was Noah himself.

She should tell him.

But she couldn't. "This is about you, not me."

"Answer my question."

"Do you want a beer?" She stood up. "They're warm, but I could put some in the freezer for a few minutes." She started toward the kitchen, but Noah came over and caught her by the arms, turning her to face him.

"Answer the question, Allie."

She looked up into his face. He was just inches from her. She could just . . . No, she couldn't. "I . . . don't know," she stammered. "What about you?"

"Definitely." He let go of her arms and turned away.

"Are you in love right now?" she asked his back.

He hesitated for a long time, then finally nodded. "Yes, I am."

Something about the way he said it was so sincere. So resigned. So achingly heartfelt, that she thought she might cry.

He was in love.

It was Vickie Freedman, but he was in love. And the depth of emotion Allie had seen in his eyes left no doubt that she couldn't sway his feelings no matter what.

So she had to step up to the plate and do the last thing in the world she felt she could do.

"Then you're doing exactly the right thing by marrying Vickie," she said, over a lump in her throat. "And I've been a shitty friend." She threw her arms around him. "I'm sorry, Noah. I'm so sorry. I want you to be happy."

He closed his arms around her slowly. He didn't say a word.

She clung to him. She didn't want to let go. She didn't realize until now how much she'd missed talking to him, even for the short time it had been.

But just when she started to think she could stay there forever, he put his hands on her hips and drew back away from her. "You're wasting away."

"It's nine pounds." She laughed. "Not a miracle."

"You didn't need to lose an ounce."

"Now you're just lying." She smiled.

He didn't. "I need to go."

No. Please, no. "Why?"

"I can't see you anymore, Al."

"Right, I'm so thin I'm invisible."

"No, I mean I can't see you anymore. We can't hang out anymore."

"What?" She felt the blood drain from her

face. "Tell me you're kidding."

He shook his head slowly. "I'm sorry."

This made no sense. "Please. Noah, tell me you don't mean this." Her knees felt weak. "Did Vickie put you up to this?"

"No." He took an uneven breath. "This is completely my decision. I doubt she even knows — well, trust me, it's best for all of us."

The doorbell buzzed.

Allie didn't care.

"Noah —"

"There's someone at your door." He moved toward it, and she knew he'd use it as an easy escape.

"No." She grabbed his arm and stood her ground. "This is more important." Desperation tasted like metal in her mouth.

He pulled free. "I have to go."

The door buzzed again.

Noah went and opened it. "Bye, Allie," he said, pushing past Sing Yee.

"Noah!" She ran to the door and looked out but he'd already rounded the corner and poor Sing was standing there with her food and a puzzled look on his face.

"Hi, Sing," she said, hoping he didn't notice the tears welling in her eyes. She gave a quick sniff and signed the paper he held out for her but in a moment were streaming down her face.

"Is everything okay, Miss Denty? Do you need me to call someone?"

"I'm fine." She tried to smile. "Thanks." She took the food and went inside, closing the door behind her.

She dropped the bag directly in the trash, went to the sofa where Noah had just been sitting, and cried until there was nothing left in her and she fell into a restless sleep.

SIXTEEN

ELEVENTH GRADE

It's gonna be an Aviance night . . .
            — ad for Aviance perfume by
                        Prince Matchabelli

They had been at the Montgomery County
Agricultural Fair for maybe ten minutes
before Olivia and Mark had disappeared,
undoubtedly off to find some quiet spot in
which to make out and God knows what
else.

This was exactly why Allie had begged
Noah to come with her, because otherwise
she would have been the third wheel and
she just *hated* that.

"You want to go see the butter cow?" she
asked Noah as they wandered aimlessly
among the strewn trash and twirling iron
rides, surrounded by neon, children, and
the smell of popcorn and cotton candy.

"The butter cow," he repeated dryly. He
was crabby. He hadn't wanted to come.
She'd had to talk him into it, with promises

of fun and rewards that she couldn't possibly provide, and now that he was here he was being more of a jerk than ever.

She didn't know what was wrong with him lately. They'd been friends for years and she'd never done anything to him, but lately he was being really chilly toward her. And she could no longer blame it on the fact that he hated her boyfriend, Tony Conversano, because she and Tony had broken up three weeks ago.

If anything, Noah had gotten even *more* icy toward her since then. Which made her wonder if he thought she was cramping his style. Maybe he thought girls wouldn't approach him if she was with him.

Maybe it was true.

And maybe Allie was just fine with that.

But for now, here she was, stuck with him and his foul mood. And he was stuck with her. And until they caught up with Olivia and Mark, they were stuck with each other because Mark was their ride home.

"Yeah, it's a huge cow, carved out of butter," she said, trying to make it sound good. Worth coming out for. "They keep it in a refrigerated case over by the livestock." It sounded lame, even to her, although the sad truth was the butter cow was the first thing she wanted to see when her parents brought her here as a child. "It's really big."

Noah looked at her. "Are you serious?"

"Yes, I'm serious!"

"Is it as big as a real cow?"

"Almost!"

"Well, then, *of course* I want to see the butter cow." He rolled his eyes. "Beats the hell out of riding the merry-go-round."

She used to love that, too, but she decided against a passionate defense of it right now.

As it turned out, the butter cow was a lot smaller than she remembered it. Standing in front of the case, seeing it through Noah's eyes, she realized it was just a big lump of fat, vaguely shaped like an animal. The August nights had been unusually hot this year, so it was possible that it had melted from a once-incredible state, but the illusion, for Allie, was shattered and she wondered if she had just glorified it in her mind all these years.

"It's really amazing," Noah said.

"It probably *was*."

"Got anything else?"

"Sometimes they have a five-legged cow in the barns."

"Anything that's not animal related?"

That ruled out the pig races, which, she was confident, *would* still be fun.

So they walked back toward the parking

261

lot, Allie hoping all the while that *something* would catch Noah's eye so he didn't spend the next month telling her what a saint he'd been for coming with her tonight.

Instead all they ran into was Vickie Freedman and her crew.

"Allison," Vickie said, with a sideways glance both left and right at her pals. They were like the battery power that kept her going. "Who's your friend?" She gestured at Noah, who had stopped several yards away to get a Coke.

"None of your business," Allie snapped.

"He's cute. So I guess he's not with you."

"He's with me."

Vickie looked her over. "I'd guess he was a relative or something but no one related to you could be that good-looking."

Illogically, Allie's thoughts flew to her mother, and she felt really sad and angry that Vickie might say something like that about her parents, who were so nice. *And* attractive. "You are such a bitch."

"You're ugly. At least I can stop being a bitch."

Vickie's friends giggled. One of them was Lela Kelly, a girl with a face like Marcia Brady *after* she was hit by the football — Allie had known her since preschool and even though they'd never been friends her laughter felt like an act of betrayal.

"I doubt you can," Allie said. Lame.

She hadn't been aware Noah had come up until she heard him ask, "Who the hell is this?"

"No one," she said, slightly louder than she needed to. But she was as proud as a peacock that Noah had dissed Vickie.

"Victoria," Vickie said, smiling as if she were the sweetest thing on earth. "Haven't I seen you around school?"

"I have no idea," Noah said, then to Allie he added, "Ready?"

She was more than ready and they started to step away when Vickie actually put a hand on Noah's arm.

"The people we're meeting are bringing some beer," Vickie said. "Why don't you stick with us instead?"

Allie rolled her eyes. Thank goodness Noah wasn't the kind of guy who'd take her up on an offer like that, because it would have been humiliating. Just what Vickie was angling for. "What people?" Allie challenged.

"Some guys that go to MC. No one *you'd* know." Montgomery College was the local community college and had students from age sixteen to seventy-five, so conceivably Vickie was meeting her grandparents here.

But Allie doubted it.

"No, thanks," Noah said.

That *thanks* really stuck in Allie's craw, even though she knew it was just a polite reflex on his part. Nevertheless, it felt good to walk away from them with him, knowing that Vickie was watching.

"I can't believe what a bitch she is," Allie said when they were out of earshot. "Actually, I can't believe she's still so seventh-grade-bitchy."

"She goes to our school?"

"She has for *years.*" Allie made a disgusted face. "You haven't actually talked to her, have you?"

He laughed, finally, for the first time that night. "No. But why do you bother?"

"I don't know," she said honestly. "Because I'm too polite to just ignore her and walk away?"

"Whatever." Noah's interest had clearly been lost and there was no way Allie was going to make this make sense for him. "What now? Are there more animals made from solid fat or do you have some sort of topiary that's sure to impress?"

"How about the Haunted House," she suggested. "That's usually pretty cool. I mean, it's cheesy and fake, but that's part of the fun."

"Fine."

They walked to the ticket booth, where Noah — in his new grudging way — insisted on buying the tickets.

Then they followed the sounds of howls and screams, past the sideshows and the insistent game runners, to what appeared to be an enormous wooden cutout in the shape of a house, painted with purples and blacks and whites of the eyes of frightened people and animals.

It was really bad.

Noah handed over the ten tickets it cost to walk through and turned to Allie. "You're not scared, are you?"

"I think I'll be okay."

"Because if you want to turn back, it's not too late."

She pushed him and they entered the façade, walking tentatively into the dark, trying to keep their footing.

The Haunted House was more of a startling house when it came right down to it. There was nothing there that might linger in anyone's dreams, but every time they took five steps forward in the weird darkness, which smelled faintly of pot, someone would jump out and scream.

And so would Allie.

It went on like this for what seemed like

ages until they were within sight of the end. This time instead of jumping out, someone reached out and grabbed Allie, dragging her into the shadows. She caught Noah's arm just in time to take him with her.

"Scared?" There was laughter and slowly the face of Noah's friend Alan Taylor came into focus. "Gotcha!"

"Alan, you asshole." Allie's heart was still pounding. "You didn't scare me, you *startled* me. There's nothing all that impressive about being able to *startle* someone."

"Is she always this much fun?" Alan asked Noah.

"Watch it," Noah said quietly.

Allie felt herself glow in his protection.

"Okay, okay." Alan put his hands up as if in surrender. "Just tell me this, are you in the mood for some *real* entertainment?"

"Why?" Noah asked. "Do you know where there is some?"

Allie wanted to kick him.

"Yes, I do, my friend." Alan slipped a bottle out from under his shirt. "Right here."

"What's that?" Allie wanted to know.

"Cuervo Gold." He shook the bottle, as if dangling a shiny bauble in front of them. "You want?"

"No —"

"*I* do." Allie took the bottle and threw back a big swig, just to defy Noah's stupid bossiness. "Speak for yourself," she added, though her voice came out in a rasp as the liquid burned its way down her throat. "What about you, Noah? Are you chicken?"

"This is stupid," Noah said. "Allie, don't be stupid."

"You're not driving," she taunted, but she really didn't know why. Yes, he'd been a dick, but she didn't need to bait him like this. It would only end up making them fight more. "Have a little."

"After you."

"Great." Keeping her eyes on him, she lifted the bottle to her lips again and took another generous swig. If this was NyQuil, and it tasted like it, she'd be knocked out.

"Great." He took the bottle from her and, holding her gaze as defiantly as she'd held his, downed a very generous amount.

"Whoa," Alan said, snatching the bottle back. He held it up to the light. "Man, you guys drank almost all of it! I said you could have *some,* not the whole fucking thing."

"Next time, grab someone less thirsty," Allie snapped and huffed out into the night air, although she did so on somewhat wobbly legs.

The air felt good.

But so did the tequila.

"He's such an asshole." Noah was by her side again and finally they agreed on something.

"He's your friend," she said. "Not mine."

"Right. *Your* friend just ditches you and disappears."

"We'll find her," Allie said, though she had some doubts. *How* would they find Olivia? There were tens of thousands of people here, spread over tens of acres. It was almost like finding a needle in a haystack.

They walked side by side through the grounds, kicking trash aside and trying to avoid bumping into people as they went. For a good solid twenty minutes after chugging the tequila, Allie felt like she got more and more tipsy. There was a lag time when you downed it like that.

When they got to the Ferris wheel, Allie was overcome by the need to sit down, and it seemed as good a place as any. Better, actually, considering that the alternative seemed to be a ground coated with beer, Cokes, urine, and the occasional cigarette butt.

"Let's go on," she said to Noah.

"No way." He looked at it. "I'm not into Ferris wheels."

"What does *that* mean? Who's not into

Ferris wheels?"

"Me."

"Oh, come *on*." She dragged him toward the guy with his sleeves rolled up over a tattoo that read GLOREA. Had he misspelled his girlfriend's name or had she? "It will be fun."

"Allie."

"Honestly, Noah, if I don't sit down I'm going to fall down, and this is the only seat I see so you've got to come with me."

He gave a dramatic sigh but handed over the tickets and ushered her into the seat before the guy with the tattoo counted them and noticed they were two short.

Allie leaned back against the cold metal and smiled as the engine cranked to life and they started to rise up into the air. As the wheel turned one exhilarating rotation after another, Allie's mood lifted with it. She loved the feeling of the wind rushing over her as they descended, only to swoop up again. She was breathless with the same flying thrill this had always given her as a child.

That is, until it got stuck.

Naturally, Allie and Noah were at the very top when it stopped. At first she didn't panic because she figured the ride was over and they were stopping to let people out. The wheel would turn, letting passengers off one seat at a time, until they finally got to the bottom.

Except the wheel didn't turn.

It didn't move.

Allie peered over the edge, the seat creaking softly, and saw the guy in charge — a guy who suddenly looked to her like an ex-con who would as likely run from trouble as solve it — pushing the button repeatedly and cranking a mechanical arm, then looking up with a puzzled expression etched on his craggy face.

"We're stuck." The blood drained from her face and chest right into her toes. Suddenly she felt chilled, though her palms were damp.

"What?" Noah moved to look down, but he wasn't as careful as Allie had been and the seat rocked wildly.

"Stop it!" She clapped her hand onto his arm, glad for the warmth of him. "Don't move!"

"Allie, what the hell's the matter with you?"

"We're *stuck,*" she rasped, as if even *breathing* would send the seat rocketing off its axis and plunging to the ground.

"Are you afraid of heights?" Noah asked.

"No." She never had been before. Then again, she'd never been suspended fifty feet off the popcorn-strewn ground, so high up that all she could hear was the wind and the faint murmur of the crowd below and her own breathing. "I'm just . . ." She swallowed. Her mouth felt dry. "Afraid of being stuck here. Now. Like this." She looked down, then immediately looked up, her fear mounting. "Oh, my God, it's so far down there. I think I *am* afraid of heights."

"It's okay, Al." He put his arm around her and pulled her close. "It'll just be a minute."

She sank against him, trying to breathe. "They bring it in on a train, you know."

"What?"

"This ride. They bring it into town on a train. It's not like Disney World or something where they build big strong things that a hurricane can't blow down. This folds up and loads onto a flatcar like something Inspector Gadget would pull out of his case. It would fall right off the tracks if they hit a cow."

Noah drew her closer still. "Lucky for you, all the cows are in the barns. Or the display case."

She gave a small laugh. He'd been such a jerk tonight, it was good to have some semblance of the old Noah back, even if it was under terrifying circumstances.

The wind lifted again, and the seat rocked,

its old hinges squeaking quietly. "Noah . . ." Her voice was small.

"We're fine."

"This isn't meant to just stop and sit here like this with all this weight on it." She pictured the wheel falling off the great steel arms that held it and rolling across the fairgrounds into traffic, maybe even continuing on across the street and through the parking lot of Lakeforest Mall, picking up momentum until finally it crashed into JCPenney and their bodies were found in piles of bras and extra-large underpants.

"It *is* meant to do this," Noah said firmly. "It's meant to do *exactly* this. Whenever it's not moving, it's sitting like this. You're not going to get hurt. You might get bored, but you're not going to get hurt. I am one hundred percent sure of it."

She turned and looked into his eyes. It had been a long time since she'd noticed how hot he was, but the way he was looking at her now, she actually felt her heart give a flip for something *other* than the possibility of death-by-carnival.

"Are you sure or are you just bullshitting me so I'll shut up?"

"Look," he said. "Can you keep a secret?"

Her eyes widened. Was he about to make some romantic declaration to her? What

272

would she do? "I promise."

He hesitated another moment before giving a single nod and saying, "I have this train set, an old Lionel that was my dad's. He gave it to me when I was little. It's sort of our thing, you know? We add onto it and set it up and —" He stopped, looking embarrassed. "Anyway, it's a simple motor, just like the one that runs this. I learned a long time ago that if you run that kind of motor too hard, too fast, or just for too long, it overheats and stops for a while."

That made sense to Allie. "I had a blow-dryer that did that."

Noah laughed. "Okay, well, that's pretty much the same thing, too. So you know it just has to cool down and then it will work again. You don't have to do anything but wait."

She nodded. Her shoulders relaxed slightly under his arm.

"So we wait. And that guy" — he pointed at the ride operator who was, unbelievably, *still* pushing the button — "will probably give up in like five minutes for a cigarette and he'll be stunned when the thing moves again. Watch him. Seriously."

"Okay." She took a long breath in. Unfortunately the effects of the tequila were completely gone. She could have used a buzz right now. Especially when she looked down and saw just how far up they really were.

Noah must have seen the frenzy return to her eyes because he put a finger under her chin and said, softly, "Keep looking up. Try and find the Big Dipper."

She did. She'd just found the handle when he kissed her.

She didn't even see it coming. One minute she was gazing at the constellations and the next minute his mouth was on hers, his hands were tangled in her hair, cupping her face, and she was responding without thought, without logic.

She was *in* the constellations.

If she'd stopped to think about it, she might have stopped him. After all, they were *friends* and this was . . . this was *not* a friendly kiss.

The weird thing was, she wasn't feeling all that *friendly* toward him. Maybe the tequila was still working on her, because she was clutching at him, opening to his kiss, and all but ripping her clothes off as if he were the hottest movie star in the galaxy instead of good old Noah Haller.

Was there more to Noah Haller than she'd given him credit for?

She kept kissing him, as if the answer

would come to her if she gave this long enough.

It felt so good.

Where had he learned to be such an amazing kisser? He hadn't had that many girlfriends. She was sure he was still a virgin, like she was. So how did he get to be so physically intoxicating?

His hand was creeping up her shirt and she was about to let him have his way with her when the Ferris wheel lurched. Allie sprang back like she'd been bitten by a snake.

"Sorry," she said, flustered. "That was . . . I didn't . . ." She was trying to say she wasn't expecting the sudden movement.

"Me, neither," he agreed.

Though she wasn't entirely sure what he was agreeing with, she had a pretty good idea that he was talking about the kiss.

The Ferris wheel moved again and they were finally descending normally, pausing to let grateful passengers out every several seconds.

"Funny what panic will do to a person," she said, forcing a laugh. "Sorry about that."

He looked at her oddly for a moment. "No problem."

"Good. I mean, I don't want to complicate things. Be a *problem* or anything." She hoped he'd object, but he didn't.

In fact, he didn't even look at her. "Yeah, it's fine."

Though she wouldn't understand it until two decades later, they didn't speak for more than a month after that.

"So how come you and Allie aren't talking to each other anymore?" Olivia asked Noah several weeks later. Allie was home sick, so Olivia had spotted Noah at the beginning of lunch and had rushed to join him before his stupid cronies did and they couldn't talk.

He gave a half shrug. "Did you ask her?"

"Yes."

"What'd she say?"

Olivia's face grew warm. "She said you were an asshole."

He gave a dry laugh. "That must be it, then."

She decided to tread carefully but ask the question that had been on her mind for weeks. "Did something happen at the fair?"

He looked at her sharply. "What do you mean?"

"Well, you guys were, like, okay before that and I don't think you've talked to each other since then." She shrugged. "You don't have to be a genius to figure out *something* must have happened."

He considered this for a moment, then said, "Yeah, something happened."

"What?"

He met her eyes. "I kissed her."

Wow. Olivia had *not* been prepared for that. "You did?"

He nodded. "As soon as it was over she said it was a mistake, so" — he shrugged — "I decided not to make that mistake again."

"But Noah . . ." She didn't know what to say. This was huge. Why hadn't Allie mentioned it to her?

"But what?" He was impatient.

"I don't know. I guess I'm sorry. I had no idea that had happened or I wouldn't have asked you. But . . . I think you should talk to her."

"I don't have anything to say."

"It sort of sounds like you do, though. I mean, do you like her? You know, *that* way?"

His face turned red, but he shook his head as casually as if she'd asked if he liked Pop Rocks. "Not anymore."

"But you *did?* Like until after the fair? Noah, seriously, she had no idea!"

"She had a pretty good idea of it that night."

Olivia didn't know what to say. She was hurt that Allie hadn't told her anything about this — since when did they keep secrets from each other? — but she didn't want to see Noah suffer for it when she knew Allie hadn't had a clue.

"I think you should tell her just how you feel," she said to him. "Maybe she said it was a mistake because she thought *you* thought it was a mistake."

He looked at her like she was crazy. "She said it was a mistake because she thought it was a mistake." Sherry Alexander walked by and caught Noah's eye. "I don't want to talk about it, Liv. Gotta go." He didn't even look back, he just went off with Sherry, making an obvious point of flirting with her.

But Olivia suspected he was making that point not for Sherry but for Olivia herself. A little piece of information for her to take back to Allie, she supposed.

But she didn't.

She never told Allie she knew a thing about it.

SEVENTEEN

Makeup for lost time.
— ad for Lancôme Rénergie Lift Makeup

It might have taken Olivia a lot longer to figure out her mother had fallen off the "I choose me!" wagon and was doing online dating if Caroline had not been careless enough to leave her entire profile on the screen before putting Olivia's laptop into hibernate mode.

It was the second Monday in June and her mother had now been staying at her apartment for three weeks and three days.

Not that Olivia was counting.

Apparently, Caroline's makeover had given her quite a bit of confidence. Instead of pursuing the path of self-growth and independence she had talked about, however briefly, once she was a hottie again — thanks to an amazing makeover at the John Barrett salon and in Olivia's own office —

she was ready to go out on the prowl again.

Well, Olivia was just fed up with that.

"Mom, what is this?" she asked, taking the computer into the kitchen, where her mother was slicing fruit and making bad coffee in a percolator on the stove.

"I was going to ask you exactly that, it's a great little computer gadget. I'd love to get one." She set the knife down, wiped her hands on the kitchen towel hanging next to the sink, and came over to Olivia. "Let's look at the bottom and see if we can figure out what it's called, shall we?"

"I don't mean the computer, Mom, I mean the dating profile. Have you posted it to a public site?"

"No."

Phew! Olivia set the computer down on the table and said, "Good. We need to talk about some *seriously dangerous* things you've put on your profile."

"Dangerous? My goodness, you make me sound like a spy."

"More like a target." Olivia scrolled through the profiles. "For one thing, you listed the name of the building here. You cannot, absolutely *cannot,* tell every Tom, Dick, and Harry where you're staying." She'd almost said *where you're living,* but she'd caught herself just in time. The last thing in the world she wanted to do was encourage her mother to stay longer.

"I see." Caroline frowned and turned the computer toward herself, poking at the keys. "I wonder how I go about correcting that."

"I think you should start a new profile. That's just one of a bunch of things I saw here that could make you vulnerable."

"How do I take this profile off the site so I can make a new one?"

"What? You said you hadn't posted it."

"I haven't posted it *publicly*. But it's on this site. Surely the site is private, isn't it?"

Olivia took a bracing breath. "Did you have any trouble getting on it and looking around before you signed up?"

"No."

"Enough said." Olivia turned the computer back to herself. "Maybe I can cancel the account. What's your user name?"

"FreeBird."

Olivia looked at her. "Like the song?"

"What song?"

" 'Free Bird.' It's a song. Like, a huge Southern rock hit from the seventies."

Caroline shrugged. "I only used it because when I had *as a* in there between *free* and *bird* it said the name was taken."

"All right, fine. FreeBird." She typed it in. "And what's your password?"

There was a long pause before she answered, quietly, "I'm too old."

Olivia stopped looking at the site. "What?"

"I'm too old. I M the number 2 and old. No spaces."

IM2Old.

God, that was sad.

"Mom . . ." Olivia felt as though she'd been sucker punched. As aggravated as she was with her mother — and she had a lifetime of aggravation built up — this small fact, this tiny admission of her true state of confidence folded up into her password, made her anger melt away and pool like rain in a puddle of guilt at her feet.

In her years of resentment, it had never occurred to Olivia that her mother harbored any personal uncertainties.

"It was all I could think of." Her mother gave a wave of the hand, and her expression once again betrayed nothing. "You have to come up with all this stuff so fast."

Olivia nodded and typed in the password, found her way to the "account" page, and deleted the entire thing.

Then she turned to her mother. "Look, Mom, if this is something you really want to do, I don't mean to put the kibosh on it. But you have to be safe. You have to understand that there are predators out there who are more diabolical than you or I can even imagine. There's no way to stay one hundred percent safe, but you've got to do everything you can. For instance, give your general location, Manhattan, instead of the specific address. Don't give out your phone number. Don't give out *my* phone number. And, for heaven's sake, don't put down your real name."

"This is so complicated."

"That's the Internet." Olivia stood up and went to the cabinet. She took out a travel mug and poured some coffee into it. "I've got to go to work now. Please, *please* be careful while I'm gone."

"I'm not a child, Olivia."

"I know. I'm sorry, Mom, it's just — I want you to be careful, that's all. More careful than you were with that." She gave a limp gesture toward the computer. "There are more important things in the world than romance, you know."

"I certainly know that." Caroline sat straighter in her chair, her face losing some color. "But romance is also important. *Love* is important, Olivia. That's something you've never seemed to understand."

"Excuse me?" Olivia couldn't believe what she was hearing. "I've never understood the importance of love?"

"No, you haven't." Caroline spoke sharply. "Not romantic love. You act like my need for companionship is some sort of vanity."

Olivia sighed. "It's more like a compulsion, Mom. It seems like it's all you ever think about."

"That is absolutely untrue," Caroline countered, though it looked like Olivia's missile had found its mark. "You're not like me. You were always fiercely independent. You didn't want my love and attention or anyone else's."

"Don't go there, Mom." Olivia held up a warning finger, and hoped it wouldn't shake with the explosion of emotion she felt. "Do *not* go there."

"It's the truth. You trusted no one —"

"Can you blame me?"

"You *never* trusted anyone. Even long before . . . we left Potomac. Before that. To be honest with you, I thought you changed when your father died, though the doctors all said I was crazy and that you didn't know any better."

Could it really have affected Olivia's whole life to lose her father when she was eighteen months old? "It seems more likely that you checked out when Dad died," she said. "And you never came back. I can remember *so well* trying to get your attention when I was little, but you kept telling me to go away, you kept handing me off to babysitters while you went out with one guy after another."

Caroline straightened in her chair. "I wanted you to have a father."

"I *did*. But he was dead." Stupid tears prickled Olivia's eyes and she blinked them back. She was *not* going to cry. "So then I didn't have a mother, either."

"You did, you always had me. We went everywhere together, don't you remember?"

"Yes, Ohio, Wisconsin, Maryland, California." Olivia ticked off the places they'd lived with Caroline's various husbands on her fingers. "Oh, yeah, we were like Bing Crosby and Bob Hope, you and I."

Caroline didn't say anything for a long moment. She sat with her hands folded in front of her, her face pale, and her eyes unblinking.

Finally, she looked at her daughter and said, "I did my best. Maybe I wasn't good at it, but I loved you, Olivia, and I tried my best for you. And now I'm alone. I'm lonely. I don't want to die in some room by myself. I want companionship, I want *love*." She looked at her daughter with watery eyes. "Is that really such a sin?"

Was it?

The seconds ticked slowly past as Olivia knew she should say something, and more important knew she should have an answer, but she didn't.

Had her mother's need for companionship been wrong?

The answer came to Olivia on a wave of guilt.

No.

It hadn't been wrong. Her choices had, heaven knew, but it wasn't Olivia's path; it was Caroline's. Olivia had no right to judge her on it.

God, she'd been such a jerk.

All this time she'd been feeling so sorry for herself, and it had never occurred to her that her mother might also be suffering. She had no idea what a poison loneliness was to Caroline.

But how stupid. Of course she should have known. She'd been suffering from it herself, only her loneliness was self-imposed, born of a steely determination not to need anyone. She called her loneliness mere solitude.

How many people had she hurt?

"No, Mom." She went to her and put a hand on her mother's shoulder. "Of course it's not a sin."

Her mother put her hand up to touch it wordlessly. She continued to look down.

And that small gesture almost did Olivia in.

"I'm sorry, Mom," she said, bending down to kiss her. She held on for a moment before letting go. "I was wrong. About a lot of things."

"I think Noah's in love with you."

The phone had woken Allie up in the middle of a dream about fending off ferocious monkeys and snakes with a whisk broom, so she wasn't sure she'd understood Olivia correctly. "I'm sorry?"

"I realize that this might sound crazy, and it's entirely possible that I'm wrong, but I don't think I am." Olivia's voice was a little hysterical. "I think Noah is in love with you. I think he has been for a long time."

Allie rolled over on her back and put her arm over her eyes to shield it from the bright light of that stupid *extra-large digits* digital clock Kevin had gotten from Sharper Image. "Olivia, have you been drinking?"

"No, and I think this is important. Don't ask me why, I have my reasons."

"Why?"

"I just told you not to ask me that."

Allie sat up in bed and blinked in the darkness, half wondering if she was still dreaming and if a monkey was going to swing at her on a vine made of licorice. "You can't just tell me to take something like this on blind faith. You need to tell me exactly what you're basing this on."

"Okay. Hold on, let me get a drink." There was the sound of footsteps as Olivia walked across a hard floor. "But don't count on me to be entirely coherent. It's been a weird night for me."

"Tell me about it."

There was the sound of clinking dishes. "First of all, remember that time at the fair?"

"The fair?"

"Montgomery County fair. In high school."

"Good Lord, I hope that drink has caffeine in it. And that you're not driving anywhere."

"Allie, I'm serious. Eleventh grade? Maybe it was tenth. Anyway, I was with Mark Grudberg and you were with Noah, sort of, and you kissed on the Ferris wheel?"

"Oh, yeah." Allie smiled, remembering. It had actually been one of the more romantic moments of her life. "That was really nice. Scary, at the time, but it's a good memory now."

"Why didn't you tell me about it, by the way?"

"Didn't I?"

"No."

"I don't know. But you know now, so who did?"

"Noah." There was the clink of glass then the sound of a refrigerator door closing. "Obviously."

"I can't believe he even remembers that!"

"He didn't *just* tell me." Her footsteps crossed the hard floor again. Eleven-thirty at night and she was still wearing high heels even though she was calling from home. "He told me at the time. When I asked him why you and he weren't speaking."

Allie remembered that part every bit as well as she remembered the kiss. She'd been desperate for him to say that calling it a mistake had been a mistake, and for him to declare his undying love, but instead he'd refused to speak to her.

She'd figured it was because he didn't want her to get any ideas about the two of them.

That didn't really sound like the Noah she knew now, though.

"And you've kept this to yourself, wondering why I didn't tell you, all this time?" she asked.

"No, of course not." There was a sound, clearly that of shoes being kicked off. "I

289

haven't thought about it for ages," Olivia went on. "Then I was talking to my mother today, and suddenly a whole bunch of things became clear to me."

"I'm not following," Allie said. "I mean, I'm glad you had a revelation that got you so jazzed, but I don't know how this leads to Noah being in love with me and the fair in high school being relevant."

The words were sort of nice, though.

Noah in love. Noah in love with Allie. Noah and Allie. Allie and Noah.

For just a split second she remembered playing the same name games in seventh grade, but that memory quickly gave way to the way he'd looked at her the other night before he left, and a twinge spun through her core.

He hadn't looked at her like a friend.

And she hadn't responded like a friend.

Then he'd gone.

"Okay, back up," Olivia said. "It began with eighth grade —"

That was enough to pull Allie's attention back. *Eighth grade!*

"Right after he started school at Cabin John and you said you liked him. But I liked him, too. Or thought I did." She clicked her tongue against her teeth. "Actually, maybe I just wanted what you wanted because you wanted it. Anyway, the point is that we were partners in geography class and he asked me about you."

"This is still in eighth grade."

"Yes. I told you this goes back. Look, you don't have a big revelation sparked by my mother without having to dig deep."

"That makes sense." Allie shuddered to think how deeply the past got imbedded in the psyche.

She could only imagine how deep and stuck things were when Caroline was involved.

"So. Noah asked me about you in eighth grade because he liked you but I told him you liked someone else."

"Really? Who?"

"I don't remember, but that's not the point. I sabotaged you! You two might have gotten together but I threw a wrench in it."

"I can't believe we're talking about this like we're still in junior high."

"This is no proud moment for me, believe me."

Allie laughed. "Liv, it was *eighth grade*. I seriously doubt Noah and I would be married today if only we'd made out in the back of Ms. Rosen's music room twenty-five years ago."

"All right, what if you'd gotten together in

twelfth grade?"

"Oh, well, twelfth grade. That would have made all the difference. We'd probably have a couple of kids and a golden retriever by now, too."

"You could have," Olivia said. "You might have."

"Look," Allie said, dismissing the idea. *After* twelfth grade they might have made a go of it. Two years ago they could have. But as kids? There was no way. "If that was really our destiny, it would have taken more than one hapless teenager to break it up."

"I wasn't hapless," Olivia said, sounding serious. "I was selfish."

"So what if you were? It would have taken more than one *selfish* teenager to break it up. In fact, I don't even know what it is you think you did."

"I didn't tell you he was upset. He was heartbroken and I knew it and I didn't tell you. And frankly, you must have had some pretty strong feelings going on there, too, because otherwise I can't believe you wouldn't have told me about it."

Allie thought back to that time. It wasn't hard. She hadn't carried a lot of high school stuff forward with her into life, but now that she gave it some thought, details were coming back to her with some clarity.

She'd had a crush on Noah for a long, long time. It didn't stop them from being friends, but the friendship stopped her from telling him how she felt. The possibility of humiliation was just too great — every week someone wrote to Ann Landers about confessing their love to their best friend and being shot down.

But then he'd kissed her. And it had been so great. The adrenaline of her fear, mixed with the surging hormones, and the undeniable romance of being suspended high in the sky with neon below and starry velvet above, had made for a potent mix.

Finally, she thought. *Finally.*

Then the ride had jerked to life. She'd been startled and drew back from Noah just as he was making his big move toward second base.

And she'd wanted him to make the move. In fact, at that point, she'd have been content if the ride had stayed stuck forever.

But when she started to apologize for gasping, he immediately agreed, he was sorry, too, it was a mistake, and so on.

Allie had gotten off that Ferris wheel so humiliated, and so *disappointed,* that she couldn't even bear to tell Olivia what a fool she'd been. Because Olivia's response would have been obvious, or so she'd thought: *Why would you think you could have a thing with Noah Haller? You've been friends too long. He thinks of you as a kid sister, not as a girlfriend.*

The dialogue in Allie's head had been written by her, but it had been easy to imagine Olivia saying it.

And she was embarrassed enough at making such a mistake without spreading the word about what a fool she was.

"You know, it's funny," Allie said to Olivia now, rolling over in bed and talking into the phone just like they had two decades ago. "I really did have the hots for him for so long, but I was too stupid to say anything to him." She anticipated Olivia's guilt and added, "And even if you'd told me you'd caught him crying into his pizza lunch, wailing my name, I wouldn't have had the balls to say anything. I thought it was the boy's job."

Olivia sighed. "I still think it's the boy's job."

"Yeah. Me, too." Allie laughed. "So even if you're right about Noah now, I just don't have it in me to say anything to him. Especially now that he's talking about marrying Vickie." She felt sick at the thought.

"But that's exactly why you *need* to," Olivia said. "Before it's too late. Look, I've been antilove all my life —"

"Who could blame you?" Allie asked. A few stepfathers, flaky mother, constantly moving from one part of the country to another. "I would have been, too."

"You weren't, and you were right. I was wrong. No matter what kind of crap relationships my mother had, or how awful it was to spend a childhood at their mercy, it was stupid to conclude that love itself sucked. It was just my mother's taste that did."

"That makes sense."

"Yeah, finally. Anyway, that's why I know that you need to talk to Noah and at least give it a shot. Like I said, *before* it's too late."

"It already is."

"No it isn't, Allie, if you just —"

"He came by my apartment and told me he can't see me anymore."

"What?"

Allie nodded, even though Olivia couldn't see her. And she was glad Olivia couldn't see her, because she felt like she might cry. "We can't even be friends anymore."

"Did he say why?"

"Isn't it obvious? Ever since he announced he was dating Vickie I've been all Eeyore about it. Then when he said he was going to marry her, I reacted like he'd announced he

295

had a terminal illness."

"Allie," Olivia said. "I'm not being a smart-ass here, but isn't that the way you've *always* been with him? Haven't you always shot from the hip?"

It was true. "I guess so."

"Then why would he suddenly be offended by that?"

"Because he was never getting married before."

"Okay, then tell me this: Why doesn't he sound happy about getting married?"

Allie leaped on that. "You've noticed that, too?"

"Yes. It's really obvious."

It stank that Noah seemed unhappy, but Allie was at least a tiny bit relieved that her impression had been true and not just colored by her dislike of Vickie.

"Then what can we do?"

"Funny you should ask that," Olivia said. "Because I think I might have the solution."

Now *that* sounded just like the Olivia of old.

Actually, it sounded even more like the *Allie* of old.

"Okay, I'll bite," she said. The solution. Maybe there *was* a solution. "What is it?"

"Can you come to New York?"

"Yes. When? Why?"

"As soon as possible. And because I have a plan and it might be the only way we can save Noah. And you."

"Me?"

"You know it."

Allie swallowed. "How's this weekend?"

"Perfect."

EIGHTEEN

This season, beauty is in color.
— ad for Estée Lauder

After work on Friday afternoon, which consisted of a bunch of dull but profitable proofreading for a defense firm downtown, Allie drove to her parents' house to wait out rush hour before driving to Olivia's in New York.

Maybe it was everything that was going on, maybe it was the fact that she was about to have a "sleepover" with Olivia for the first time in twenty years, and maybe it was just the old Madonna song playing on the radio when she got in the car, but by the time Allie pulled up in front of the brick Colonial she'd grown up in, her mood was terribly melancholy.

The storm door was open when she arrived, like the warm glow of a candlewick. The lights were on inside. Straight ahead she could see the shadows of her mother's movements in the kitchen, and to the left there was the flicker of the TV lights. Her dad watching ESPN, undoubtedly, and waiting for dinner.

She walked right in, just like always. "What's for dinner?" she asked as she walked into the kitchen and saw the steaming pot on the stove.

"Five-cheese penne. Are you staying?" her mom asked.

She loved that. It was a Barefoot Contessa recipe and it would blow her points off the chart today, but she'd been saving up for a special occasion. "Yes, please."

"I thought you were off to New York."

Allie reached for the hunk of Parmigiano Reggiano her mother had to the side of the stove and pulled off a piece. "I thought I'd pass the time here until rush hour is over." She popped the cheese into her mouth, where it melted into pure flavor like only the best Parmesan can.

"Good thinking." Peggy poured the penne into the pot. "So what's behind this trip anyway?"

"Nothing's *behind* it. I'm just going to see Olivia."

"Whom you haven't seen or talked to in years. Then, suddenly, when Noah's getting married you two are close as peas in a pod again." Peggy raised an eyebrow. "If you don't want to talk about it, that's fine, honey. But I know my girl well enough to know when something is going on."

"Nothing's going on, Mom."

"All right." Peggy ladled some chicken stock into the pot and stirred.

"Nothing bad, anyway."

"That's a relief. Hand me the cheese, would you?"

Allie handed her the block of cheese and watched her shave it over a microplane into the pot. "I just don't think Noah should marry Vickie."

"So you've said." Her mother raised an eyebrow again. "Is there more to it now?"

Of course. "I think I have feelings for him. I think . . . I might really have feelings for him."

Peggy set the cheese down, wiped her hands on her apron, and looked at Allie. "It's about time you figured that out."

"Am I the only one who's just finding out?"

Peggy gave a laugh. "Allison, Noah has come by every Thanksgiving dinner, every Christmas morning, every family cookout for the past I don't know how many years unless one of you was with someone else at the time. No matter what else happens, or who else you have a relationship with, you always come back to each other."

"But we never . . . *did* anything."

Peggy shrugged. "I'm not speculating as to whether you did or not. I just know you've spent more time with each other than a lot of married couples. Then when things ended with Kevin, you were angry but you didn't really seem upset. But as soon as Noah got engaged you were moping around, crying all the time."

It was all true. "But do you think I'm just jealous?"

"Actually no, I don't."

She was strangely relieved to hear her mother say that. It was like validation. Proof that this was real.

"I don't, either."

"So the question is, what are you going to do about it? Are you trying to stop him from marrying Victoria?"

"I've got to try."

"And if you can't? Have you thought about what you'll do then?"

"No. I can't think about that." It must have been the effects of being home, because without any warning at all, Allie began to cry.

"Oh, honey." Her mother put warm arms

around her. Suddenly it didn't matter how old she was, it felt like her mom could fix anything. "Then you do what you need to do."

A few hours later, on the road to New York, what Allie had to do was dial Noah's number twice — with star 67 each time for anonymity — just to hear his voice before hanging up and disappearing back into the night and the New Jersey Turnpike.

"I'm going to Aunt Cassandra's tonight," Caroline said, shortly after Olivia got home from work. "Do you want to join me?"

Olivia dropped her keys and purse on the table in the foyer and headed for the kitchen, where her mother was sitting and writing up some sort of list. "You're going to Aunt Cassandra's *again?*"

"Mm-hm. She wanted some help going through her clothes and donating the ones she doesn't wear anymore to charity."

This didn't compute. "That's great, Mom, but I don't get it." She took the coffee out of the freezer. "You can't stand Aunt Cassandra, yet you're going over there like two, sometimes three times a week all of a sudden."

Caroline sighed. "We have had our share of disagreements in the past, that's true, and she can be a callous old goat."

"But . . . ?" She put coffee into the filter.

"Oh, I don't know. She needs the help."

"She can *hire* the help." Olivia put water in the machine, pushed start and turned to face her mother. "Come on, I know there's more to this. What has she got on you?"

"As far as I know, nothing." Caroline laughed. "But I wouldn't be completely surprised if she came up with something."

"I'll bet she has an entire dossier."

"Olivia, that's not quite fair."

"I cannot believe you're my mother." Maybe coffee wasn't strong enough, she thought, as it started to percolate. "Seriously, what have you done with Caroline?"

Caroline smiled. "People change."

Olivia poured her coffee into a mug and took it to the table, sitting down and taking a moment to assimilate this. There was something her mother wasn't saying. "I seriously doubt she's going to put you in her will at this point."

Caroline looked so genuinely surprised that Olivia immediately felt terrible for having said it.

"I wouldn't dream of accepting a penny from her," Caroline said, practically clutching her pearls. "I can't believe you'd suggest such a thing! You are the sole heir to that fortune."

"*Me?*"

"Of course. Cassandra never had children and you are your father's only child, so naturally the family inheritance goes to you." Caroline took a demitasse cup from the cabinet — she'd purchased them herself a few days ago — and poured herself a thimbleful of the coffee. "Who did you think would get it?"

"I never thought about it." Ever. She'd *never* thought about the money. All she'd ever thought about with regard to her father was that she wished she could remember something, anything, about him. He'd died when she was about eighteen months old, and though her mother had never talked much about him, it was Olivia's impression that her father was different from her subsequent stepfathers.

Maybe it was just wishful thinking, but she wished she'd known the one good man in her and her mother's lives.

"Perhaps you should start thinking about it," Caroline said, then took a dainty sip. "An inheritance that size will need some clever investing. You should be prepared."

"I have a feeling Aunt Cassandra is more the I'm-leaving-it-all-to-my-cat sort."

Caroline shook her head. "She can be

304

stern, but she's not crazy."

"We'll see."

"Also, she hates cats."

Olivia sighed. "That figures."

"Anyway, I think I may stay overnight, so don't wait up for me."

"Overnight," Olivia echoed. "You and Aunt Cassandra are having a slumber party?"

Caroline sighed. "The charity truck is coming for the pickup first thing in the morning. I can check that they make out the charitable donation slip correctly."

This was just hard to picture on so many levels. "That's a shame. You'll miss Allie."

Caroline took another sip and set her cup down. "I thought you two might enjoy being alone after all this time."

"That's nice of you." Olivia got up and refilled her coffee cup. "I think we might be up late."

"And what will you two be doing tomorrow?"

"I'm hoping Allie will take me up on some of the appointments I've set up for her." And she really hoped Allie wouldn't be insulted that she'd done it. "Meanwhile, I'll be at work."

"Olivia Pelham, you cannot work another weekend! I've been here a month and you have taken exactly four days off in that time. That's not healthy."

Olivia shrugged. "I love my work." She did, she loved her work. It kept her from having to ponder all of the questions other single women her age were pondering. New York was a big city, with lots of people, but it was probably the crappiest place in the world to date.

Luckily for Olivia, she didn't have to think about that right now.

She could worry about that later.

"It's funny, but you used to say that about school, too, to the exclusion of almost everything else."

"I did?"

Caroline nodded. "Even when you were young and carefree and should have been boy crazy, you always said you'd rather do your homework."

"Oh, yeah." She *had* said that. And when the choice had been homework or hanging out with her mother and Donald, homework had won every time. "I guess I've always had a good work ethic."

Caroline looked unconvinced. "Or maybe you just like hiding from real life. In any event, I hope you won't leave your friend sitting here alone in the apartment while you toil."

Olivia laughed at the mental picture of her *toiling*. "No, Mom, I won't." With the class-A treatments she'd set up, Allie was going to be busier than she was.

Fortunately her mother let the conversation drop there, but Olivia kept thinking about it long after her mother left. There was some truth to her mother's contention: From an early age she had learned she could dive into the things that were expected of her — school, work, homework — and thereby escape the stuff that she found truly hard: socializing, friendships, boyfriends.

In fact, if it hadn't been for Allie, Olivia might never have come out of that shell.

Interesting. She'd never looked at it that way. Despite the problems they'd had in the end, Allie had contributed quite a bit to what Olivia's life had eventually become.

"I can't believe you're really here," Olivia said over wine and cheese at eleven o'clock that night.

They were sitting in Olivia's opulent living room. One entire wall was full of windows looking over the Upper East Side. It was gorgeous. Allie kept worrying that she'd spill something on the snow-white sofa or carpet, but she loved the feeling of sitting in the middle of someone else's glamorous life.

"Me, neither," Allie said, leaning back against the plush sofa cushions. "This is all sort of surreal."

"In a way, we have Vickie to thank for this."

"True." It was a sad thought but to the point. A long moment passed before Allie screwed up the nerve to ask, "Do you think we should talk about what happened?" She was testing cold waters with one timid toe.

She'd thought for a long time she needed to nudge the issue, because they were talking again, forming a tentative friendship. But, on the other hand, she wondered if it might not be smarter just to let that sleeping bear lie.

"What happened? You mean back in high school?"

Allie nodded.

Olivia sighed and looked toward the windows. Clearly it wasn't something she particularly wanted to leap into, either. "We could, but what would be the point? We were both young. I really can't blame you for what happened. We were seventeen. I heaped a big, heavy secret on you and expected you to be more mature than most adults I know."

Allie bristled. Old feelings still lingered in her psyche like tea leaves left in a cup.

"Listen, Olivia, I don't want to hammer the point or defend something so old it's no longer relevant, but I have to say this: I honestly didn't tell anyone."

Olivia looked at her with sad eyes, as if she'd expected this denial but didn't buy it. "What can I say to that?"

"I don't know. I know why it's hard for you to believe. To this day I wonder how everyone found out. It's like one of the great mysteries of my life, but I swear to you, Olivia, it didn't come from me."

There was a very long silence. Allie filled the time by slicing off a piece of the Brie she shouldn't have been eating.

"I've thought about it, too," Olivia said. She worked her hands nervously in her lap. This was still a hot issue for her, but who could blame her? "Maybe I wasn't as discreet as I thought I was."

"What do you mean?" Had she told someone else? Who? Who else could she possibly have trusted as much as she'd trusted Allie at the time?

Olivia set her wine down. "We talked about it in between classes at school, do you remember?"

"Of course." How could she forget?

"In the bathroom."

"Right."

Olivia shrugged. "Obviously we weren't shouting, but I suppose it's possible some-one overheard in the hall."

"It would have to be someone pretty evil to go spreading it around. You were so up-set."

"I don't know about *evil*, necessarily. Just crappy. There are as many crappy people as nice ones in high school." Olivia swallowed and lifted her wineglass again, with a hand that shook slightly. "Let's change the subject and let that one rest finally."

"Okay." Allie wondered if it was really go-ing to rest, and if Olivia really believed her, but she knew better than to push the issue right now. She'd said what she needed to say and she believed she'd finally been heard. "Let's talk about your life in New York."

Olivia shook her head, but a light came into her eye. "Better still, let's talk about *your* life in New York."

Allie raised an eyebrow. "The reason you told me I had to cancel everything, no mat-ter what, and come as soon as possible."

Olivia smiled. "Exactly."

"Hit me with it, I'm ready. What's the plan?"

"You are going to have a makeover. Now, before you get all up in arms, thinking I'm saying you *need* one, let me just say that, for all the times you did it for me, I thought I owed you one. Here you've lost all this weight —"

"Only twelve pounds." Allie was thrilled with twelve pounds gone, but the battle was far from over. She was well aware that she was the only one celebrating when her jeans were fractionally easier to button.

"Here you've lost all this weight," Olivia stressed again, "so I think it's time you treat yourself."

"That's so nice of you," Allie said, but she was still puzzled. There was more to this. And as much as she wanted to enjoy this time with Olivia after so long, she felt cautious. It wasn't that she was necessarily picking up on a hesitation from Olivia so much as she was afraid to trust this, to truly give herself to it, in case it didn't work.

She'd lost Olivia as a friend once before and it had hurt like hell. Good as it felt to start to share confidences with her again, it wasn't worth it if it was all going to end up going down the drain again.

"It's nothing," Olivia said, her voice betraying no hidden agendas or volatile feelings. "I've got all these resources but I very rarely have anyone who would appreciate them. You used to be the makeover queen,

311

so I thought you'd get a kick out of it."

Allie smiled. "And how does this save Noah?"

"Mmm?"

"Your plan was to save Noah. And me. How does it save Noah for me to get a haircut?"

The question remained suspended in the air for a moment before Olivia's posture sank and she gave in and told the truth.

"Because I *know* you guys have the hots for each other, even though *you* have remained mysteriously unaware of that fact, and I think if you had the confidence you *should* have, you might be a little more open to the idea."

Allie laughed.

"It's the truth," Olivia insisted. "People have all kinds of ways to boost their confidence; I'm not saying my way is the only way, but you" — she gestured with her wine — "are a makeup and hair girl. That's the key to your happiness, and I can give you that."

"Who says that's the key to my happiness?"

"Oh, Allison Denty, it has *always* been the key to your happiness. You were never more joyful than when you were leaving Montgomery Mall with a Woolworth's bag full of

Aziza, Maybelline, and Flame-Glo."

There was no point in denying it. The mere memory of it made her feel warm. "It's true."

"Remember that time we bought Village Naturals beer shampoo and sat by the penny fountain pretending we were drinking beer?"

Allie gasped. "And that old woman walked by and *actually* wagged her finger at us and yelled at us for drinking beer!"

"Right!"

Allie closed her eyes for a moment and sighed. "That was about the coolest I ever felt," she said sincerely. Then, "That's sad, isn't it?"

"Yes," Olivia agreed. "But as nervous as I was that she was going to call my mom or Donald, I also felt cool."

"We were such losers." Allie laughed.

"But we had fun!"

"We did." Allie took a moment to linger in that misty feeling of the past before saying, "And now here we are in cahoots all over again. Only this time, you're the one with the plan. What do you want me to do?"

"Glad you asked," Olivia said, getting right back to business, though this time with a smile in her voice. "Because *you* have the hard part."

"Which is . . . ?"

"You have to go to Noah and tell him the truth about how you feel."

Nineteen

"Remember that green face mask we used to get?" Olivia asked as she unlocked the door to her office on Saturday evening.

Allie had spent the day at the stylist, getting cut, highlighted, colored, styled, and tipsy from all the free champagne they'd served. Then she and Olivia had had a long and fattening dinner at Patsy's restaurant and had just enough garlic and wine in them to keep going a few more hours.

"Queen Helene's Mint Julep Masque?"

Olivia nodded. "That's it."

"Oh, my God, did you know they still make it?" Allie was clearly thrilled by this revelation. "I bought some at Bed Bath and Beyond the other day. I couldn't believe they had it."

"Chuck it."

"*What?* Are you kidding?"

"Nope. You're moving on."

"To what?"

"The good stuff." Olivia opened the door and flipped on the lights, illuminating her large corner office.

"But I love that green stuff! It's pretty good."

"Follow me." She led Allie to an alcove in the office, which had shelves stacked with products to sample.

Allie's eyes widened as she walked in. "Oh."

"Exactly."

"This is incredible," Allie breathed, looking around like a kid at Disney World for the first time. "If I'm Cinderella today, this is the castle."

She still didn't quite get that she *was* Cinderella today. After her visit to the salon, Olivia had had her assistant take Allie down to the sample room to pick out some more figure-flattering clothes. Allie had lost a good chunk of weight, but she hadn't bothered to dress like it. Not everything in the sample room had fit, fashion being what it was, but there was enough good stuff to boost Allie's self-esteem.

"Now that you're old," Olivia said, tongue in cheek, "those cheap masks will dry out your skin and make you look like Grannie on *The Beverly Hillbillies* instead of Ellie May."

Allie's face fell. "Really?"

"Not to worry." Olivia went to the shelf and took out glycolic acid dermabrasion pads. "This is ten thousand times more effective and not nearly as painful. In fact, it's not painful at all." She handed the jar to Allie. "They look like Stridex pads, but they are so much better. Rub one on your face and neck, wait five minutes, and rinse."

"And?"

"And behold a miracle. At least if you do it a couple of times a week, and stay out of the sun, and drink lots of water, and do everything else I tell you to."

"Yes, ma'am." Allie unscrewed the top and took out a pad. "Just rub it on?"

Olivia nodded. "Rub it on." She went to the shelves and took down some more products. This was much more fun than when she'd done the same thing for her mom, partly because Allie was so much more interested in it.

But also, Allie was young. Olivia knew this, even though they were the same age and sometimes she felt as if she were a hundred, particularly in a business in which models over the age of twenty-two were regarded as old, crippled football players.

"Now what?"

"Now wait."

Allie sat back on a secretarial chair Olivia had brought over to the product closet. "So this is your office, huh? Pretty nice digs."

Olivia nodded. "It'll do."

"I bet there are hundreds of people working here who would claw you to death if they heard you talking like that."

"You're right."

"So why don't you seem happier about it?"

"I'm happy," Olivia said, but the words stuck in her throat. It wasn't a lie, really. Not a big lie. It was just . . . She sighed and amended, "I'm not *un*happy."

"But you should be happy," Allie said. "Everyone should be, but especially someone who seems to have the world in the palm of her hand. What's missing for you?"

"Nothing's missing! When did you become a psychologist?"

"Actually, Liv, you haven't changed so much that I can't read you anymore. There's something you're not saying, so you can either spit it out or we can chitchat about your view."

Olivia sank down into the chair opposite Allie's. "You're right, there's something missing."

"What is it?"

Olivia met her eyes. "I don't know. Do you want some wine?"

Allie looked surprised. "Is there a bar in here, too?"

"Sort of." Olivia opened a drawer and took out a bottle of Veuve Clicquot champagne that had a red bow tied around the neck. "The editors of French *Elle* are always sending this stuff and I'm always squirreling it away for a special occasion. I'd say this qualifies, wouldn't you?"

"Absolutely!"

"I'm going to get ice. Could you open this?" She handed it over to Allie and went to the break room and filled a Tupperware container someone had left behind with ice. She also grabbed two tumblers.

When she got back, Allie had gotten out the coffee machine.

"Do you prefer coffee?"

"No, it's a little trick I learned in college." Allie took the ice, put it in the basket of the coffeemaker, and poured the champagne over it slowly. Then she took the carafe out and held it up. "Voilà! Cold champagne! The French would never approve, of course, but I can't tell much difference."

"Perfect." Olivia poured the champagne

into the tumblers and handed one to Allie. "Cheers. Now go wash your face."

Allie took a sip of the wine, then dutifully went to the sink and rinsed her face, blotting afterward with paper towels.

"Now, moisturizer." Olivia took out her own container of Philosophy's Hope in a Jar. "This is the best."

"The Oprah stuff."

"That's it." She handed Allie the little white jar with plain black type. "But forget Oprah. It works on everyone. Have you used it before?"

Allie scoffed. "If they don't have it at CVS, I haven't used it."

Olivia sighed. "So much educating to do, so little time."

They clinked their glasses again and Olivia ushered Allie back to her chair. "Now — makeup. My favorite part."

"You know, it's really ironic that now you're the makeup expert and I'm the rube."

"You're not a rube."

"Oh, yes." Allie looked around at the embarrassment of wealth Olivia had in the form of costly cosmetics, creams, potions, and supplements. "Yes, I am. I can't even *pronounce* half this stuff and it's not because it's foreign. It's all science these days.

Money and science."

Olivia nodded. "So you can see how they lured me in."

Allie gave a shout of laughter. "Oh, my God, you're right! You were always the science and math girl!"

It was true, she had been. The more straightforward, the better. Olivia had never wanted to be creative, or to think too much, or delve into her innermost thoughts. That was painful. English composition had been a nightmare. But math and science had always been her friends.

"I still am," she said, brushing mineral foundation over Allie's still perfect skin.

"It seems to have served you well." Allie drank from her glass.

Olivia paused to do the same. The champagne was tickling down her throat, warming her inside. Loosening some of the internal ties that bound her. "This is nice," she said. "I'm glad you came."

"Are you kidding? This is fabulous! But I still don't know why you suddenly wanted to give me a makeover. This isn't some sort of hidden-camera thing for the magazine, is it?"

"Oh, God no. I would never ambush you like that. This is just for fun." But she had her reasons, all right. Allie needed the

confidence to go for what was really important to her: Noah. And Olivia still knew
enough about Allie to know that confidence
was the thing that was keeping her from going for it.

So Olivia went on, touching her cheeks
with blush, lining her eyes with the perfect
complementary colors, shading them to
enhance the nice shape that had always been
there. It was easy to put makeup on Allie
because her face, the canvas, was so good.

Though Allie never would have believed
it.

Finally, she took out mascara. "Look up."

Allie did. "What kind is it?"

"Lancôme. It's the only one you can cry
in and just wipe it off instead of looking like
a raccoon. Look down."

Allie did. "Thank God I can cry safely
now."

"I don't think you're going to want to."
Olivia brushed on a few more swipes, then
stepped back and said, "Okay, take a look."

Allie looked into the mirror and broke into
a wide smile. "Damn, Liv, you are *good!*"
She squinted and scrutinized her image,
turning from side to side, checking it out. "I
can't believe what you've done." She looked
at Olivia. "You have to move in with me!"

"I'm not going back to D.C.!" Olivia

laughed.

"Then I'm moving in with you." She looked back into the mirror. "You've performed a miracle."

"No I didn't. Everything you're looking at was already there. I barely had to put any makeup on you at all."

Allie rolled her eyes. "That is so untrue."

"It's not untrue at all." Olivia sat down and poured more champagne into each of their glasses. "Let me tell you a little secret I've learned from years of being in this industry: There are no miracles. Sure, you can use stuff that will make your skin look and feel worse, and there's certainly stuff that can make your skin look and feel better."

Allie touched her cheek. "Clearly."

"Yes. But what you're looking at in the mirror is you. Right? It's you."

"It's Ideal Me."

"Well, that's what everyone wants, isn't it? Even these people who go out and have their noses shaved down to pencil erasers, and who get implants, and fillers, and who Botox their faces into immobility, they're all in search of the miracle that's going to make them feel like . . ." She searched for the word. "Like themselves."

"That's right!" Allie gasped. "That's

exactly it! I don't go out looking for products that will make me look *young* or like some perfect ideal, I just keep buying the fantasy, hoping I'll end up feeling comfortable in my own skin."

"That's exactly it. So keep your skin at its best, use the things that help and don't hurt, but accept yourself all along the way."

"Easier said than done."

Olivia nodded. "I know. All the good stuff takes work."

Allie looked at the shelves full of products. "So the *What Now* senior beauty editor says there is no real Hope in a Jar."

"Not other than that." She gestured at the table in front of the mirror. "The hope has to be in you."

They were silent for a moment.

"That's really corny," Allie said at last.

"I know! But true."

"Definitely true."

"So let's talk about what you're going to do when you get home."

"Uh-oh. Are you up to something?"

"Me?" Olivia put a hand to her chest. "Of course not! But I *do* have an idea . . ."

"What?"

"Go see Noah. Tell him how you feel. Wrestle him away from Vickie's clutches."

"This *was* an ambush!"

"You know you want to."

Allie didn't answer.

"I know you want to, too," Olivia added.

"What if he rejects me?"

"He won't."

"Okay, you think he won't. So humor me. What if he does?"

Olivia thought about it. "If he did, which he wouldn't, you would dust yourself off and move on, knowing you had done your best. Knowing you'd been true to yourself."

Allie was silent for a moment. "Eventually I suppose that *would* feel better than never having tried."

"You would," Olivia said, with feeling. "Honestly. You're in a rut, Al, you've told me so yourself. You're not satisfied with your life, your job, or your love life. It's time for a change."

Allie lifted an eyebrow. "What are you proposing?"

"I don't know. A makeover. Change your look, change your life." Olivia thought about that for a moment, then nodded. "Yes. That's it. A person doesn't need to tackle *everything* all at once in order to push the dominoes over to start change going."

Allie laughed. "When did you get so philosophical?"

"I don't know. It's come on me rather suddenly lately. I'm kind of scaring myself."

"Afraid you might have to turn the microscope inward?" Allie laughed.

Olivia laughed, too, but the truth was, that was exactly what she was afraid of. "Let's stick to one basket case at a time, okay? What do you say to a little change?"

TWENTY

TWELFTH GRADE

I told two friends and they told two friends
and so on and so on and so on and so
on . . .

> — ad for Fabergé Organics
> Wheat Germ Oil
> and Honey Shampoo

Olivia hated the winters here in Washington.
Springs were beautiful, with cherry blossoms and azaleas; summers were all blue skies and pool weather; autumns came alive with red leaves and golden sunsets; but winters — that deadly stretch from January to April — were relentlessly gray and damp and bone-chillingly cold. It always seemed to be cloudy and there was a lot of miserable coastal rain but it never seemed to snow.

Even Norman Rockwell couldn't have done anything with a Washington, D.C., winter.

So by the middle of January this year,

Olivia was already feeling desperate. For what, she couldn't say. She never could. Sun, warmth, blue sky, maybe all of that.

Hope.

That was the thing. She was without hope.

Everyone else was talking about college, visiting colleges, getting their applications in and their results back. But Olivia's mother was short on resources, and there wasn't a chance that Donald was going to kick in, so Olivia was facing nothing more than Montgomery Community College.

Allie was going to Rutgers, as her father had.

"It's close," Allie had assured Olivia. "I'll be back all the time. And maybe you can even get a scholarship or a grant or something and go there, too!"

But Olivia's ambition wasn't to follow Allie to New Jersey any more than it was to stay here and go to junior college.

Olivia's ambitions, though she had only a slippery grasp on them at this point, were to pack a backpack, get a Eurail Pass, and travel around Europe for a few months, taking pictures.

She'd found she was pretty good at photography, actually. By the time her guidance counselor had figured out that she needed to take another elective instead of another math, photography had been one of the only faintly appealing classes left, so Olivia had signed up only to find that she liked it.

Now she loved the idea of recording slices of life with her camera and maybe selling them to magazines or newspapers. Someday maybe she could even do her own book of photos or a show at one of the galleries downtown.

Meanwhile, it was the perfect excuse to, as Donald disdainfully put it, "bum around Europe."

However, once Donald had proclaimed that to be a stupid idea, Olivia's mother had mindlessly agreed, so Olivia was stuck here, going to MC until . . . what?

Until she got a job and earned enough money to make her own choices, she supposed.

This was what she was thinking about every night, including January 20. She'd had dinner with Donald and her mother, done her homework, and gone upstairs to call Allie as usual.

Around nine o'clock she heard her mother and Donald bickering downstairs. She couldn't tell what it was about, but she didn't care. This seemed to happen all the time lately. And as usual, around nine-thirty, her mother came up the stairs and walked down the creaking hallway to her bedroom.

Around ten, Olivia had finally given up trying to keep her wandering mind on a book, so she turned out the lights and lay in the dark, hoping for sleep to come.

It took ages. She felt like she tossed and turned and looked at the clock every five minutes. Now and then she drifted off but then she'd wake again, agitated.

Finally, shortly after one-thirty A.M., she decided to go downstairs and make a cup of hot chocolate or hot milk or maybe some chamomile tea. Anything that might help relax her.

She went out into the chilly hallway and made her way down the stairs in the dark so the light didn't wake her mother and Donald. When she got to the bottom of the steps, the house lights and streetlights coming through the window provided enough light for her to get to the kitchen, where she turned on the light. Flicker, the bird, stirred in his cage but didn't squawk, thank God.

She took a mug out of the cabinet, filled it with water, and put it in the microwave and waited for it to heat.

At first she didn't take any notice of the reflection in the microwave door because the light was on, but when the timer went off and the oven went dark, she could see, with crystal clarity, that Donald was standing in the kitchen behind her.

It was hard to say what instinct guided her to pretend she didn't notice him, but that's what she did, rifling through the cabinet, looking for a tea bag, opening it with great deliberation, then dunking it in the water.

When she finally couldn't think of anything else to do that would require her to keep her back to him, she turned around and pretended to be surprised.

"Oh! Donald! I didn't know you were there."

"I've been watching you." His words were slightly slurred.

That was no surprise. He'd been drinking a lot in the past year. When they'd first moved in, he didn't drink at all, but now Olivia was positive he was an alcoholic.

But he rarely reached the point of slurring.

"Sorry if I bothered you," she said, trying to keep her voice normal. "I'm just going up to bed now." She moved forward, keeping her eyes on the tea, dreading the moment when she'd have to pass him in order to get through the door and bolt upstairs.

Sure enough, as soon as she got within an arm's reach, he grabbed her arm, shaking the hot tea onto her and himself.

Olivia recoiled, both from his touch and the scalding liquid.

"Let go!" She wrenched her arm free, but he was fast, and grabbed her again.

Harder this time.

"Don't you raise your voice at me, young lady."

The stench of alcohol rode on his breath and settled between them.

"Please don't grab me," she said, more quietly, although part of her thought this would be a good time to raise the roof.

But if she did, what would he do to her then?

"You live in my house," he rasped. "You do as I say."

Something told her this was not a time to argue back.

"Can I please go?" she asked quietly, not meeting his eyes. "I have school tomorrow."

"Maybe we should have a little talk first." Again, he slurred his words. How could his reflexes be so fast when he couldn't even talk? "Come on into my den."

That would be like following a spider into its web.

"I really need to sleep," she said, swallowing hard because her throat felt like it was closing. Dread. Fear. "I have a test tomor-row."

"You have a test tonight." He pulled her out of the kitchen and down the single step to his den, a room that had originally been a garage and, as such, felt far from the rest of the house. "I'm going to test your loyalty."

"To who?"

He chuckled. "That's a good one. You're a smart kid." He opened the door and pulled her in. "Say we start by testing your loyalty to your mother. You wouldn't want to tell her about our little meeting tonight."

"What's to tell?" Olivia's entire body trembled. "I just want to go to my room."

"Then again, there should be a little loyalty to me, too, don't you think?" He went on as if she hadn't said a word. "Be-cause I've given you a roof over your head and food and everything else you needed for six and a half years."

Olivia stood tall, hoping he couldn't tell how she shook. "It wasn't my choice."

"You were the beneficiary, though, weren't you?" He released his grip on her arm and rubbed a knuckle over her breast, watching with obvious pleasure when her nipple rose at his touch.

It was cold and fear and she knew it, but she knew just as well that he took that as a sign of her wanting him.

She stepped back, pulling her nightgown tighter around her, wishing it was newer or warmer or made of steel. "I'd be glad to leave."

And she would leave. She would leave tomorrow. If Allie's family would let her stay with them, that would be the best, but if not she'd find something else.

She'd sleep in Cabin John Park if she had to.

Anything but this.

"Come on, now, Miss Livia, you don't need to play games with me. I know you want this, too."

"I don't know what you're talking about." She backed up, still hoping that somehow, by some miracle, she could get out of this by pretending it was some kind of big mis-understanding.

That would require Donald to have some conscience running in the back of his mind, though, and at the moment he didn't seem to have anything like that.

"Sure you do." He touched her breast again, and licked his lips. "You've been wanting this as much as I have." He tugged her nightgown down, exposing her breast, then bent down, coming at her with his mouth open.

She turned to run, but he turned her back.

Still, she scrambled backward, feeling for the door behind her. She caught it, finally, in her hand, and was about to pull it open, when he slammed his fist right next to her head, banging the door shut.

"This isn't how this is supposed to go," he said, and his foul breath made her feel like vomiting.

"If you let me go up now, I won't tell anyone," she promised.

"I don't think so."

"Then" — she thought fast — "can I at least go brush my teeth?"

He laughed outright at that.

And why not? It was a stupid attempt to get away and even he knew it.

"Where was I?" He pulled her nightgown down again and clasped his mouth onto her breast.

His face was hard against her skin, the stubble of his beard rubbed her like sandpaper. She went to scream, but he clapped his hand over her mouth.

"Shut up," he rasped. "You owe me this." He yanked her nightgown up and tore her underpants off, then pushed his hand roughly against her.

"Stop it!"

"You can make this easy or you can make

this hard, but you can't make it stop." He jabbed his fingers into her. "So make your choice."

If she screamed, what was the best that could happen? Her mother would come? If he'd do this to Olivia, God only knew what he'd do to her mother to keep it quiet.

No one could help.

Later, she didn't remember anything past that point. In her mind, it was a blur of pain and fear and anger, all taking place in the dark, surrounded by the semifamiliar shadows of her daytime life.

She only remembered it as the night that changed the rest of her life. The night she learned that she was made of weak stuff and needed to live her life as safely as possible because she didn't have the strength to go out and take on the world by herself.

"What is *wrong?*" Allie followed Olivia out of gym and into the bathroom.

Stupid Mr. Bredicca had yelled at her and told her that there was only one bathroom pass and she'd have to wait, but she ignored him. What was he going to do? Kick her out of gym? She wished!

"Nothing." Olivia was a mess, tears streaming out of her eyes and down her very pale face. "Leave me alone!"

"No! Something is obviously really wrong and I'm not going to just go off and leave you here." Allie followed her through the open door of the girls' bathroom and stood barricading it. "What's going on?"

"I can't tell you," Olivia whispered.

A frisson of fear tripped through Allie. This was weird. Olivia always told her everything.

Especially the bad stuff.

"Liv, you can," she said, walking toward Olivia. She reached a hand out to touch Olivia's shoulder and Olivia flinched. "Oh, my God, what is going on?" Allie didn't want to make this about her, but Olivia was acting so strange it was really scaring her.

"You wouldn't understand." Olivia dissolved into hard, staccato sobs.

"I would." Allie put her arms around Olivia and held the cold, shaking figure.

"N-no, you wouldn't. You couldn't. I don't even understand."

Allie knelt in front of Olivia and met her eye to eye. "You are not going through this alone, whatever it is. I'm here and I'm going to stand right here next to you until you let me help you. I don't care how many classes we miss or if we have to sleep in here."

Olivia gave a halfhearted smile but it

wilted into tears immediately. "You'll hate me."

"Oh, my God, no I won't. Ever. I don't care what you do. Just tell me why you're so upset."

So Olivia did. She told Allie everything she could bear to say.

That afternoon, Allie went with Olivia to her house and stood outside waiting while Olivia told her mother what had happened.

By the next afternoon, it was all over the school that Olivia Pelham was having sex with her stepfather.

TWENTY-ONE

We're all washed up.
— ad for Fostex Soap

The clock seemed to be ticking awfully slowly today.

"Olivia." Tim poked his head in her office. "I'm afraid you're needed at the studio for a photo shoot."

Despite the fact that she'd been sitting there thinking about absolutely nothing in particular, Olivia had to fight to bring her attention to him. "What?"

"The studio." Tim gestured. "We have a model who's not feeling well." He pantomimed drinking. "And we don't have time to get a new one."

Olivia sighed. What the hell was she supposed to do? Go there with tomato juice, egg whites, Tabasco, and a blender to concoct some sort of hangover remedy?

Where in her job description did it say

she had to fix people who couldn't manage to be professional enough to do their own jobs?

But she knew where. It was between the lines.

There was a *lot* of stuff between the lines of her job description. And she'd been working between those lines long enough not to be surprised by them.

"Go to Starbucks and get a coffee traveler. Bold." It usually came with multiple cups. She'd pour the entire damn thing down the model's throat if she had to.

It wouldn't be the first time.

"Got it." Tim popped a finger gun at her. "The usual routine."

"The usual." She sighed, then added to herself, "It's always the usual."

That was the first catastrophe of the day. By nine-thirty A.M. they'd sobered the model up enough for her "before" pictures. By ten-thirty, Tim reported, she'd rallied for the "after." And they'd only lost forty-five minutes.

Which translated to several thousand dollars.

Which came up a couple of hours later, when Olivia was in a meeting with the editor in chief, Gil Marshall.

"We're getting our asses handed to us by

Allure and *In Style,*" he barked. "Circulation is down across the board, costs are up, and the biggest celebrity we had this month was Tara Reid. I mean, *shit.*" He threw his hands in the air. "Is this the best we can do?"

"I had Katherine Heigl lined up but you didn't want to rush production to coincide with her Donate Life America campaign," Olivia pointed out. She was ready to back it up with more of Gil's willfully missed opportunities but he cut her off.

"We can't move our entire schedule around, change the focus of dozens of employees, just to accommodate one charity!"

"We have to if we want sales," Olivia said. "We had to use a completely anonymous cover model that month, and that issue sold particularly badly, whereas a *People* magazine that came out at the same time had *huge* sales. It was a mistake, Gil. A stingy mistake."

It didn't matter what he said. Later, she couldn't remember it at all. What mattered was that, despite how right she was, Gil Marshall had bulldozed over her point and acted as if it had no relevance at all.

And the fact that she knew it was *completely* on point didn't matter one whit.

What mattered was that Gil Marshall had a scapegoat for every decision he made that went wrong. That was what had mattered above all else for all the years Olivia had worked there.

The rest of the meeting went on in a similar way. Just like tens of other meetings had gone in the past. Once, Olivia had risen to the challenge, trying to make right all the things Gil said were wrong.

But lately she'd gotten tired of the futile exercise. Lately she'd looked out the window during these meetings and contemplated the clouds drifting past, forming and unforming familiar shapes.

Sometimes it felt as if someone were giving her a sign way up high.

But when the sign looked like a smiley face with no other explanation, what was she supposed to do with that?

"Olivia, we have a problem and it's already gone to press."

Olivia put her call on hold and asked Tim, "Is this urgent?"

"Sort of. Yes."

She finished her call, hung up the receiver, and asked her waiting assistant, "What is it?"

"So . . . you know how we had that article on feminism and how women are portrayed in the media and how powerful words can be?"

Olivia thought for a moment. "Yes. It was called 'Bad Words,' right?"

Tim colored and cleared his throat. "That's right. And you said you loved the word *legend* because of all the dignity and accomplishment it implied without being sexist."

"Right." Yes, she'd meant that. It was a good, strong word. She stood by that.

"And then you said you hate the word *pussy* because of how demeaning it is to women's sexuality."

"Yes." She hated the word entirely. There was never a flattering or even benign use for it. If one wasn't referring to a cat — and for decades one really hadn't used the word in reference to a cat — there was no positive or flattering use for it. "Was that too racy?"

"Not exactly." Tim looked down. "At least, not until now."

Her nerves tightened. "What do you mean, *'Not until now'*?"

"Well, there was a typo." Tim referred to the copy he had in his hand. "Where you said, 'I hate pussy,' they accidentally left off the *h.*"

Olivia had to think for a moment. There was only one *h* in the sentence Tim had

343

said, and its elimination changed the sentence entirely.

"So we're going to press with me saying 'I *ate* pussy.' "

Tim grimaced. "That's about the size of it."

"That changes the meaning of what I said."

"Um . . . completely."

"In fact, without a correction, it changes the entire slant of the article."

Tim sucked air in through his teeth and nodded. "It kind of does. Yes. Although it *was* about feminism. Maybe that will just give it a 'sisters are doing it for themselves' vibe."

Olivia considered the ramifications. She wasn't really all that concerned about how the change reflected on her, but there was the potential for — no, the likelihood of — a huge reaction and potential backlash from the public. Either Olivia could stand by her statement and face the misunderstanding of thousands of people, or she could run a correction and risk alienating a huge percentage of readers who might have been delighted at her "coming out."

And most of the readers would probably realize it was a typo.

"It's okay," she said to Tim, although there

was nothing he or anyone else could do now that the issue had gone to press. "If anything, this will make me seem more interesting than I am."

Which was true.

But all Olivia could think was that she just couldn't get worked up about this kind of mistake anymore.

She just didn't care.

"David Weiner is on line two," Tim told Olivia shortly before five o'clock.

David Weiner! She looked at her calendar. Did they have an appointment?

They did.

She pressed the button and lifted the receiver, trying to come up with an excuse to get out of it. "David! I was just thinking about you!"

"I'm flattered. I hope I don't blow your nice thoughts with what I have to say."

"What?"

"I need to cancel our date tonight."

Thank goodness. Olivia slumped in relief, then turned the page of her diary. "Would you like to reschedule? I have a couple of hours on Tuesday night."

"Actually, Liv, I don't think I'm going to be able to get together for a while. Maybe not ever."

Her heart lurched. Did he have a communicable disease? Had he passed it on to her before finding out? When was the last time she'd seen him? Four weeks, maybe. He'd canceled last time, too. "Why not?" she asked. "What's going on?"

"You're not going to believe it."

AIDS? Would he introduce HIV-positive results this way? "Try me," she said, her voice tight.

"I've met someone."

It took a moment for Olivia to register what he'd said. "You've met someone? A woman, you mean?"

"I hope I haven't made you doubt my sexual preferences that much!"

"No, no." She let out a relieved breath.

"It's okay, I know it's a shock. It's a shock for me, too. Everyone always says when you meet the One you know it, and I wasn't even interested in meeting a One, so imagine my surprise when Brenda turned up."

"Brenda." Did Olivia know a Brenda? She didn't think so. "That's great, David." Then, because she didn't think she sounded convincing, she added, more firmly, "Really. I'm so happy for you."

"Thanks, kid. I hope I didn't disappoint you tonight."

"Not at all. I actually needed to cancel

346

anyway."

"Then it's worked out fine." He sounded like he didn't believe her. "Look, I'll give you a call sometime, see how you're doing."

They both knew he wouldn't.

"Great! I hope you will."

They both knew she didn't.

They said their good-byes and she replaced the receiver slowly.

What now?

Even her fuck buddy — a term she hated, regardless of how apt it was — had found someone he was willing to change his ways for. David Weiner had, like Olivia herself, been one of the last holdouts, a single professional who didn't want to muddy the waters with a relationship. David had, until now, been singly focused on his career, which had made him the perfect convenience for Olivia.

She almost couldn't believe he'd changed. Not that she wasn't happy for him — she was. She sincerely hoped things worked out the way he wanted them to. Oddly, she felt not an iota of jealousy or regret.

What she felt was lonely.

Now virtually everyone she knew seemed to have someone or something that made their lives more meaningful and Olivia felt more lost than ever.

■ ■ ■ ■

By the time Olivia had to leave — there was no choice, the office had emptied of even the stragglers who'd stayed to do the last-minute rush to get the issue out — she was completely exhausted.

No, maybe *exhausted* was the wrong word. Maybe it was simply that she was worn out from trying to make straw into gold all day, every day. Gil made things nearly impossible, with his constant picking at words and intentions, and his insane desire to make the magazine turn magically into a bestseller without any effort or sacrifice on his part.

She left the office with the intention of walking the fourteen blocks to her apartment. It wasn't something she'd have suggested anyone else do at this hour, but Olivia was indomitable.

Unfortunately, once she got to the street and into a driving rain she wasn't expecting, she tried to hail a cab, only to find out she was also apparently invisible. It seemed like forever that she stood there with her arm out, but all the cabs that passed were occupied.

Finally she decided to just pound her way

home on foot, despite the fact that, at that point, she'd been at work for more than twelve hours, awake for more than fourteen, and she was completely exhausted.

Walking felt better than standing curbside with her arm in the air, trying to stop a cab that might or might not come.

So she walked. It felt good to be alone and perhaps a little bit aimless. And although she felt safe, despite multiple CNN reports to the contrary, she was not content. This — the bright night, the polluted air, the blast of cab horns even at ten P.M. — wasn't what she wanted for the rest of her life.

She longed for peace. As a child, she'd had a good dose of it — at that time, the suburbs of D.C. were quiet, even dark and star filled, and she'd spent many balmy nights enjoying the quiet and the stars. Just enough to make her want more, enough to make her *imagine* more.

By the time she was a teenager and read books by Beryl Markham and Isak Dinesen and even Ernest Hemingway on the dark, mysterious continent of Africa, she wanted to escape into that faraway land. But that was a secret fantasy. She knew, even then, that it wasn't practical. She knew she needed to get a degree in some sort of business administration so that she could be financially independent.

In other words, she wanted to be the opposite of her mother.

She *never* wanted to end up like her mother.

Yet she had, in a way. Like her mother, she was living in circumstances that she didn't want. She was living a life she didn't particularly like.

And it was all because instead of running toward a future she believed she'd love, she'd backed away from a future she feared.

Now she was living it.

So she'd succeeded in what she tried: She was financially independent. She was not afraid. She was not locked into a marriage or a relationship by a fear of being alone.

But she wasn't happy.

Something needed to change and she was pretty sure that something was *everything.*

TWENTY-TWO

Boys go sweet on girls who go soft.
— ad for Love's Baby Soft

The drive home from New York flew by. For some reason, Allie kept finding herself thinking about Marianne's revelation at Weight Watchers.

She wanted her own revelation. Some simple, correctable reason for everything that ever went wrong in her life. Including, but not limited to, getting fat.

Allie, of course, had rejected the notion that everyone who overeats does it because of some deep psychological trauma, but at the same time, she wondered why it was so hard for her to just whip up some willpower to lose the weight.

For her, *that* seemed to be the question.

And as she drove past the newly refurbished rest stops on the Jersey Turnpike — each one offering something more delicious

351

than the last: Nathan's, Dunkin' Donuts, Roy Rogers — she realized that she had trouble sticking to a diet because she *resented* the fact that she had to.

One thing Allie had always been able to take for granted when she was growing up was that she was strong and fit. She had a pile of Presidential Physical Fitness Awards in her School Days memorabilia books, and she hadn't even been aware she was being tested.

She'd been on the swim team, the softball team, she'd played tennis, ridden horses, and every time she'd gotten a whim to change her room around — which was often as a teenager — she'd been able to move her bed, her dresser, and everything else in her room, without any real effort at all. And certainly without help.

What had changed? She'd kept on eating the way she always had, moving the way she always had, she swam in the summer, walked year-round, so what the hell was up with the extra pounds?

And why should she have to work extra hard and give up the undeniable pleasure of food just to lose them?

The answer, which came to her as she willfully passed the Nathan's, etc., at the rest stops, was that she just *did.* She just had to. Life wasn't always fair, and this was a good example of that.

There wasn't anything physically wrong with her, there was no mysterious reason she had packed on the pounds, and thus there was no magic pill that would melt them off. She knew that because just following the basic diet and exercise principles of Weight Watchers had made her lose weight at a completely predictable and average rate.

Life was unfair and this was one perfect illustration of that.

In a way, this epiphany came as something of a relief to her. Thinking there was something physically wrong, or that this was somehow out of her control, was a huge burden.

Now she knew she could make the right changes just by taking one sensible step after another in the right direction. That was all. It was plodding, perhaps, and certainly slow at times.

But it was the same method that had won the race for the turtle.

So it was an approach she was going to take in all of life.

Which was the thought that led her, inevitably, back to Noah. Because Noah was never far from her thoughts — he never had been. Two years ago, if she'd seen the president shopping at Georgetown Park — which she did — the first person she'd call was Noah. If she saw a "Where are they now?" article on the cast of *The Love Boat,* she'd tell Noah. If she got a flat tire or if her fuel line filter got clogged — again, true story — the person she would call was Noah.

So it wasn't new for her that she would be thinking about Noah during an ordinary drive on an ordinary road.

What was new was the *way* she was thinking about Noah. Because these days her thoughts were tinged with longing and loneliness. Was it simply because he was suddenly unavailable? No. She didn't even need to think about that — it wasn't a matter of him becoming the unattainable dream.

It was a matter of her coming to understand if she wanted to keep him around — and there was no doubt at all that she did — she needed to tell him how much she loved him.

Then, if he didn't want to be with her, she'd accept it. Not gracefully, probably. There would be whining, and a lot of self-pity, and there was a distinct possibility that her next few weigh-ins would be ugly, but she would accept it.

With that thought guiding her, she drove straight to Noah's house despite the fact that by the time she parallel parked right outside his building — a miracle in and of itself — it was almost midnight.

She didn't let herself stop and wonder what she'd do if Vickie was there. If she did, she'd turn back and go home and she didn't want to do that.

So she marched up the stairs to his door and rang the bell, then waited, with a pounding heart, until he opened it, ruffled and sleepy looking.

"Are you alone?" she asked.

"Yes. What the —"

"Good." She pushed past him and kicked the door closed behind her, right out of his hand. "We need to talk."

"Is everything all right?" he asked, then shook his bleary head. "I guess not, huh? Dumb question. What's wrong?"

"I want coffee," she said. "Do you want coffee? Do you have anything besides that instant crap?"

"No. And no."

She didn't want instant-coffee breath. This was a talk that required confidence. "Then I'll get water. Do you want some?"

"Does it matter what I say at this point?"

"Not really."

"Then sure." He gestured weakly toward the kitchen and went to the couch, where he plunked down like a rag doll. "What are you doing here, Allison? I thought we weren't going to see each other for a while."

"Yeah." She dropped some ice cubes into a glass and took water from the tap. "About that. What the hell does it mean? Did Vickie tell you that you're not allowed to see me?"

He gave a faint smile. "After all these years, do I seem like the kind of guy who's going to let someone tell him how to feel? Besides, I don't think Vickie's thinking about you nearly as much as you think about her."

"Oh." For a moment she was offended, but she had bigger fish to fry. "Then it was just you."

He nodded. "Just me."

"After all these years, our friendship is over. Kaput. What the fuck is that? Who breaks up with friends?" She sat down next to him. "I don't even know if that's the right expression. Do you *break up?* Or is it more like *severing ties?* Or maybe —"

She didn't finish her thought because he cupped his hand around her face and drew her to him in a kiss.

At first she was shocked into stillness, but

that only lasted about two seconds, after which she dropped her glass of water on the floor and coiled her arms around Noah, pulling him closer. Or her closer. Or both. It didn't matter; his mouth moved against hers in a way that sent desire like she'd never felt racing through her.

How had she missed out on this for so long?

He moved his hands up her back, his touch definite. There was no question in it. When he traced down her spine, it tickled, and she arched toward him. When she did, he unhooked her bra with one quick flick of his fingers.

Her inhibitions fell apart just as easily.

He spanned his palms against her, which pressed her body against his. She went willingly: If she could have, she would have climbed right into his soul.

"Noah," she breathed, as he traced his mouth along her jaw and down her throat.

His only answer was to kiss her mouth.

He was as hungry for this as she was.

Noah yanked at Allie's shirt, ripping the buttons off. They ticked to the floor like little raindrops, as his hand moved across her skin.

Then, suddenly, they both drew back and looked at each other.

It was the obvious time for one, or both, of them to give a final warning, to point out that if they didn't stop now they were going to tumble over the point of no return.

But neither of them spoke. There was no need.

Instead they both smiled, and crashed back into each other, their need even more urgent than before.

They didn't stop.

Not until much, much later, when the sun was beginning to peek out on the horizon through the east windows.

"I should go," Allie said, but what she meant was that she should stay. She didn't want to move. It would be easy to imagine lying right here, with Noah, forever.

Never in her life had anything felt so right or so completely unconflicted.

Until he said, "You probably should."

Even though she was tired, a rush of adrenaline shot through her like a bullet. "What, no *thank you, ma'am?*"

He laughed. "I didn't mean that."

"What did you mean?"

"That things changed last night." He sat up, and the pathetic "blanket" she had made of his shirt dropped off his shoulders. "I have business I need to attend to now."

"Business." She rolled her eyes. "Try

again, Noah. The way you really talk to me."

"I need to talk to Vickie." He yawned and then dropped his face into his hands. "I needed to anyway. This isn't about you. Or it's not *because* of you. It's because that whole thing wasn't right anyway."

"Tell me about it. I don't know how you lasted as long as you did without killing her."

He looked at her seriously. "It's complicated."

"How can it be complicated, Noah? You haven't even been seeing her for that long."

He stared straight ahead. "Three or four months can be a long time."

She laughed. "On what calendar? Noah Haller, you and I are both entering what we used to think of as *parent age.* Ten years fly by like two months. How in the world can you say that three or four months can be a long time?"

He met her eyes. "Trust me."

"Okay, fine." She shrugged. "I guess if spending fifteen minutes talking to Vickie seems like forever, dating her for three months could seem even more like forever."

"That's not what I meant." He clasped and unclasped his hands in his lap. "The relationship went further than I expected it to."

This was making no sense. "What are you talking about, Noah?" Genuine fear coursed through her. "Did you get married in some Vegas chapel or something?"

He hesitated just long enough for her imagination to get on a horse and gallop off for several seconds.

"No," he said finally. "But . . ."

"But what?"

"There's a problem. A . . . condition you need to know about. I should have told you before" — he gestured behind them — "we did that."

"You didn't seem to have any conditions, Noah." Her joke fell flat.

She always joked in tense situations and those jokes almost always fell flat.

"Here's the thing." He tried again. He didn't meet her eyes. "I'm trying to do the right thing. That's why I said we shouldn't see each other. It wasn't for Vickie, it was for me. And for you." He met her eyes. "For *you.*"

She shook her head. "I'm not seeing it, Noah. How the hell is cutting me out of your life some big favor to me?"

"My life comes with a lot of shit you might not want to deal with," he said.

"Like what? Architectural talk? Historical preservation conditions?" She was flummoxed. "The fact that you snore? Hate vanilla ice cream? Pee all over the toilet seat when you stumble in the bathroom in the middle of the night? What on earth could you be hiding, Noah, that I haven't seen at some point over the past twenty years?"

"A pregnant ex-girlfriend," he answered so quietly that for a moment or two she languished in the idea that she might have actually misheard him.

"I'm sorry?"

He met her eyes now and nodded, his expression so somber she couldn't help understanding him without doubt or question. "Vickie's pregnant."

Twenty-Three

They're not as innocent as they seem.
  — ad for Maybelline Kissing Slicks

"Oh, my God," was all Allie could say when Olivia answered the phone. "I just can't believe it."

"What is it?" Olivia's nerves were instantly taut. "What's wrong?"

"Noah."

"Is he okay?"

"Yes. Well, *no,* of course, but he's not hurt or maimed. He's just . . . screwed."

Olivia, who had been pacing in front of the window holding the phone with white knuckles, finally took a breath and sat down. "Okay, I could have done without the scare, but why don't you start at the beginning and tell me what the hell you're talking about."

"All right." She heard Allie take a deep breath. "Here goes. I drove home from your

362

house yesterday, and I wasn't going to go to him, I really wasn't, but in the end I did. I just couldn't stop myself. I *had* to see him."

"So far I understand completely. Was he glad to see you?"

"Yes! I mean, he took some persuading, but we finally broke through some of those stupid barriers and were able to talk honestly. He told me he's loved me for years."

"I knew it! I told you that, too."

"Liv, it was hard enough to believe coming from *him.* There was no way I could have invested myself in a secondhand report."

"Good point. I'm with you on that. So where does the bad part come in?"

Allie made a shuddering sound. "Oh, it's coming. Anyway, we talked and finally got it all out in the open, and . . . things happened."

"Say no more."

"Thank you. *But.*"

"Uh-oh."

"Yeah, *but* afterward when we're talking about how he's got to dump Vickie, he lays it on me."

"What?"

"Vickie's pregnant."

Olivia had heard the expression *my heart skipped a beat* all her life but until now it had never actually happened to her. This was so completely unexpected that if Allie had told her Noah was planning to have a sex-change operation, she couldn't have been more surprised. "How the hell is that possible? What is he, sixteen? Didn't he take some damn precautions?"

"All things I wanted to know," Allie agreed. "And he said he was *extremely* careful, and always, um, *confirmed* that there had been no mishaps afterward, but somehow something, well, slipped through the cracks."

"Really." Always really careful. That sounded like Noah. Accidents happened, of course, they happened every day. But Noah had managed to go, what, twenty years — maybe more — without having one, but now suddenly, when he was with the most manipulative woman Olivia had ever known, his fail-safe methods failed.

This didn't add up.

"How pregnant?" Olivia asked.

"What do you mean, how pregnant? Completely. One hundred percent."

"I mean how far along."

"I didn't ask."

"Maybe we should."

"Why?"

Olivia thought fast. What she was going to say had the potential to be complete slander to Vickie Freedman, but, on the other hand, if she was right, it might save Noah.

And Allie.

"What are you getting at?" Allie prodded.

Olivia took a deep breath, as some yoga instructor had taught her years back. "You can't tell Noah. Not yet, I mean. Before you fly off the handle, or even believe me — because I am not sure of *any* of this — you and I have to formulate a plan."

"You've got me completely confused."

"I know. I'm sorry. Okay, here it is, I'm just going to say it: I think Vickie's sleeping with someone else."

Allie gasped. "You *do?* Who? How do you know?"

Olivia explained to her about Vickie and Todd Reigerberg's strange interaction the night of the reunion.

"Lucy Lee is married to Todd Reigerberg?" Allie asked when she'd heard it all. "And Vickie is *sleeping* with him? Are you sure? *Todd Reigerberg?*"

"Yes. Why is he any more surprising than anyone else?"

"I guess he's not, he's just such a cheesy anchor on what has to be the lowest-rent news show on the East Coast."

That was consistent with the not-so-slick exchange Olivia had seen. "You're missing the point. Or, actually, maybe that's just consistent with the point. The guy is married, he's got something of a high profile, if he was the real father of her baby, there's no way she'd want to make *that* announcement."

"You know I'm ready to jump on this," Allie said. "But Vickie has money. She doesn't need any man to step in and take care of her. Why would she bother to lie, or worse, to tell one man he was the father when she knew another man was? Don't get me wrong, I'm not saying she's a really moral, principled person, but . . . what if she is?"

"That's why I didn't want either one of us flying off the handle at this. I think we need to come up with a really careful, measured response."

"Good. I like that. How?"

"Vickie's left me about ten messages saying she wants to come up and get together for lunch. Or have me down. I think she imagines I can introduce her to celebrities or something."

"Deep."

"I know. So what I'm thinking is that I will take her up on that. Go down, have lunch with her, try to feel her out on the whole pregnancy thing, while you take some private time with Noah and *calmly* tell him what I've told you. Because ultimately this really is his choice. If he wants to pursue a paternity thing, which I hope he does, it's up to him."

Allie was silent for a minute, then said, "He better."

"Right, but if he doesn't, I don't think we can bully him into it," Olivia said. "I don't think we should. Once you give him the facts, if he opts to move forward as if Vickie's telling the truth then that says right there that he's made his decision."

"Or he's crazy." Allie sighed. "But we'll have to see what happens. So how soon can you get here?"

Olivia clicked on Outlook and checked her calendar for the rest of the week. It was full. "Can you wait until the weekend?"

"I don't think so! Are you kidding?"

"All right, all right, give me a second." She checked her appointments for the next couple of days to see which were the least urgent. "Day after tomorrow," she announced. "Wednesday. Can you wait until Wednesday?"

"It won't be easy."

"Bear up, Allie. Keep yourself busy." She smiled to herself. "Watch the news."

"Very funny."

"E-mail me your address and directions from the nearest metro. I'm staying with you. See you Wednesday!"

Olivia hung up the phone. It was going to be a long forty-eight hours.

She had no idea how long, though, until she got home and found her mother was there with a thin, spindly woman dressed entirely in black, from her high-necked blouse to her ankle-length skirt.

"Aunt Cassandra," Olivia said, setting her keys down. She half wondered if it would be wiser to keep them in hand so she could run if necessary. "How nice to see you."

"Who's that?" the older woman barked, turning a stiff neck in Olivia's general direction.

"That's Olivia, Cass," Caroline said, bringing in a tray with glasses of water and sliced cheese and apples on a plate. She set them down in front of Cassandra and handed her a water.

"Oooh, is it?" Cassandra was interested. "Let me see what my little brother's daughter looks like now, come on." She strained to turn to Olivia but her movements were limited.

When Olivia stepped into her line of vision she gave a thin smile. "There you are.

368

And, oh my, you look so much like your father."

"Doesn't she?" Caroline agreed.

Olivia had seen only a few pictures of her father, a lean young man with freckles and sandy hair, though it was hard to tell his true coloring because the prints had faded.

"Indeed. Though he didn't reach her age, did he? Bless his heart." There was genuine regret in Cassandra's voice. "I miss the boy Hank was. And the man he became, too. However briefly."

Olivia hadn't expected that.

In fact, she'd never thought about the fact that her father had died at an age younger than she was now.

"Do you think about him often?" Olivia found herself asking as she sat down in one of the chairs opposite the sofa where Aunt Cassandra sat.

"Now, Olivia, it's been a long time," her mother started, presumably to prevent hurt feelings if — as they both expected — Cassandra would bark that he was dead and gone.

But she didn't.

Instead she said, "I think about him every day." Her pale blue eyes grew watery. "Every day. I will never forget when they brought that boy home. I was thirteen years old and thought I was far too adult to have a baby as a sibling."

Olivia remembered herself at thirteen and tried to imagine how it would have felt to have a baby move in. "Did you babysit for him?"

"I didn't want to," Cassandra said. "Every time our parents asked me to take care of him, I kicked and screamed. But when they'd gone and we were alone" — she paused — "I loved his pudgy arms and legs and those fat cheeks. Nothing was greater fun than to make him laugh. It was always like that with that boy. He loved to laugh. And he was smart as a whip, too. Got every joke" — she snapped her fingers — "like that."

Olivia noticed her mother look down, and there was a deflation in her shoulders that told Olivia this touched her deeply.

"As he got older, he just got smarter," Cassandra went on. "My goodness, he could do the most complicated mathematics when he was just eight years old. By the time he was a teenager, he was ready for any university in this country."

"He was so intelligent," Caroline agreed, looking at Olivia. "You got that from him. You truly got so much from him."

"She did, didn't she?" Cassandra looked

back to Caroline. "I see what you mean now."

"Striking, isn't it?" Caroline asked.

"Indeed."

Olivia didn't know what they were talking about, but it was clear that it wasn't the time to ask. They were in a different place, talking about a different person and a different time.

And frankly she was more interested in hearing about that person in that place at that time than interjecting her own present into it.

"What do you remember as your favorite thing about my father, Aunt Cassandra?" Olivia asked, then sat back and, for the first time in as long as she could remember, enjoyed the long answer about her heritage and her father.

"He knew how to make or fix just about anything. One time, I'll never forget it, I was going to the country club and my car wouldn't start. Hank came out with a Popsicle stick and a paper clip and damned if he didn't make the thing run better than it ever had before . . ."

It was late when Caroline, who had been stifling yawns all night, finally said, "I think it's time for us to hit the hay. What do you think, Cassandra?"

Cassandra glanced at Olivia. "I'd like to spend just a little more time with my niece, if she's up to it."

"Absolutely," Olivia said. Then, to her mother, she assured, "I'll see to it she gets to her bed in the den."

Caroline hesitated, and Olivia knew it was because she was afraid Olivia didn't mean her offer, but when Olivia gave her a nod, she reluctantly went on her way.

"Your mother worries a lot," Cassandra said, when Caroline was gone.

"I know." Olivia looked toward the hall to the guest room, as if her mother were standing there. "She has a lot of stresses."

"I don't believe she ever got over Hank's death."

Olivia hesitated, then had to ask, "You don't? Why not?"

"Because she's come over to the house so many times now but, unlike the other relatives who want this and that from me, she only wants to hear about him. She only wants to see pictures from his youth. It's as if she can't think about anything else."

This shocked Olivia. She had never gotten the impression her mother thought about her father much at all. "And do you tell her what she wants to hear?"

"I tell her what I remember," Cassandra said. "I can't do any more than that, though it isn't very much. I don't lie, if that's what you're asking."

"No." Again, Olivia looked toward her mother's door, fighting an urge to go to her and ask what she really felt. "No, I don't think either of us would ask for that."

"You and I both know she's not coming to see me."

Olivia smiled. "I would have agreed with you there a few weeks ago, but now I'm not so sure."

"I offered her money," Cassandra said suddenly.

Olivia turned to her sharply. "I beg your pardon?"

"You're no dummy. You know what I mean. I thought she wanted money. I thought she asked about Hank so she could get her hands on some inheritance from his only living relative."

Olivia felt sick. "And?"

Cassandra raised her eyebrows and shook her head. "And nothing. Refused me flat-out. She didn't want a penny. Not even money for the train. I believe she was even insulted."

Olivia felt shame because this surprised her. "But she kept going back? To hear more about my father?" Not *my dad.* Never *Daddy.* She'd never known him at all, much less known him well enough to assign an affectionate nickname to him.

"That's all she wanted. So you see, I think she's grieving still, though there's little you or I can do about it."

That was the moment that the clouds lifted for Olivia. Her mother hadn't moved from man to man because she was desperate for romance; she'd moved away from the painful memories again and again, always hoping to find something that would distract her enough to make the grief go away.

But she never had.

Instead she'd had a child in her dead husband's image, a child she had to somehow care for on her own, even though she didn't know the first thing about how to do it.

"You're seeing what I saw," Cassandra said.

"What?"

"A sad and lonely woman." Cassandra lifted her brow. "You're not like that. In fact, you have no man in your life. Are you a lesbian?"

This was so completely unexpected that Olivia had to laugh. "No, I'm not."

"There wouldn't be anything wrong with it if you were, you know. I'm not as behind the times as you might think."

Olivia was fascinated. "Would you like a drink?"

"Love one. Do you have something stronger than that prissy wine your mother kept trying to push on me?"

"Bourbon?"

"Two fingers. Neat."

"No ice, right?"

"I like you, girl."

Olivia thought that if she had some straight bourbon she might just warm to Aunt Cassandra, too.

"Let's not talk about your mother anymore," Cassandra said, after a generous gulp of the fiery liquid. "I want to hear about you. It sounds as if you work in an office building all the time, almost every day of the week, is that true?"

Olivia smiled faintly. "Yes, but I enjoy my job."

Cassandra narrowed her eyes. "No wonder you're so pale."

"I'm not pale —"

"*Deathly* pallor."

Olivia couldn't help laughing at the woman's complete lack of social niceties. "I use some of the most expensive cosmetics in the world to ensure I *don't* have a deathly pallor."

Cassandra gave a nod. "But it begins in the eyes, my dear. Your eyes look dead."

"Really." Under other circumstances, Olivia might have left this conversation right here, but this was her father's sister insulting her. It wasn't hard to step back and listen without taking it too personally. "Tell me more."

"Very well. I think you should quit your job before it kills you. You look far more adventurous to me than you would let on."

Now she'd touched a nerve. "I don't know about that."

"Of course you do. It's written all over you that you know I'm right but you're afraid."

Olivia took another sip of bourbon. It was starting to go down easier now. "How would a woman who's spent so many years avoiding human contact be able to read anyone?"

Cassandra gave a bark of laughter. "You're a smart one." She tapped her forehead. "More clever than most. But then, you already know that."

"Yes."

"Then you're smart enough to take the good advice of an old woman."

"Of course."

"So let's figure out what your adventure should be, shall we?" Cassandra regarded her with some thought before asking, "Did you ever hear about my trip to Africa with Karen Blixen and that pig, Ernest Hemingway?"

Twenty-Four

Makeup optional.
— ad for Hope in a Jar by Philosophy

"Wow, you look different," Allie said, when she opened the door to Olivia.

"What are you talking about?" Olivia entered Allie's apartment. "I don't look any different than I did last week."

"Yes you do. It's like you have sort of a glow. Did you —"

"You are *not* going to ask me if I got laid."

Allie didn't blush, but her expression itself was an admission. "I was, actually."

"Just because you're doing it doesn't mean I have to." Olivia laughed. "Anyway, I didn't. But I guess you can say I have a new lease on life."

"Interesting. Go on."

Olivia shook her head. "No time for that now. I've got lunch with Vickie in forty minutes. Where do you and Noah stand?"

378

"Well, apart from the fact that he's tortured and feels like his life is falling apart, we haven't gotten very far."

"Stuck at the pregnancy, huh?" Olivia went into the kitchen and inspected Allie's new coffeemaker.

"Do you want me to make coffee?"

"Would you?"

"Outta the way." Allie shouldered her way through. "In answer to your question, yes. We're stuck at the pregnancy thing. And I don't see any way around it."

Olivia leaned on the counter and watched Allie make coffee. "You know it would be a bad idea for him to get married just because of the baby even if it *is* his, right?"

"Oh, *I* know that." Allie scooped grounds from a Dunkin' Donuts bag into the filter. "And I think he's heading there, too. Noah's not fool enough to willingly ruin the rest of his life. In fact, I think the whole marriage thing was a knee-jerk reaction to being faced with something you don't expect to be faced with once you've stopped counting your age in halves."

"I still can't believe *Vickie* did something so stupid."

Allie poured water into the machine and turned it on. "Maybe it wasn't stupid," she said simply.

"How?"

"Maybe it was actually very smart of her to time it just right. I'll tell you, if half the people who told me I was getting old at the reunion told her the same thing, she probably started thinking about her biological time bomb right then and there."

Olivia's expression hardened. "I don't care how old she's feeling, she doesn't have the right to trick someone else into accommodating her life-altering plans."

"Hey" — Allie took out a travel mug — "you're preaching to the choir. I'm just pointing out that this might not have been a long-term diabolical plan."

"It might not have been a plan at all. She might have just found herself knocked up and picked the more available fuck buddy to name as the daddy."

Allie held up the coffee carafe. "Cream or sugar?"

"Black."

She poured. "I guess we'll know more in an hour or so."

Olivia nodded and took the steaming travel mug Allie handed her. "Wish me luck."

"You know I do." Allie gave her a quick hug, careful not to slosh the coffee. "Thank you for coming."

"Are you kidding? You two are the best friends I've ever had. There was no way I wasn't going to help."

"You look horrible," Allie said, walking into Noah's apartment.

He was bare from the waist up and, frankly, apart from the pale face and weary eyes, he looked pretty damn good.

"Thanks." He pulled her against him and kissed her forehead. Then her lips. "You don't."

"Thanks a bunch, sweet-talker."

"You know it."

They went into his bedroom and she sat on the bed while he rummaged through the closet.

"Vickie called," he said, his voice muffled. "She wants me to go to the doctor with her for an ultrasound."

"An *ultrasound,*" Allie repeated. "Already?"

Noah poked his head out. "What does that mean? *Already.*"

"First ultrasounds aren't usually done until eighteen weeks. I mean, they *can* do it sooner, but eighteen weeks is the big one where they can find out the sex and everything."

He grabbed a Beatles T-shirt and pulled it

over his head. "Since when are you an expert on pregnancy?"

"It's called *What to Expect When You're Expecting,*" Allie said. "You should check it out. Especially since your girlfriend is claiming to be pregnant."

"She's pregnant, Allie. Come on."

"Fine. That doesn't mean she's not a liar."

He sat down on the bed next to her. "I'm not up for games. What are you getting at?"

She needed to back up. "First of all, tell me this: Have you thought about what you're going to do?"

"Yes. I'm going to tell Vickie I'm in love with someone else and I can't marry her under those circumstances."

"And if she hits the roof?"

He shrugged. "I think she might, but what can I do? It was idiotic of me to agree to the marriage thing in the first place."

"So it was her idea."

He looked at her. "Allie, a month ago, I wasn't thinking about marrying Tori any more than I was thinking about marrying Hillary Clinton."

"You did have that dream once —"

"Drop it. God, you'd think I could tell you one little embarrassing thing without it flying back in my face over and over like a gnat."

"You'll never hear the end of it," Allie assured him. She was feeling pretty good about the way this conversation was going. Noah had his head on straight, he wasn't planning on making any rash moves in reaction to the pregnancy. He was being logical.

Way more logical than Allie could have been if she were him.

So she had to hand that to him. So far this was going well.

"But back to the point," Allie went on. "You're planning to tell Vickie that the relationship is over?"

"I'm going to tell her that I will be there for her and the baby any time they need me and I fully expect to be a part of the child's life."

"Admirable. But what if the baby's not yours?"

Noah looked at her. "It is mine."

"How do you know?"

"Because Tori told me it was. We're not teenagers, Allie, I don't think she's trying to trap me."

She looked at the beige carpeting next to the bed. Berber. She liked Berber as long as you didn't have a dog walking around snagging it all the time.

"Allie." He touched her arm. "You're not

383

too good at hiding stuff so why don't you tell me what's going on?"

She looked him in the eye. "I don't think the baby's yours."

He drew back. "Why not?"

"For one thing, she's eighteen weeks along. What did she tell you?"

"Three months. More or less." He frowned. "Maybe fourteen or fifteen weeks. I don't know, though, I didn't pin her down on it. And I can't take your pregnancy information to the bank, since you don't exactly have a lot of experience with it."

"What if she is eighteen weeks along?" Allie asked. "Were you even seeing her then?"

"We must have been."

"*Think* about it, Noah. Were you? Because if you weren't —"

"Are you kidding me?" He cocked his head. "You don't need to explain where babies come from, Al, I get it."

"And?" she pressed.

"We didn't exactly hold out on sex, but I don't really want to get into that with you."

"Look, Noah, I'm not that eager to talk about it, either, but it might be important."

"Okay. That's it. What are you not saying?"

"That she's sleeping with someone else. I think. Well, we're almost sure."

"We?"

"Olivia and I. Actually, it was Olivia who first figured it out." That age-old impulse to give herself credibility by adding someone else still kicked in. "She saw Vickie sneak off with Lucy Lee's husband during the reunion. They were apparently pretty . . . familiar . . . with each other."

"Is that right." He looked off into space, as if trying to see the movie of the reunion night way off in the distance. Then he met Allie's eyes. "Why didn't Olivia tell me this?"

"She didn't think it was her place. She's not a busybody like me, she just thought you and Vickie must have a casual relationship and that you knew you might not be the only one she was seeing."

"Why didn't *you* tell me?" Noah said, and now he looked hurt. "You of all people know I'm not that kind of guy."

She nodded. "I do. But Olivia didn't even tell me. Not until I told her about Vickie's pregnancy."

He looked as if he considered this for a few seconds before giving a reluctant nod. "I guess this gives me something to talk to Tori about, then." He moved for his phone.

"Wait," Allie said. "Olivia's talking to her now."

He stopped in midmovement. "She's *what?*"

It was funny, it hadn't even occurred to Allie that this might not be a good idea until now. "She's — they're having lunch. You know how Vickie's been leaving messages again and again wanting to meet up with Olivia. So Olivia figured this would be a good time to, you know, try and figure out what's what."

Noah's expression was dark. "Where are they?"

"I don't know, they were meeting at Vickie's."

"When?"

Allie looked at her watch. "About now."

"We are way too old for this, Allie." He stormed around the room, pulling on socks, shoving on his shoes. "I can't believe you two."

"Wait!" Allie scrambled after him as he left the room. "What are you doing?"

"I'm going to talk to Tori myself," he said, turning on her furiously. "It seems to have escaped your notice that we're not in high school anymore. You and your cohort don't need to double-team me and my girlfriend to try and drive a wedge between us."

What? Wasn't there already a wedge between them? And, "Girlfriend?" was all Allie could say.

He rolled his eyes. "You know what I mean. This isn't Olivia's business and frankly it's just barely your business."

"We slept together!"

"And I'm being honest with you." He stopped and turned to her, putting his hands on her shoulders. "That wasn't just a fling, or a mistake. But it was between you and me. Only. I had no intention of being with Tori again, but that conversation was for *me* to have with her. Not you and not Olivia."

"I'm sorry!" He was right. Completely right. She could see that now. She, or better still Olivia, should have had a conversation with him and then let him take care of it himself.

Instead they'd acted like children in the middle of a good, juicy drama.

He stormed out of the apartment with Allie close on his heels. "Go home!" he barked at her.

"No, I'm going with you."

"How many ways do I have to tell you this is none of your business?"

"I won't say anything to Vickie," she promised. "You're right, that's none of my business. But I have to go and help Olivia out of this mess I helped her into."

He considered for a moment. "Fair enough. But I want her out of there and the two of you gone. Tori and I are going to have to talk this over alone."

"Fine." She didn't mean to sound petulant but she did. "And, Noah."

He turned angry eyes on her.

"I'm really, really sorry. I can't tell you how sorry I am. I wanted to help. I know that sounds hollow and stupid now, but it's true. I love you, Noah. I wanted to help you, not hurt you."

His expression softened slightly. "I love you, too, Al. But damn if you're not going to drive me crazy." They reached his car and he unlocked it. "Get in. And for God's sake, try and resist the urge to help me any more between now and the time we get there."

Twenty-Five

Because you're worth it.
— ad for L'Oréal

Olivia arrived at Vickie's town house in Kalorama ten minutes late, thanks to a cabdriver who didn't seem to know north from south.

"Come in!" Vickie threw open the door and leaned in to kiss the air by Olivia's cheek. "I'm so thrilled you could come."

"I thought it was important," Olivia said carefully. This was not the time to bait Vickie or play any unfair head games. She was going to approach this in as straightforward a way as she could manage.

"This way." Vickie led her through a short hall and up a flight of stairs to an ornate living room. "Our reservations aren't for twenty-five more minutes so I thought we'd take our time."

"Perfect."

"Have a seat." Vickie gestured toward a black leather sofa positioned in front of a fireplace over some sort of animal-print rug. It was ghastly. "Would you like a drink?"

"As a matter of fact, that sounds like a good idea. I'd like to talk to you about something."

Vickie nodded knowingly. "The baby?" She patted her stomach.

"Yes, actually."

"Noah couldn't wait to let everyone know, I guess." She took two glasses out of a polished wood cabinet, then lifted a blue bottle of Tynat drinking water.

Olivia was careful not to agree. "He told Allie. Allie told me."

"Whatever. Good news always travels one way or another." She appeared unperturbed. "Water?"

"Yes, thanks."

Vickie poured into the two tumblers. "Is it the wedding you want to talk about?" she asked eagerly. "Don't tell me you have some great connection that could get us into St. Patrick's."

"No —"

"Because I would move the wedding to New York in a heartbeat for that, believe me." She handed a water glass to Olivia.

"No, Vickie, please. It's not about that."

"Call me Tori." Her voice hardened almost imperceptibly as she sat down on the sofa with Olivia. "Please."

"The thing is," Olivia said, "I wanted to talk to you about the reunion."

"The *reunion?*"

Olivia nodded. "And Todd Reigerberg."

Vickie set her glass down on the coffee table very deliberately. "Todd Reigerberg. The anchorman."

"I think you know him as more than that."

Vickie lifted an eyebrow. "Yes. He's Lucy's husband."

This was harder than Olivia had anticipated. It was one thing to tell Allie over the phone that she thought the two were having an affair, but now, face-to-face with Vickie, she got the distinct feeling she might have a real fight coming.

So Olivia took a gamble. "I saw you two that night," she said, setting her own glass down, half anticipating a hasty exit. "Outside . . ." She let the word linger in the air, hoping it would sound as if she had more solid evidence than she did.

Apparently it worked, because all the color drained from Vickie's face. "You were spying on me?"

"Of course not! I went out to get some air. Obviously I didn't think I was going to see . . . that."

It was easy to see the thoughts whirling around Vickie's mind. Finally, whether it was part of the ploy or just crazy hormones, Olivia didn't know, but Vickie's face crumpled and she started to cry. "It was the only time."

Olivia was instantly uncomfortable. "Is Noah really the father?" she asked quietly.

Vickie whirled on her. "How dare you ask me that!"

"I dare because Noah's my friend and I don't think you're being honest with him."

"This is none of your business."

Olivia's hackles rose. If Vickie had nothing to hide, it would have been so easy to put an end to this. "I guess I'm making it my business."

Vickie narrowed her eyes at Olivia. "Have you gone to Noah with this?"

"No," Olivia answered honestly. "I wanted to talk to you first."

Something in Vickie relaxed fractionally. "No one's said anything to Lucy or Todd?"

Funny, that hadn't even occurred to Olivia. Or, as far as she knew, Allie. "No."

"Then I'll tell you something. Yes, I've been with Todd a few times. We knew each other a long time ago, and you know how those things go sometimes. You have a few drinks and one thing leads to another."

Olivia thought about it for a moment. "You weren't drinking at the reunion."

"Obviously, I had the baby to consider."

"So you knew you were pregnant even then."

Vickie paled. "I wasn't feeling well."

"That's not the same as being worried about the baby."

"Well, *now* I know there was a baby."

This lying was absurd.

"You've probably already had CVS or amnio," Olivia said. "So can they do a paternity test from what's already been done or do you have to have a new test?"

"I don't intend to have *any* testing." Vickie stood up. "I think you should leave."

Olivia stood, too. "That's fine, Vickie. I think you've given me my answer."

"How do you figure that?"

"Good-bye." She started toward the stairs, but Vickie grabbed her by the shoulder and turned her around.

"I said, how do you figure that?" Vickie's eyes were flashing with some very ugly emotion.

It was obvious she was nervous, and it was equally obvious that she wouldn't have been nervous if she didn't have reason for it.

"You're scared," Olivia said. "I can't think

why you would be if you were confident Noah was really the father. In fact, if he were, you probably would have told me to go to hell and sent me on my way as soon as this conversation started, but instead you needed to find out what I knew first."

"Spoken just like Nancy Drew."

Olivia shrugged. "Unlike Nancy Drew I'm going to leave this investigation to the experts now." She took another step away.

"I can't believe you're doing this to Noah!"

She stopped and turned back. "I beg your pardon?"

"He's looking forward to being a father. This gives his life *meaning.* Can't you see that?"

"His life already had meaning!"

"He *wants* this. Are you really going to take it away from him because of a biological technicality?"

"A biological technicality?"

"Yes. He's going to be a great father. Responsible, upstanding, active in this child's life. Why do you want to screw that up?"

"I'm not trying to screw anything up, I just want Noah to know the truth."

Vickie scoffed. "I hardly think you're the kind of person who needs to go around telling other people how to live."

"Probably not," Olivia agreed, not rising to the bait. "But I'm the kind of person who thinks that however people decide to live, they should do it armed with the facts."

"Funny, as I recall, you didn't want your mother to know *the facts* about her husband. And you."

Olivia froze.

"Aha." A mean glint came into Vickie's eyes. "You can dish it out, but you can't take it, huh?" She sauntered forward. "It's been a long time, but as I recall, when your mother's husband made the moves on you, all you did was snivel in the bathroom to Allison about how you didn't want to tell her. Interesting that now you're this great arbiter of truth."

Olivia didn't know what to say. She couldn't move. That Vickie could be this callous was shocking and proved Allie's point more than any of the rest of this could have.

Vickie had overheard Allie and Olivia in the bathroom that day, and she had been the one who had spread it all over school. Then — and this was the most incredible part of it — she'd held on to it in some little pocket of her mind for all these years so that eventually she could pull it out, just like this, and use it.

"You are amazing, Vickie," Olivia said. "But none of that changes the fact that Noah needs to know this child isn't his."

"You know what I've noticed? I've noticed *Noah* hasn't asked this question. So clearly *Noah* doesn't want to know. And what he doesn't know" — she had the gleam of triumph in her eyes — "won't hurt him. Unless *you* decide to tell him."

"You stay here," Noah ordered Allie outside Vickie's. "You're not coming in to the middle of this."

"I have to! What if she's hurt Olivia?"

Noah stopped and looked at her. "Really? Do you think she's hacked her into little pieces and put her in the freezer?"

"You don't know Vickie like I do."

"Likewise." He took out a key and unlocked the front door.

She hated that he had a key to Vickie's even though, obviously, he would. Still, there was something so . . . *shared* about it. Almost intimate.

He pushed the door open.

Immediately they could hear raised voices.

". . . as I recall, when your mother's husband made the moves on you, all you did was snivel in the bathroom to Allison about how you didn't want to tell her," Vickie taunted. "Interesting that now you're this great arbiter of truth."

Allie gasped. She felt as though she'd been punched in the gut. So it had been *Vickie!* God, that totally figured. Vickie was the only person Allie knew who might be cruel enough to take that kind of information and turn it on someone without a second thought.

Had she just done it for her own amusement? Was it satisfying for her to hurt other people so severely? Or had she for some reason been jealous of Olivia, even back then?

"You are amazing, Vickie. But none of that changes the fact that Noah needs to know this child isn't his."

Allie was impressed at how calm and cool Olivia sounded on the heels of that bombshell.

Vickie, on the other hand, was getting shrill. "You know what I've noticed? I've noticed *Noah* hasn't asked this question. So clearly *Noah* doesn't want to know. And what he doesn't know won't hurt him. Unless *you* decide to tell him."

Noah went up the steps. "I want to know," he said, in a hard voice.

"Noah!" Vickie looked shocked. "I didn't

hear you come in."

Allie followed close behind him. "I cannot believe what a bitch you are," she said heatedly. All the rage from all the years collected in her and burst forth. "You ruin lives like it's *nothing!*" She moved toward Vickie without thought, except to hurt her as much as she'd hurt everyone else.

Noah grabbed her arm, hard. "Go, Allie."

"Did you *hear* what she said?"

"What business is this of yours?" Vickie snapped, turning on Allie like a wild animal. "My God, Allison, you have *always* tried to horn in on my life."

Allie stepped back. *"What?"*

"Oh, sure, like you don't know *exactly* what I'm talking about."

For a moment, Allie was more baffled than offended. "I have *no idea* what you're talking about!"

"Does the Enchanted Forest ring a bell?"

The Enchanted Forest? This was getting seriously weird. "That park, near Baltimore? That closed like thirty years ago?"

"And you just *had* to have your birthday party there on the same day I was going to have mine."

Allie glanced from Noah to Olivia, but they were looking at Vickie with the same slack-jawed incomprehension she was feeling. "Vickie, that was more than three decades ago —"

"It's *Tori,*" Vickie fumed. "And that's just one example. You did a thousand little things to try and one-up me."

"Me?" Apart from the accuracy of the location of her eighth-birthday party, Allie had the feeling Vickie had her confused with someone else.

"Yes, *you.*" Vickie made an impatient gesture. "And here we go with the innocent act. You know, you're also the reason I can't water-ski —"

"Enough!" Noah stepped in, though Allie was *dying* to know how she was to blame for Vickie's landlubber status. "Let me talk to Tori," he said to Allie.

"No, I just want to know —"

"Yes. Now, you have to go. Olivia." He nodded at Olivia and she came over.

"Come on, Al," she said, her voice soft, but her grasp firm. "They need to talk."

"She's crazy. She can't get away with this," Allie objected, staring Vickie down.

"She won't. She already hasn't. That's why she's just a miserable old cow, holding on to ancient grudges." Clearly Olivia wasn't without her share of vitriol. "But this is between them now."

Allie finally looked at Olivia. "So we can

kill her later?"

Olivia gave a tense laugh. "I think she's got what's coming to her already." She threw a hostile gaze Vickie's way. "I have a feeling there's a long line of people who will want to give her what she's got coming. Starting with Lucy Lee."

"He should have called by now." Allie sat at her kitchen table, pulling the label off her second beer.

"I think he's got his hands full," Olivia said, leaning back against the hard kitchen chair.

"But it's been two and a half hours. That relationship wasn't long enough to warrant a two-and-a-half-hour postmortem."

"There was a pregnancy."

"Not *his*."

"Which, arguably, makes the postmortem even more involved. If it was his, he wouldn't be severing all ties." Olivia shook her head. "Ties take time to sever."

Allie gave half a laugh. "Yeah, I think I saw that on *America's Test Kitchen.* They need a sharp knife."

"There you go."

Her door buzzer sounded and Allie sprang to her feet and flew to the door, throwing it open.

Noah stood there, looking like a boxer who had gone twelve rounds. But a hot boxer, like Oscar De La Hoya.

"Noah!" She put her arms around him and held fast. "Why didn't you call?"

He gave a wisp of a smile. "I thought a visit would be better."

"I've been worried sick."

"Why?"

"Are you kidding? That woman is crazy!"

He sighed. "Am I going to stand here all day or are you going to move aside so I can come in?"

"Oh!" Allie stepped back. "Sorry."

"Hi, Noah." Olivia came into the foyer and handed him a beer.

"Thanks." He took it gratefully and downed half of it in one long gulp.

"Come in, come in." Allie held his hand and pulled him into the living room, sitting right next to him on the couch. She couldn't get close enough. "Tell us what happened."

"Tell us what you want to tell us," Olivia corrected, always the calm one. "Because it's really none of our business. Or at least" — she looked over the two of them — "it's none of *my* business. Maybe I should leave the two of you alone."

"Are you kidding?" Allie asked. "If it weren't for you, Noah wouldn't even have found out the truth at all. At least not until the kid came out with bad anchorman hair and the perennially confused expression of his biological father."

"I hope you're not disappointed about the baby," Olivia said to Noah gently. "I realize this might not be good news."

He gave a brief smile. "I'm not disappointed, Liv. That wasn't what I wanted." He gave a quick glance in Allie's direction.

She flushed with warmth.

"I just can't believe I didn't see who she was right away," Noah went on. "The whole situation is so messed up."

"Well, she looked good," Allie admitted grudgingly. "Your gender can't help being blinded by that sometimes. More often than not."

"As a matter of fact, *our* gender counts on that more often than not," Olivia added.

Noah raised his beer. "We're happy to comply, apparently."

"You wouldn't have for long." Allie studied his profile until he turned and met her eye.

Heat rushed through her and he held her gaze.

"Look, kids," Olivia said, standing up, "this has been fun, but I have to go."

"What?" Allie asked, dragging her attention away from Noah. But as soon as she

looked at Olivia, she knew Olivia thought Allie and Noah should be alone.

And that she was right.

Olivia nodded. "I'm actually going out of town in a couple of days and I need to get back to the city and do some major packing."

"But you just got here," Allie said, her argument weak. "We have so much more catching up to do."

"You and Noah have some catching up to do yourselves," Olivia said, smiling. "We can do it later. When I get back to the U.S."

"Back to the U.S.," Noah said. "Where are you going?"

"It's a long story," Olivia said. "But basically I'm taking a leave of absence from work so I can do some traveling. I've always wanted to see the world from the ground, not from a hotel room, so I'm going to go do that. Maybe take some pictures."

Allie remembered that conversation from a long time ago. Olivia wanted to travel the world, be a photographer. She didn't want a real job, a desk job she had to go to every day.

"Write," Allie said. "Call. And promise me you'll come stay for a week when you get back."

"I promise." Olivia came over and gave

Allie a big hug. "Better late than never, eh?"

Allie held on tight. "Yes," she whispered.

Olivia drew back and smiled at her. "I'll see you soon." She moved to Noah and kissed his cheek. "Take care."

"We'll be fine."

Olivia gave a laugh. "This has been a long time in coming," she said. "I had no idea the happy ending would still be so much fun."

"It is," Allie said. "It's so much fun." She turned to Noah. "I'll be right back. I'm going to walk Olivia out."

"Take your time."

The implication, and the truth, was that they now had all the time in the world.

For a couple of minutes, Allie and Olivia walked in companionable silence.

Finally Allie spoke. "I hate that you're going so far away now that we've finally gotten back in touch."

They stopped and Olivia turned to her. There were tears in her eyes. "These past weeks have changed my life," Olivia said. "I'm on a roll now. I can't interrupt the momentum and stay in my old routine. I think it would kill me."

"Well, we definitely don't want that."

"But you're starting something new, too," Olivia said, gesturing toward the building where Noah waited for Allie. "You and I are back. We can talk, we can e-mail, we can write. We won't lose anything again. But there's a certain guy you're going to want to give your time and, er, *physical presence* to a lot more than me." She smiled.

Allie laughed. "Not that I'm the kind of girl who disses her friends in favor of a guy."

Olivia shook her head. "You never were."

They looked at each other for a moment and Allie had the strange impression of the years melting away. In a way she was looking at the friend she had known so well, so long ago.

"*Promise* you'll keep in touch," Allie said. "No getting distracted by elephants and tigers and thinking we're too small-time to bother with."

"Are you kidding? I'm going to *love* hearing about what's going on with you two."

"You will. You'll hear every detail."

"And I'll know if you're holding out."

Allie crossed her heart. "I won't hold out."

Olivia smiled again and gave Allie a hug. When she drew back, the tears were spilling down her cheeks.

Just like Allie's were.

"I'm so sorry I blamed you for so long —" Olivia began.

"I understand," Allie insisted. "We can't

go there. We can't go back and change it. And unfortunately we can't actually *kill* Vickie, so all we can do is move forward from here."

"Okay." Olivia took a shuddering breath. "Now. Go back in there and start making some interesting stories to tell me."

"You got it. And you do the same. Send me a picture of you on an elephant."

Olivia gave a nod. "I'll make a point of it."

Allie returned to her apartment with a mix of melancholy about the past and excitement about the future.

Her future with Noah.

She still almost couldn't believe it.

They sat down on the sofa together, and silence bounced between them.

Then Allie said, "This is weird."

"It *is* weird," Noah agreed. "But good."

"Definitely good."

More silence.

"The thing is," Noah went on, "that it should have happened . . . better. I should have swept you off your feet."

She scoffed. "Imagine what that would do to your back."

"Cut it, Al, I'm serious. I should have figured this out ages ago."

"That's true."

"Not that I'm the only one at fault. You've been a complete idiot about it, too."

She nodded, then said, "Well, not a *complete* idiot. I, at least, had the foresight to come up with the when-we're-forty plan."

"The what . . . ?"

"You have to marry me when we're forty if we're not already married to other people. That's the deal."

He looked at her and a light came into his eyes. "That's right, we have a plan."

"Yes, we do."

"A verbal agreement." He frowned. "That's binding in court, you know."

"I didn't know that."

He nodded. "Trust me. It would be very sticky for you to try and get out of it. Or me. Either of us."

She twined her fingers in his. It was impossible not to smile. "Better not try, then."

"I think that's wise." He raised an eyebrow. "And, really, Allie, it's about damn time we got wise."

EPILOGUE

Winston Churchill High School — 25-Year Reunion — Who's Coming?

Peter Ford: Totally! Cant wait!

Marlene Newman: I will definitely be there. We're doing an 80s theme. BTW, does anyone have Vickie Freedman's e-mail address? I need to know if she wants to be on the committee this year.

Noah Haller: Won't be there, will be on vacation with gorgeous wife, sends regrets.

Allison Denty-Haller: Will not attend, has no regrets!

Yancy Miller: Vickie is now Victoria Reigerberg. I saw her husband (with his niece) at the Marriott the other day when I was having dinner. He said he didn't think they'd be coming to the reunion.

Lucy Lee: Todd doesn't have a niece. Let me guess: Was she a blonde? LOL. I'll be at the reunion if I'm not on assignment. See you there!

Olivia Pelham: I'm working on a book of photos in Kenya. Probably won't be back in time. Allie and Noah, see you in a few weeks!

ABOUT THE AUTHOR

Beth Harbison is the *New York Times* bestselling author of *Shoe Addicts Anonymous* and *Secrets of a Shoe Addict.* She lives with her husband and two children near Washington, D.C., where she enjoys a large collection of impractical shoes and purses, and a small group of friends who are always there to help save her from the occasional Really Bad Decision. Visit www .bethharbison.com.

The employees of Thorndike Press hope you have enjoyed this Large Print book. All our Thorndike, Wheeler, and Kennebec Large Print titles are designed for easy reading, and all our books are made to last. Other Thorndike Press Large Print books are available at your library, through selected bookstores, or directly from us.

For information about titles, please call:
 (800) 223-1244

or visit our Web site at:
 http://gale.cengage.com/thorndike

To share your comments, please write:
 Publisher
 Thorndike Press
 295 Kennedy Memorial Drive
 Waterville, ME 04901

30.95